CLASS
MOM

CLASS
MOM

A Novel

Laurie Gelman

HENRY HOLT AND COMPANY
NEW YORK

Henry Holt and Company
Publishers since 1866
175 Fifth Avenue
New York, New York 10010
www.henryholt.com

Henry Holt® and ⬚® are registered trademarks of Macmillan Publishing Group, LLC.

Distributed in Canada by Raincoast Book Distribution Limited

Library of Congress Cataloging-in-Publication Data

Names: Gelman, Laurie author.
Title: Class mom : a novel / Laurie Gelman.
Description: First edition. | New York : Henry Holt and Company, 2017.
Identifiers: LCCN 2016052495| ISBN 9781250124692 (hardcover) |
    ISBN 9781250124708 (electronic book) | ISBN 9781250169983
    (international edition)
Subjects: LCSH: Middle-aged women—Fiction | Middle-aged mothers—Fiction. |
    Domestic fiction. | CYAC: Schools—Fiction.
Classification: LCC PS3607.E465 C57 2017 | DDC 813/.6—dc23
LC record available at https://lccn.loc.gov/2016052495

Our books may be purchased in bulk for promotional, educational, or business use. Please contact your local bookseller or the Macmillan Corporate and Premium Sales Department at (800) 221-7945, extension 5442, or by e-mail at MacmillanSpecialMarkets@macmillan.com.

First Edition 2017

Designed by Meryl Sussman Levavi

Printed in the United States of America

10 9 8 7 6 5 4 3 2 1

*This book is dedicated with love to my husband,
Michael, and our daughters, Jamie and Misha.
Without the three of you, I would never
have been a class mom.*

CLASS
MOM

To: Parents
From: JDixon
Date: 9/4
Subject: Getting to know me—your new class mom

Hello, parents of Miss Ward's kindergarten class!

My name is Jennifer Dixon and I have "volunteered" to be your class mom for this coming year. Since this is a thankless job, don't expect warm fuzzy emails like you probably got in preschool. Wake up! You're in kindergarten on the mean streets of William H. Taft Elementary School, and it's time to face a few facts. The main one is that I'm in charge and I have some strong suggestions to make this an easy year for all of us, especially me.

First and foremost, read the school's @#$%& weekly email! It may seem boring, but it actually gives good information and keeps me from having to answer questions like "When is curriculum night?" (See below, by the way, for the answer to that one.)

Second, when I ask for something, volunteer! If I say we need doughnuts, say, "How many?" not "Can I bring cups?" I don't want to have to assign stuff, so please be among the first to email me back. I will be testing you on this very soon because curriculum night is . . . (see below).

And finally, if there is an event . . . show up! They may seem dull and tedious but let's never forget we are here to build a community. It can't just be the same five people showing up, because they'll get sick of each other.

Important Dates to Commit to Memory
My Birthday: April 18. No gifts necessary, but I do enjoy Starbucks.

Curriculum Night: Tuesday, September 27—6:30 to 8:30 p.m.

This will be your first chance to see the effects of alcohol on your fellow parents. I'll be asking for refreshment contributions sometime next week.

Parent Dialogue Coffee—October 7—Location: The Lounge—no idea what the "dialogue" is, but don't be surprised if it's about coffee.

Parent Social, K–6th Grades: January 18—6 to 8 p.m.—Location: Cafeteria. It's been my experience that these are a bit awkward, kind of like a 7th-grade dance. Go at your own risk.

Miss Ward has also requested that you drop off a photo of your child before the first day of school. Let me repeat that . . . before the first day of school. I'm not sure, but I think she plans to use them in some sort of Wiccan ritual to "cleanse" the classroom.

    That's it for now.

    Any questions?

                           Jennifer

P.S.: By the way, if any of you consider yourselves "crafty," let me know. This year all gifts for the teacher have to be homemade, so for this and only this, I am open to suggestions.

I click Send on my laptop, sit back in my chair, and grimace.

"Well, that should give them something to think about," I say to absolutely no one.

Rubbing my tired eyes, I wonder for the fiftieth time that day why I ever agreed to be a class mom again.

My first instinct had been the right one.

"Absofuckinglutely NOT," I told Nina Grandish when she asked me. Nina is the reigning high priestess of the school's PTA. In spite of that, she is my best friend. "It's the worst job I've had since I worked customer service at Allstate."

"Please!" she begged. "I really need you."

"Nope. I don't have time."

"Yes, you do. Vivs and Laura have already gone back to school."

"I'm starting my mud-run training."

"That's unlikely," Nina scoffed.

"I'm thinking of getting a dog for Max and I'll be busy with that."

"No, you're not. You hate dogs. Come on! Think of all the *experience* you bring to the job."

"Oh, wow," I said. "Thanks for reminding me how much older I am than all the other parents."

"Not older," Nina cooed, *"wiser."*

And I am, by almost fifteen years. The nineties were a bit of a lost decade for me. After a blistering four years at the University of Kansas (Go, Jayhawks!) I found myself with a super-useful degree in art history and not a chance in hell of finding a job with it. So, I decided to hit the road and see a bit of the world. Some people go to Paris to look at great art; some go to Rome to look at great architecture. Me? I went to Amsterdam to see a great band. INXS was just starting to ride their wave of international success, thanks to the album *X*. Luckily for me, they weren't *so* famous that they would only date supermodels. I got picked out of the audience thanks in part to the "no bra" phase I was going through, and lo and behold I ended up a groupie.

You know that Cameron Crowe movie *Almost Famous,* where the girls are called Band-Aids and they travel with the band and keep the musicians', um, *morale* up? It was kind of like that but not nearly as glamorous. I was with INXS for a little over a year, then moved on to a folksinger named Greg Brown. Yeah, I had never heard of him either, but he could certainly draw a crowd, albeit an unwashed one. In those three years away, I somehow ended up with two kids, one of whom may or may not have been fathered by Michael Hutchence. Thanks to his untimely death in 1997, poor Vivs may never know. But Laura's sperm donor was most definitely Greg Brown's banjo player. I'm 65 percent sure.

To quote the poet Steve Perry of Journey, "They say that the road ain't no place to start a family." So I took my two kids from two different fathers and made my way home to Kansas City.

Actually, by that time my parents had fulfilled a lifelong dream and moved to Overland Park, which is a fancy suburb of KC. I was sad that I didn't get a chance to say good-bye to our old house, but thrilled that I had such a nice place to bring Vivs and Laura home to.

Let's just say I had a bucket load of explaining to do to Kay and Ray Howard, my extremely Catholic parents, when I landed on their swank new doorstep with Laura and Vivs both still in diapers. My mother's face went from confused to horrified to delighted so quickly that I thought she was having a stroke.

Luckily, they are more the forgiving kind of religious people and less the judgmental kind. So after a few dozen Hail Marys and one excruciating afternoon at Our Lady of Unity doing the Stations of the Cross, I moved in with them and started what I now call the normal years. With their help, I raised the girls, worked for a while at Allstate, and, yes, was class mom seven endless years in a row. It's a record that I believe still stands at William Taft. I hope it's not what ends up as the most noteworthy thing in my obituary, but you never know.

It was while working at Allstate that I met the man who would become Baby Daddy #3 and Husband #1, Ron Dixon. By the way, I still have had only one husband. I just think it's funny to introduce him that way. Ron called to file a complaint with the people with whom he *thought* he was in good hands. As was my job, I took the call and tried to talk him out of canceling his policy. Ron has an amazing voice. Even when he's complaining, it sounds like he just swallowed liquid velvet. I could have listened to him all day. It was around the time he called me a soulless bitch that I decided I wanted to meet him. To this day, he thinks I took all my disgruntled phone callers to lunch.

What can I say? I had him at hello. I'm not unattractive, considering my age and the mileage I've put on my body, and Ron happened to be single, having just gone through a soul-sucking divorce. In fact, when he called the insurance company he was trying to put in a force majeure claim for a fallen tree that had clearly been hit by a car. I later found out that the tree was the victim of domestic abuse, having been plowed over by his ex.

As a member of the sisterhood, I take exception to men always calling women crazy, but in this case I can say unequivocally that Ron's ex-wife, Cindy, is nuts. Not fear-for-your-life nuts, just garden-variety nuts. The biggest problem is that you never know in what form the nuttiness is going to rear its ugly head. Like one day, a few months after Ron and I moved in together, six Costco-sized crates of diapers appeared on our doorstep with a card from Cindy saying, "Get the message?" I figured she was either calling us babies or suggesting that we have a baby. Ron said she was telling us we are full of shit.

Ron is a good fit for me. He's what my father would call a solid guy, both physically and emotionally. He's about five eleven (although he tells people he's six feet, for reasons that are not quite clear to me) and fit without looking bulked up, and he has short dark hair that is thinning at the temples. He's not what I had typically found attractive in the past—I mean, he doesn't even have a tattoo—but he has immense charisma and just about the kindest face on the planet. Combine that with the voice, and I was a goner the moment I saw him. Our courtship was short and sweet, because when it's right, it's right, and why screw around? And thanks to crazy Cindy's fear of vomit, they never had any children. So when he dropped the B bomb on me on our first anniversary I shouldn't have been surprised.

We were having dinner at Garozzo's, and over penne Victoria he casually mentioned that he would really like to have a baby. I stifled my first thought (*Well, good luck with those labor pains!*) and told him of course we would try. I pretty much counted on my aging womb to keep anything from happening, but wouldn't you know it? I had one good egg left. And thank goodness for that, because Max is the dessert of my parenting life.

So now at the ripe old age of forty-six, I have two girls in college and one boy starting kindergarten. And I'm the oldest mom in the grade. Oh sorry, the *wisest*.

✦ ✦ ✦

"Max! Get down here. Your toast is getting cold."

I sit back down at my kitchen-counter office and slam out an email to my class parents that I hope they read before drop-off this morning.

To: Parents
From: JDixon
Date: 9/6
Subject: Questions answered

Dear Parents,

Wow. When I said, "Any questions?" at the end of my previous email, it was what is known as a rhetorical question, as in one that doesn't need a response. Oh, well. Allow me to answer them in the order they were received.

  1) No, I'm not kidding.
  2) Yes, I'm serious.
  3) No, beer making is not a craft.
  4) The date of curriculum night is on the original email—just look.
  5) No, you can't be fired from a job you volunteered for.

Thank you for the feedback.

Jennifer

Max rounds the corner to the kitchen wearing an outfit that bears no resemblance to the one I picked out for him.

"Wow. Love the red pants. Aren't they part of a costume?"

"Yup. Pac-Man."

"And the purple top?"

"Nana gave it to me, remember?"

"I do. Are you sure you want to wear them together on the first day of school?"

"Ya. I want to stand out."

"Well, mission accomplished." I quietly thank the heavens that he didn't wear the matching Pac-Man hat.

Max smiles and takes a bite of his toast. Ever since he was old enough to pick out his own clothes, he has exhibited a, shall we say, *unique* taste in fashion. You never know what ensemble he is going to come up with. Sometimes I think he uses a blindfold and a dart to put his outfits together. I'd left him a pair of khakis and a white polo shirt on his bed in the hopes he would embrace his new school uniform, but I guess he didn't.

Ron comes in from his run all sweaty. I love him this way.

"Hey!" I grab his butt. "I need you ready to go in ten minutes if you want in on the first-day-of-school fun."

"I'm ready now." He grins and dashes up the stairs.

"Mom, what's my teacher's name, again?"

"Miss Ward."

"Is she nice?"

"I haven't met her yet, but she seems nice from her email."

"I hope she likes purple."

"Who doesn't?" I smile. "You know you have to start wearing the uniform tomorrow, right?"

He nods, his mouth full of toast.

"I'm going to pick you up at noon and we can go out for lunch anywhere you like."

"Can Dad come?"

"I don't think so. He needs to be at the Fitting Room." I'm referring to the sporting goods store Ron owns.

Before I can even yell, "What the hell is taking you so long?," my husband is showered and ready. It really must be nice to be a man. I'm not a very high-maintenance woman, but I do need more than six minutes to shower and look presentable.

"Who's ready for kinderga—"

Ron stops mid-word as he takes in what Max is wearing.

"Is that what you're wearing, Max?" he asks.

I give him a look across the kitchen table that says, "Don't be an asshole about this."

"Ya. I want to stand out."

"I thought there was a dress code." Ron looks at me.

"Not on the first day." I shoot him another warning look. They usually work. I must be misfiring. "And it's only a half day today, so let's get going!"

THE FIRST DAY OF SCHOOL. Yup, all caps, bold and italicized. That's how epic it is in my mind. Everyone is so clean and excited! Backpacks are fresh, sneakers are squeaky, and pencils are sharp. Take this same snapshot mid-November and it's a whole different story.

We make our way down the well-worn hallways of Vivs's and Laura's old stomping ground, William H. Taft Elementary School. When we get to room 147, we find the prettiest and preppiest person I have ever seen standing at the classroom door greeting people. She has long blond hair, which is kept back by a pink headband. She is wearing light-pink-checkered pants and a white blouse with ruffles. I hope she owns a smock.

As we approach, she hits us with a dazzling smile and holds out her hands.

"Is this Max? Oh, my goodness, Max, I have been so excited to meet you! Is that a new shirt? Purple is my favorite color!"

Well, color me impressed. Miss Ward is a real charmer. She has obviously studied the pictures we all sent in at the end of the summer. Max hasn't said a word, but wears the goofy smile of a man smitten. So does Ron when I look over at him.

"Hi, Miss Ward, so nice to meet you. I'm—"

"No, no!" Miss Ward interrupts me. "This is not about Max's

parents. It's all about Max today. Come on in and find your name on your desk, sweetie." She ushers Max into the room and he eagerly follows without a backward glance.

Ron and I look at each other. I shrug.

"It's all about Max."

As we head out of the school, Ron asks what I'm up to.

"I'm going to meet my new trainer."

He looks at me skeptically.

"I know what you're thinking, but after that debacle at your store I feel like I need to step up my workouts."

"Or, just, you know, start them." He smiles and gives my shoulder a squeeze.

Here's the thing. Ron's sporting goods store is one of the biggest in KC. A few months ago, they hosted a mini mud run to promote our governor's "Get Fit" initiative. When he mentioned that he needed participants, I volunteered. That was my first mistake. I thought I was in shape, thanks to my twice-weekly visits to our neighborhood Curves, which I had joined shortly after Max was born. So when I got to Ron's store that day and saw the course setup I was, like, "No problemo." That was my second mistake.

Let's just say that the upper-body strength you get from hauling a toddler around for a few years doesn't exactly prep you to climb a rope or swing from monkey bars or even drop to your belly and crawl through mud, although that was the easiest part.

It was weeks before I could show my face down at the store again. I mean, it's not great when the wife of the owner breaks down and cries because she can't get over the wall. Plus I was sore for days in areas I didn't know existed.

"Who'd you get to train you?" Ron asks when I don't acknowledge his dig. I can tell he is annoyed that I hadn't consulted him on the decision.

"Someone my mother recommended. He comes to your home and works you out. I figured I'd finally start using Ron's Gym and Tan." That's my nickname for the home gym Ron has set up in our basement.

Ron gives a fake gasp. "You mean you're going to give up Curves?" He's never been a fan. Ron's kind of a gym snob.

"See you later." I give him a sly smile and head to my minivan. "Hot new trainer's awaiting."

Ron frowns. "Hot? You didn't say he was hot."

I laugh as I open my car door. I actually have no idea what he looks like. But with a name like Garth, I have high hopes.

✦ ✦ ✦

My mom has actually told me very little about Garth, just that he used to be a trainer at the local Lucille Roberts gym. He had to stop for a while and is now getting back into it. He's very cheap for an in-home personal trainer—$30 an hour. I just hope this isn't a case of "You get what you pay for."

I pull up to the house and see a white Prius parked in my driveway. My new trainer is ten minutes early. Me likey. As I get out of my car, he does the same, and I get my first look at the man I will be spending two hours a week with.

I wish I could tell you that everything turned to slow motion and "Dream Weaver" started playing in my head as he whipped his hair around and flashed me a dazzling smile, but that would be lying.

Garth is about 5'6" and mostly bald, and he looks like he's in his midfifties. He reminds me a bit of the actor Michael Chiklis from *The Shield*.

As I rearrange my expectations in my head, he walks over and guess what? He *does* have a dazzling smile! It makes me like him immediately.

"Hi, Jennifer, I'm Garth." He shakes my hand and nearly crushes it.

"Ow. Hi, Garth. That's a good grip you've got there."

"Oh, good gravy, I'm sorry," he says and lightens up his vise grip immediately. "I always forget to take it down a notch for the girls."

"No problem. Clearly I need to toughen up a bit."

"Well, that's what I'm here for." He smiles and follows me to the front door.

"Can I get you something to drink?" I ask while throwing my purse on the hall table.

"Nope. Thanks. I always bring my own." He proudly holds up a gallon jug full of water. Clearly Garth is old school, and fancy water bottles are not his style.

"Umm, why don't I show you our workout area and then I'll run up and change."

"Sounds good." Garth smiles again. "After you, my good woman."

As I lead him down to the basement, I wonder just how old school he is. Not for nothing, but I've been at Curves for five years. That's some pretty advanced stuff.

Ron's Gym and Tan is located in a corner of our basement, right next to the laundry room. It consists of a treadmill, a bench press, free weights, a mat, and one of those big exercise balls.

"This is fantastic!" Garth declares, and it only takes me a second to realize he is not kidding.

"Really?" I ask. "Do we need any other equipment?"

"No. This is perfect. Why don't you get changed, and I'll lay out a workout plan." He actually sounds excited.

"Okay. I'll be right back."

As I run up the stairs to my bedroom, I wonder what I've gotten myself into.

✦ ✦ ✦

I'll admit I have a somewhat acerbic way of presenting myself, but I had no idea how many parents I could offend with just one email. Actually, it wasn't that many, but it only takes one to stir the pot. Nina calls me just as I am getting out of the shower after my workout.

"Oh, my God, what did you say in your class email?" she screams.

"Just the usual stuff. Why?" I toss my wet towel in the hamper and head toward my closet.

"I just got off the phone with Asami Chang and she is pi-issed!"

"About what?" I ask, rifling through my T-shirts.

"She says it was an inappropriate way to address kindergarten parents."

"So?"

"So, was it?"

"Probably. But I can't believe anyone took it seriously."

Nina sighs. "That's what I thought. But you know your, um . . . humor is sometimes lost on people. Asami wants you to step down as class mom and let her take over."

"Well, I think she is absolutely right. I am not fit to liaise with parents." I make a mental note to send Asami a basket of fruit.

"Not so fast, funny girl. You promised me you would do this."

"Yes, well, the people have spoken. I'm not wanted on the voyage."

"*I* want you on the voyage. I think it will be good for you to meet some people, and I know Max loves it."

"Ooooh. Good one, bringing Max into it. What about what's-her-name?"

"Asami Chang. I'll deal with her. So we're good?"

"Define 'good.'"

"And you'll tone down your emails?"

"Not a chance."

Nina laughs. "There's my girl. How was your new trainer?"

"Interesting," I say. "Different from Curves, that's for sure."

"Different, good, or different, bad?"

"Well, I certainly haven't done a burpee in a long time."

Nina cracks up. "A burpee? What the hell is that?"

"I'd really have to show you. One thing's for sure, my ass is going to be sore tomorrow."

"Well, that's a good thing. Okay, I gotta run. Remember, play nice with the parents!"

I hang up and pull on my jeans. I admire Nina for the way she successfully navigates both sides of the fence. She is the perfectly perfect ideal of what the PTA president should be, but she can also slum it with hoi polloi. She is this cute little five-foot-tall dynamo with skin the color of cappuccino and a very short Afro that she keeps threatening to take "native." She's like the bunny that never runs out of batteries. I don't know where she gets her energy. Being president of the PTA is not a job for sissies. It's a full-time, relentless piece of crap that very few people would want to inflict upon themselves. But year after year Nina manages to squeeze it into what I know is a full schedule running her graphic design business.

She and I met about ten years ago at a bicycle shop. It was so random. I was looking at cycling gloves and she was getting a new tire rim. A man walked into the store and announced to no one in particular that he had a loose nut. I swear to God, at the exact same moment we both said, "Well, you should see a doctor about that." And that was it, soul mates for life.

Nina is a single mom, but you'd never know it. She is totally on top of things and never complains about being alone although I can tell she still carries a torch for Sid, the father of her daughter, Chyna. He left her two weeks before Chyna was born and basically fell off the face of the earth, but she still hopes he will come back. I'm not sure I understand why because he sounds like a total skeeze. But the heart wants what it wants, so she has kept the candle burning for lo these twelve years. I've tried to set her up with a few guys—mostly customers from my hubby's sporting goods store—but no one has caught her fancy. I guess it's hard to measure up to the stellar example that was Sid.

Chyna is just like her mom—petite, dynamic, and full of shit. I can't wait till she's old enough to babysit for me.

We bonded as single moms, but even after I hooked up with Ron we stayed close. In fact, Vivs and Laura used to tag-team babysit for Chyna.

To: Parents

From: JDixon

Date: 9/18

Subject: curriculum night party

Hello, fellow parents,

Now that the awkwardness of last week's attempted coup on my class mom fiefdom is behind us (no hard feelings, Asami; I understand your people's need for power), let's get on to some serious business, like who is bringing the wine.

September 27th (aka curriculum night) is fast upon us. It's my favorite night of the year, because it answers burning questions such as "Who has the hottest husband?" and "Who spent a little too much money at the ice cream truck this summer?" Plus, I want everyone to think that Miss Ward's class is the place where people PAR-TAY! To that end, we need some provisions.

2 kegs (I'll bring the funnel)
Jell-O shots (lime and cherry, please!)
"Special" brownies—Wolffe family, I'm counting on you for these.

If you're still reading and haven't yet speed-dialed Principal Jakowski, here are a few other things we MAY need.

Mini quiches (the microwavable kind)
Small cheese platter
Small veggie platter
Yummy cookies or brownies
Cups, small plates, cocktail napkins
Sparkling and flat water
Red and white wine

The phone lines are now open, so run, don't walk, to your keyboard and volunteer to bring something. Don't be shy!

Thanks in advance for what I'm sure will be an overwhelming heed to the call. Response times will be noted.

Jennifer

✦ ✦ ✦

Just as I close my laptop, my two favorite men come in the back door.

"Mom! The tent is up!" Max yells even though I am sitting right there.

"Already? Wow. Are you guys sure you want to do this?" My question is really for Ron—he's the one with the fifty-year-old spine.

"Camping out is a time-honored tradition among Dixon men," my husband says.

Max nods solemnly. I know he is all in on this camping adventure, but it's hard to take him seriously when he's wearing a sombrero and poncho.

"And besides," Ron adds, "we have the Kodiak Canvas Flex-Bow Deluxe out there. We could go to base camp with that baby, right, buddy?"

I roll my eyes. I know it's what he does for a living, but I still can't believe how jacked up Ron gets about any type of sports gear. Max, on the other hand, is putting on his game face. He's not really an outdoor sporty kind of kid, but he's trying to be one for his dad's sake. I worry about that sometimes. They are planning to camp out in the backyard this Friday.

I shrug. "Okay. Just don't be surprised if it's a bit chilly out there. You guys should have done this in August."

"August, Shmaugust," Ron scoffs. "We're Dixon men. Besides, we'll be sleeping in the Nemo Nocturne 15." He looks to me for a reaction, but I really don't have one.

"Well, I'll leave the back door open that night, just in case." I wink at my boy. I'm not sure, but I think he looks relieved.

To: JDixon

From: Sasha Lewicki

Date: 9/18

Subject: curriculum night party

I am out of the office until September 20.

Thank you,

Sasha

To: JDixon

From: Shirleen Cobb

Date: 9/19

Subject: curriculum night party

Dear Jennifer,

You didn't mention anything about food allergies. My son, Graydon Cobb, is VERY allergic to peanuts, dairy, wheat, grass, wheatgrass, chocolate, and airborne dust. Please don't allow any of these things in the classroom.

Shirleen Cobb

To: Shirleen Cobb
From: JDixon
Date: 9/19
Subject: curriculum night

Dear Shirleen,

Since curriculum night is for parents only, I wasn't going to worry about food allergies, but from your note I can see that Graydon's situation is very serious and he could hive up at any moment. Just how big is the bubble he comes to school in?

Jennifer

Why, oh why, is it always the mother with the most allergic kid who is, herself, a nut? I mean, I get it, allergies are serious. Life-threatening, even. They're nothing to joke about. But when did this all happen? When did peanut butter become the grade-school equivalent of anthrax? When I was in second grade, I sat beside a kid named Alan Ervine who smelled like peanut butter all the time. I'm convinced he dabbed it behind his ears like cologne. No one in our classroom had a problem with it. The banishing of PB is a problem for us because PBJ sandwiches are the only ones Max will eat. In the name of peanut butter, someone needs to figure this thing out. I would, but you know how busy I am being class mom.

To: Parents
From: JDixon
Date: 9/21
Subject: Hello? Did anyone read my last email?

Dear Miss Ward's class,

Shocked? Appalled? No, "disappointed" best describes my feelings after the less than adequate response to my call for help. Only two people got back to me. Sasha Lewicki, sending an out-of-office autoreply, was the first, with an impressive turnaround time of 11 seconds. And Jackie Westman stopped me in the parking lot to say she'd bring cups. Listen, people, we are going to be in that classroom for TWO HOURS. Don't you think we're at least going to need water, to say nothing of alcohol? So get your fingers on the keyboard and start volunteering to bring stuff pronto.

Geez!
Jennifer

P.S. Response times will be noted.

I click Send. This is the part of being class mom I hate the most—begging people to do stuff for the classroom. Everyone always thinks someone else is going to volunteer, and the class mom gets stuck with all of it.

"Well, not this time, my little kindergarten parenteers," I say to my reflection in the computer screen. "This is the year I shame you all into participating. Mwa ha ha!"

"Are you talking to yourself again?"

I jumped at the unexpected sound of my husband's voice.

"What are you doing here? I thought the Dixon men were going to tough it out in the backyard."

"We were until a squirrel jumped on top of the tent. Max freaked out, so I brought him in."

I could see Ron's disappointment.

"He's in his bed?"

"Fast asleep. And look at us. Ten p.m., and nothing to do."

He saunters over to where I'm sitting on the bed with my computer.

"Who says I have nothing to do?"

Ron takes my computer and puts it on the dresser.

"I do," he says as he leans in for a kiss. "I want to see what Garth's thirty bucks an hour is getting me."

"Well, not much yet except for a bag of sore muscles." I dodge his kiss and roll to the other side of the bed. Ron follows me.

"What are you doing?" I ask.

"What does it look like?" He stalks me across the bed.

"It looks like you're not getting the hint," I snipe back.

He sits up with a mix of hurt and curiosity on his face.

"What's wrong?"

That's actually a good question. My handsome husband wants to have sex with me and I'm being kind of a bitch. But here's the thing. I was really looking forward to this night. I adore Ron, but sometimes it's nice to have a little break. I was so juiced up to be all alone in our Cali-king bed—no one beside me snoring or stealing the blankets. And now it's not happening and I'm pissed off. No, I'm disappointed, but it reads the same as pissed off sometimes.

"I just wasn't expecting you, that's all." I know my explanation is weak.

"You weren't *expecting* me?" He pushes himself off the bed. "Would you rather I go back out to the tent?"

Well, actually I would, I think but do not say. Instead, I get up and walk to the door.

"I'm going to check on Max."

As I leave, even I am wondering where the hell that all came from.

To: Parents
From: JDixon
Date: 9/23
Subject: Well done

Dear Miss Ward's class,

Thank you so much for finally responding to my call for help. Who knew so many of you have "special" brownie recipes?

Okay, this is how it is going to shake out.

Mini quiches—Dixons, Elders
Cheese platter—Changs (please include crackers)
Veggie platter—Wolffes
Wine—Batons (who are French so we're expecting some good stuff)
Cookies—Kaplans
Sparkling and flat water—Zalis
Brownies—Fancys
Plates/napkins—Aikenses
Cups—Westmans
The rest of you are off the hook for this party but don't suppose a slow

response time is going to get you out of supplying snacks at some point.

Please drop everything off BEFORE 6:30 on curriculum night. Miss Ward wants it all out before her presentation starts.

Okay. That's it. Move along.

xo

P.S. Response times were weak, people, WEAK! I'm not going to embarrass everyone by posting them THIS TIME. Just know I'm keeping a list. A list you really don't want to be on.

✦ ✦ ✦

I look at my watch and realize I have exactly four minutes until Garth is ten minutes early for our workout. I like how consistent he is. As I turn to get my workout clothes on, I'm reminded of how hard he worked me in our last session. Everything hurts just a little bit. Not enough to debilitate me, but enough that I'm aware of what my body has been doing. It's as though Curves never even happened for me! I intend to write them a strongly worded letter about their false promises.

I'm a little on edge, because tonight is parents' night at school. It's my first face-to-face as class mom, and I'm nervous. I know I've done it before, but this time it's different. This time I actually give a crap what the other parents think of me. Don't ask me why, but I do. Oh, to once again be twenty-six and so full of your own sense of what is right that you can give a virtual finger to the establishment.

The doorbell interrupts my thoughts and I run down to let Garth in.

✦ ✦ ✦

"What has gotten into you today?" Garth enthuses as I complete yet another set of burpees.

I shrug. "Nervous energy, I guess." I'm really in a zone.

"What are you nervous about?"

"It's curriculum night at my son's school."

"So?" says Garth. Clearly he has never been to one.

"Well . . ." I start.

"Tell me while you're doing crunches," Garth suggests.

I get down on the mat on my back. Garth is sitting on the big exercise ball. I start to do my ab work.

"It's just that I sent out an email at the start of the school year and it was supposed to be funny but I guess it confused and offended some people. Things like that didn't used to bother me but now they do." I'm basically grunting out my explanation as I crunch my core.

"Eighteen, nineteen, twenty. Okay, rest. Why does it bother you now?" Garth asks from the ball.

I lie there and think for a minute. "Well, I guess—"

"Tell your story crunching," he interrupts.

"Jesus, okay!" I grunt. "I guess I care more now because of Ron. When Vivs and Laura were small and I was a single mom, I think I felt I had something to prove. I was also young and stupid." I flop to my back.

"One more set, but take thirty," Garth says.

I roll on my side and look up at him.

"I realize now that the things I do and say and *write* have a direct reflection on Ron and Max, too. I didn't really think about Vivs and Laura when I was waging war against the world. But I'm starting to see why they were always upset with me."

"Sounds like you're growing up," Garth says, with more than a bit of wisdom in his words.

"About time, I guess." I smile and start crunching.

4

I am just finishing printing out the class lists I'm going to hand out at curriculum night when I get the call.

"Mrs. Dixon?"

"Hey, Ashley. Are you on your way?"

"I can't babysit tonight. My mom says I need to focus on school work and that you should just get over it."

I roll my eyes. Gotta love Ashley. She is the most inappropriate babysitter ever. Reminds me of me.

"Uh, kinda leavin' me hanging tonight, girlie. We have something at Max's school."

"Yeah, I know, but my mom told me to tell you I'm sick. Wait, I think I was supposed to say that first."

"Okay, well, you tell your mom I said thanks."

"Okay, bye."

Damn. Ashley is so good with Max. Too bad I'm going to have to fire her seventeen-year-old ass.

"*Ron!*"

"Jesus, what? I'm right here."

Things have been a little tense with us since the camping-out night. I can tell he's still waiting for some kind of explanation. I'm still waiting to think of one.

"Ashley just canceled, so one of us has to stay home. I vote for me."

"And I vote for me," Ron countered. "And I know somewhere in the prenup we established that a tie goes to me."

I want to argue, but I know he's right. As class mom, I have to be there to press the flesh, kiss some babies, and talk about world peace. Oh, wait, that's POTUS. I just have to be there.

"Max!"

"Mommy, I'm right here. Why are you yelling?" He is standing behind me wearing a pirate hat and a feather boa.

"Sorry, just a habit. Ashley is sick or doing her homework or something, so Dad is going to stay home with you while I go meet your teacher."

"Okay. Can I watch TV?"

"I'd say your chances are pretty good."

"Yes! Say hi to Miss Ward for me. I love her."

"You do?"

"Yup."

"Okay, then."

I kiss Max five times, grab the two platters of mini quiches I said I would bring, and head out the door.

✦ ✦ ✦

Miss Ward's classroom must be seen to be believed. Think Pee-wee's Playhouse and then vomit Disney crap all over it. There isn't one inch of space that isn't covered in colorful, um, stuff.

I almost don't recognize Miss Ward, who is sitting on her desk putting on lipstick. She is wearing a purple leather miniskirt and a pink low-cut V-neck sweater that couldn't possibly be any tighter. Her blond hair is in a messy ponytail. The best part of her getup is the thigh-high black boots. They're not quite stilettos, but they make her look like a life-sized Bratz doll.

As I approach her I can't help but wonder what happened to Sister Mary Perfect.

"Hi, Miss Ward."

She leaps up and hugs me.

"Jenny! I'm so happy you're here! Are those mini quiches? Yum. What time is everyone coming? I've been ready for an hour."

"They should be here any minute." I put my trays on a table next to an impressive platter of sushi. "Wow, did you bring this?" I ask, a bit too loudly

"No. Nadine Lewicki's mom sent it. Wasn't that sweet of her?"

"Very." I'm actually impressed. I didn't think Sasha read my emails, what with all the out-of-office replies. Not that I asked for sushi, but still.

"Max says Nadine has never been in class. Is she okay?"

Miss Ward seems taken aback by the question.

"Well, it's not something I can really talk about. But her mom and I are in close contact."

"It seems like her mom works a lot. Oh, by the way, Max wanted me to tell you hello. He says he loves—"

"Um . . . Jenny?" Miss Ward suddenly has the "I'm the teacher, take me seriously" look on her face. "Can you just respect that tonight is a getting-to-know-you party and not the time to get into personal issues about your child?"

I open my mouth and close it again. I am speechless, and believe me when I tell you that does not happen often. But it wasn't until that moment that I noticed the crazy eyes. Miss Ward has crazy eyes. I recognize them from Ron's ex-wife, Cindy. It doesn't make her a bad person, but it's definitely noteworthy.

"I'm sorry. You're right. I'll save my thoughts for conference day."

At this point, other parents start to trickle in and I get busy playing hostess.

"Are you the class mom?" a breathy voice from behind me demands.

I turn, and a large woman with short red hair is standing there, huffing and puffing like she's just run from the parking lot. She is wearing an orange ribbed sweater and a brown skirt. Pinned to her sweater is a big button that says, "It's No Joke."

"Yes, hi, I'm Jennifer Dixon, and you must be Shirleen Cobb."

She looks shocked. "How did you know?"

"The pin. Allergies. 'It's no joke,'" I say solemnly.

"Well, exactly. That's what I want to talk to you about. I think you need to—"

Thankfully, I am saved from finding out what I "need" to do by another parent, this one asking me where to put the brownies. I excuse myself from Shirleen and show a skinny blonde dressed all in black where to put her goodies.

And so it begins, my first evening with my fellow kindergarten parents. I am definitely the most, shall we say, marinated of the group. Most of the couples look to be in their early thirties.

As I scan the room, I notice a really tall couple over by the birthday calendar. I think it's nice when tall people find each other. Short people, too, although I feel sorry for their kids because, let's face it, they don't have a shot. I see the blond woman with the brownies talking to another woman also dressed entirely in black, their heads bent together as they take in Miss Ward's ensemble. The two men at their sides must be their husbands. One of them is very good looking. Hmm . . . I notice he's checking out Miss Ward, too. The other husband seems to be picking wax out of his ear.

Across the room, a couple is looking at the turtle tank. They have their backs to me, and I can't help but notice that the guy sure can fill out a pair of jeans nicely. As I'm admiring his butt, he turns around and I get a look at his face. *Ho-ly shit!* Goose bumps spread across my body as I recognize him. Don Burgess. *He's such a fox.* The words come to my head before I can stop them, because back in high school you never heard one without the other. "Don Burgess he's such a fox." It's like it was his full name. Today it would be a hashtag. #donbur gesshessuchafox.

Every high school has a Don Burgess—the one guy that every girl wants to be with and every guy wants to be. But Don took his coolness to another level. It was effortless. His jeans never looked new, but never looked old, either. He drove a lime green Dodge Charger and brushed his hair with his fingers. Best of all, he was sooo rock 'n' roll. Not in a skeezy way, just a super-cool way. The permanent expression on his face let you know he was in on some cosmic joke that you would never be groovy enough to understand. If he smiled at you in the hallway, it was as though the angels had come down from heaven for that brief moment and filled you with light. If he *talked* to you, forget it. The first time for me was junior year, when he bumped into me in the cafeteria and said, "Whoops! Sorry, Jen." I felt as though I'd been hit by a truck. *He knew my name!* You'd think he had asked me to prom by the way I reacted. I was high on life for a week.

"Don't I know you?"

I look up and he is standing right in front of me—dirty blond hair, green eyes, and just the right amount of stubble. Holy crap. Why does age look so damn good on some men?

I let out a nervous giggle, like the total tool that I am.

"Hey, Don, it's me, Jen Burgess. Uh. I mean, Jen Howard." I can't even imagine how many shades of purple I am right now.

"Jen! No freakin' way!"

I giggle again and attempt to moderate my pulse.

"Wow. You grew up gorgeous!"

He leans in to give me a hug, and a whiff of Polo by Ralph Lauren immediately transports me back to the hallways of East High. That was his scent, and it always lingered for a good thirty seconds after he had passed by. Now it was on my clothes. The normal me would be thinking how weird/pathetic it is that he still wears his high school cologne, but clearly normal me is nowhere to be seen. I back away and take a stab at acting cool.

"Do you have a child in this class?" I find asking the obvious is always nice.

"Yep. Lulu. Who's yours?"

"Max." I start looking around to see if anyone is watching me talk to Don Burgess (*he's such a fox*). Like anyone would care.

"So, are you married?"

"I am. My husband's at home with Max. Our babysitter canceled on us so I had to come alone. But he totally would have been here." *Shut up, diarrhea mouth,* I think to myself.

"Cool. Ali—that's Ali over there." He points to the woman still looking at the turtles. She waves.

"We're not married, but we co-parent Lulu. It works, I guess." He shrugs and gives me his trademark Don Burgess *he's such a fox* smile.

I feel dizzy, like I've been out in the sun for too long. I realize I'd better keep moving; otherwise, I risk making a complete fool of myself.

"Well, I'm paid to mingle . . ." I say, and start to walk away.

"Hey remember the P.E. laundry room?"

Of course I remember the P.E. laundry room! I want to scream, but instead I respond with that witty giggle I have recently adopted and, get this . . . *a thumbs-up.* Could I be any dorkier?

I get back to the job at hand and leave my high school crush to charm someone else. I glance around, and over by the book nook I notice a shortish woman with mousy brown hair and a guy who is a total hunk. They can't be together. I don't want to generalize, but let's face it, hot goes with hot, average goes with average, and so on down the line unless there is a large amount of money involved. But that would mean *she* has the money. I wonder if that's why Miss Ward is all tarted up tonight. Between Don Burgess and this guy, my time would have been well spent putting on some lipstick.

After Miss Ward's presentation about all the "super-fun" things the kids are going to learn this year, it is time for me to give my spiel. I stand up on a chair for maximum effect.

"Hi, everyone. I'm Jennifer Dixon, your class mom. Perhaps you have seen my emails?" I smile at the hunk, but notice that he's holding hands with his Mrs. She must be loaded. Don is standing behind him and gives *me* a thumbs-up.

As I continue, I get a few grins, but mostly blank stares, plus one toxic glare from Asami Chang. Tough room. Luckily I was planning to make my remarks brief. I'm much braver in writing than I am in person.

"I have brought copies of the class list for everyone. I also sent it to you in a PDF. If you have any questions, you can always call or email me. All my contact information is at the bottom."

At this point, I look up and see Nina walk in, wearing a megawatt smile and a fabulous aqua blouse that really brings out the blue in her eyes. I feel like I need to end with a bang to impress the woman who put me in this power position, so I add, "Here's to a great year!"

As everyone turns to the refreshment table, Nina walks over.

"Way to whip them into a frenzy."

"Yeah, well, I'm better in print."

"Have you made any friends yet?"

"Shirleen Cobb and I had a moment."

"Ah, the allergy mom."

"And, oh my God!" I drop my voice to a whisper. "The hottest guy in my high school is a parent in this class! I just made a total idiot of myself talking to him."

"Which one is he?" She looks around. "That guy?" She motions toward the guy with the rich wife.

"No. He's over by the food. Dirty blond hair and jeans."

Nina spots him and raises her eyebrows in approval.

"Not my flavor, but he's pretty damn cute."

"Are you kidding me? He's totally hot."

She shrugs. "I can see how he would have been gorgeous in high school."

For some reason, this irritates the crap out of me.

"Shouldn't you be bothering your own classroom instead of checking on mine?"

Nina laughs. "Nope. It's my job as PTA president to visit everyone. Oooh! Is that sushi? Nice touch." She makes a beeline for the California rolls.

As she leaves, the two women in black approach me minus their husbands. They both have long straight hair and are dressed in turtleneck sweaters, black jeans, and over-the-knee boots. They are both as skinny as I believe a woman can be and still be called a woman. Their only difference is one is about six inches taller than the other, and one is blond, the other brunette. In my head I immediately dub them Dr. Evil and Mini-Me. Dr. Evil speaks first.

"Hi, I'm Kim Fancy, Nancy's mom."

Seriously, her daughter is Nancy Fancy. Who would do that?

"Hi, Kim. I think Nancy and Max sit at the same table."

"Oh, really? Nancy never said anything."

"Well, neither did Max, but their names are on their seats."

I turn to Mini-Me.

"I'm Jen."

"I'm Kit's mom, JJ Aikens."

"O-KK," I joke. Nothing. Mini-Me just stares.

"When are you planning the parent cocktail night?" she asks.

"Sorry? The what?"

Dr. Evil looks at me like I have two heads.

"Every year the class mom organizes a cocktail party so the parents can get to know each other."

"Really? Is that new?"

"Uh, no," Mini-Me says condescendingly. "We started it in preschool."

"Well, okay. I'll start thinking about it." In my head I'm counting the ways I'm going to exact my revenge on Nina. Mini-Me interrupts my thoughts.

"We both have really busy schedules, so the sooner you can pick a date, the better."

"Okay. Good to know."

"Can't wait!" Dr. Evil says, and they both smile and walk away. I make a mental note to get the backstory on them.

I turn away, looking to rip Nina a new one, when I bump into the extremely tall couple.

"Hi, Jen? I'm Peetsa and this is my husband, Buddy."

"Pizza?"

"Yup. Just like the food. We're Zach Tucci's parents."

"Oh, my gosh, Max talks about Zach T. all the time."

"Same here," Buddy says, and then he blushes. "I mean, Zach talks about Max."

I think I like these two despite their intimidating height. Buddy has jet black hair that he wears brushed back, dark eyes, and a nose that might just be a little too small for his face. Peetsa can only be described as a classic Italian beauty. Think Sophia Loren, but with smaller boobs and lips.

"We should set up a play date," I suggest.

"Your place or mine?" Buddy says, and immediately blushes again. Oh, jeez, this guy is going to be fun to tease.

Peetsa rolls her eyes. "He means we'd be happy to host. By the way, we love your emails. It's the first time I've ever laughed out loud reading something from a class mom."

"Thanks. I try to have fun with them. I'll host the play date. Max just got a remote-control helicopter and he's dying to show someone."

"Is Max your only child?" Peetsa asks me.

"No, I have two older daughters."

"Oh, do they go here?"

"Well, they used to. Do you have any besides Zach?"

"Our daughter Stephanie is in sixth grade. Kinda crazy how long we waited between kids, huh?"

I decide to hold off telling her just how not crazy six years between kids sounds to me.

"I'll call you tomorrow to set up a play date. By the way"—she leans in to me—"is it me, or does our teacher look like a hooker?"

It's official. I love this woman.

"Maybe she has a paying gig after this?" I offer.

"Buddy can't take his eyes off that sweater."

"What?" Buddy blushes. "It's a nice color."

Peetsa laughs and pulls him away.

I turn to grab something to eat, and bump into two women, one tall with short blond hair and the other even taller with *really* short brown hair, scoping out the brownies. Encouraged by my last parent encounter, I put on my friendly face and say hello.

"Hi. I'm Jen."

They both smile.

"Hi, I'm Carol, Hunter's mom," says Blondie.

"And I'm Kim, Hunter's other mom," says Short Brown Hair.

I don't know why, but the two-mommy thing takes me by surprise. Unfortunately, when that happens, my ability to rebound isn't stellar. I start to babble.

"Oh, wow! How great. Good for you! We should have a play date. Does Hunter like helicopters? Or do you guys try to keep him away from gender-specific toys?"

SHUT UP! SHUT UP! SHUT UP! I scream in my head. Boy, this night is one for the record books.

They look at each other and start laughing.

"Breathe, Jen," says Kim . . . or Carol. I've already forgotten who is who. "We know you're cooler than this. Unless someone else writes your emails."

"Sorry." I blush. "I *am* cooler than this!"

"Want to tell us how some of your best friends are gay?" asks Kim or Carol with a smile. I start to laugh.

"Yes, thanks. That was next on my list of stupid things to say."

"Don't worry. We've heard worse. But a play date sounds good. Should we email you?"

"That would be great. See you later and again, I'm sorry."

As they walk away, the blond one says loudly: "What's that you say, Jen? You had a lesbian experience in college? How wonderful!"

Nina sidles up to me. I'm actually sweating now.

"Look at you, making friends," she coos, as only Nina can.

"Oh, my God. Why didn't you walk over here two minutes ago?"

"And miss the train wreck that was you meeting Hunter's two mommies? No way."

I shake my head, trying to push the whole thing out of my mind. I turn to Nina.

"Hey, what can you tell me about the turtleneck twins over there?" I nod toward the book nook, where Dr. Evil and Mini-Me are pretending to look at *Wild About Books* while obviously assessing every parent in the room, kind of like I'm doing.

Nina rolls her eyes and picks a sesame seed out of her teeth.

"Well, the taller one, Kim, moved here two years ago from New York—or *Manhattan,* as she always calls it just in case we think she means any other part of New York."

"Someone should tell her there's a Manhattan, Kansas. That'll shut her up."

Nina laughs. "The shorter one is JJ Aikens—I've known her for years. She used to be seminormal, but ever since Kim turned up all she wants to be is another Kim. I think she's even convinced herself that she's from New York, too."

"You mean *Manhattan,*" I correct her.

"Sure I do."

"Well, that explains a thing or two. Kim's husband was checking out Miss Ward."

"Oh, hell, Jen, who wasn't? I haven't had sex in so long, Miss Ward is looking good to *me.*"

"Do you know that tall couple?" I ask her.

"Peetsa and Buddy? Sure. Their daughter and Chyna have been in the same class on and off for years."

I am about to say something, but Miss Ward is waving an empty garbage bag at me, which I guess is her way of asking me to start cleaning up.

Nina sighs. "Well, I'm off to Mr. Greely's class to check in. No sushi there, I can promise you that."

As I'm grabbing cups and plates, I find myself glancing around the room, looking for Don Burgess. Our eyes meet over the large recycling bin.

"Hey, are you trying to take my job away?" There's that smile again.

"Sorry?" This time I manage to suppress the giggle.

"Waste management. That's what I do." He hands me some used napkins to put in my trash bag.

"Really? That's . . ." I stop because I don't know what to say. *That's interesting? That's cool? That's disappointing?* Who knew Suchafox would end up a garbageman?

"I know." He laughs at the look on my face. "It's not what you'd think I'd be doing, but there's a lot of money in garbage."

"Well, that's great. Good for you. Helping to keep KC clean."

"I do what I can," he says. As he walks away, he turns back to me and says the last thing I thought I would ever hear Don Burgess say:

"Don't forget to recycle those cups!"

✦ ✦ ✦

When I get home that night, I find Max and Ron in our bed, both fast asleep. Max is wearing his Spider-Man costume as pajamas, of course. As I pick him up, I realize he's almost too big to carry, and my heart hurts a little bit. I remember when the girls got too heavy for me. It's just one more step away from you that they take without even knowing it. As I lay him down in his race-car bed, I put my nose into his hair and take a deep breath. He never lets me do that when he's awake.

I sit down on the bed and look around Max's room. A stranger would think that two completely different children share it. One is a diehard sports fan, evidenced by all the posters of Chiefs and Royals superstars papering the walls. The other is a techie/wizard fan who has a flair for fashion, shown through all the gadgets and drawings littered about.

When I get back to the bedroom, Ron is sitting up, squinting at his iPad.

"How'd it go?" he asks.

"It was a real barn burner. You would have loved it."

"Really?"

"No." I stretch out on the bed. "What did you guys do?"

"We had hot dogs and watched hockey on ESPN Classics in bed. Perfect manly-man night."

"For our perfectly unmanly little boy," I add.

"He loved it."

"Ron, please stop trying to make him love sports. If he does, he does. If he doesn't, it's not the end of the world."

"I'm just trying to show him all the options. I've given up on football and soccer, but I have high hopes for hockey."

I shake my head.

"You know that kid Zach T. he always talks about?"

Ron shrugs. "The one he ate lunch with that day?"

"No, that's Zach B."

"The one he says picks his nose?"

"No, that's Zach E. Zach T. is the one who is really into gadgets. I met his parents tonight. They seem like nice people."

Ron gasps. "Don't tell me you actually met someone you like!"

"Ha, ha. Their names are Peetsa and Buddy."

"Pizza?"

"Just like the food."

"God, can you imagine going through high school with that name? 'Hey, Pizza! Can I have a slice?' I would have tortured that poor girl."

"I'm sure she's heard them all."

I'm about to tell him about Don Burgess *he's such a fox* when the phone rings. I roll onto my side to answer it.

"Hello."

"Hi, Mom." It's my older daughter.

"Hey, Vivs. What's up, baby?"

"Not much."

"How's school?"

"Good."

Vivs is my show pony. She came out of the womb just knowing the right thing to say and do, which is pretty much a miracle considering Michael Hutchence and I were less than stable people at the time of conception. There were a couple of dark years during puberty when Vivs thought she was Marilyn Manson and, I'm not going to lie, I was terrified of her. But we got through it. Currently she is a junior at KU, majoring in human ecology, whatever the hell that is.

"What's going on?"

"Nothing."

"Jesus, Vivs, really? Do I have to drag it out of you? What's up? Do you need money?"

"Mom! No. I just called to say hi. Jeez. Why so bitchy?"

"Sorry. I just got back from curriculum night at Max's school." Vivs laughs. She knows how much I hate school functions.

"How's he doing?"

"He's good, but I think Ron traumatized him tonight by making him watch a hockey game."

"He loved it!" Ron yells.

"Still on the sports thing, huh?"

"Yeah." I sigh. "How is Raj?"

"He's okay."

Raj is Vivs's on-again off-again boyfriend. I can't really get a handle on what their problem is but they seem to break up and make up an awful lot. Ron and I really like him. He's an engineering major at KU, which means he will actually leave school with a useful degree, which is more than I can say for either of my daughters.

"Have you heard from Laura?" she asks.

"Not for a couple of days. You?"

"Yeah, I had lunch with her today. She's freaking out because she was snapped making out with two different guys on the same night. Someone posted the pictures on Instagram and now she looks like the campus slut. She didn't call you?"

"Oh, my God. No, she didn't."

Ron raises an eyebrow at me.

"I'll call her tomorrow."

"Don't tell her I said anything."

"I won't. Thanks for giving me a heads-up."

"K. Love you."

"Love you too, baby." I hang up.

"Oh, my God!"

"What happened?" Ron asks.

"I guess Laura's taking a page out of her old mom's handbook." I can't help but smile.

"What, is she pregnant?"

"Nooo, that comes *after* college. Haven't you been paying attention?"

"Obviously not."

I roll on my side to face him.

"It seems she made out with two different guys at a party and someone took pictures and posted them on Instagram."

"Our Laura? Didn't-have-a date-until-she-was-seventeen Laura?"

"The very same. Poor baby. Vivs says she's freaking. I'll call her tomorrow."

5

To: Parents
From: JDixon
Date: 10/25
Subject: Parent/teacher conferences

Hello, fellow parents!

Ever wondered what Miss Ward really thinks of your child? Oh, I know it's all smiles and compliments on curriculum night, but prepare yourselves for brutal honesty as we sally forth into parent/teacher conference season.

And best of all, I'M IN CHARGE OF THE SCHEDULE! Oh, I'm just drunk on the power I have now! Who wants the coveted 12:30 Thursday spot that allows you to take a long weekend? Cuz there's a super-cute coat sitting in the window at Macy's with my name on it . . . first person to get that for me wins their pick of times.

OR we could do it the old-fashioned way and have you email me 2 times that work for you from the list below and I will "try my best" (wink) to accommodate you.

Thursday, Nov. 17, p.m.

12:30, 1:00, 1:30, 2:00, 2:30, 3:00, 3:30

Friday, Nov. 18, a.m.

8:00, 8:30, 9:00, 9:30, 10:30, 11:00, 11:30, 1:00, 1:30

Let me know as soon as you can, so I can get on with my life. Early birds will be rewarded with primo spots.

Dixon out!

To: JDixon

From: Sasha Lewicki

Date: 10/25

Subject: Parent/teacher conferences

I am out of the office until October 27.

Thank you,

Sasha

To: Jen Dixon

From: Carol Alexander

Date: 10/25

Subject: Parent/teacher conferences

Hi, Jen,

Any time on Thursday works for us. Kim and I have a big lesbian conference to go to on Friday. Want to come with us? The theme this year is Dykes or Bikes: Which Would You Rather Ride?

Kidding, of course. Except for the part about any time on Thursday.

Thanks,

Carol

To: Jen Dixon
From: Jill Kaplan
Date: 10/25
Subject: Parent/teacher conferences

Hi, Jen,

I'm Rachel Kaplan's mother. I'm so sorry I didn't say hello at curriculum night, but I wasn't feeling very social. My asshat of a husband wouldn't come with me and I was too pissed to be friendly to anyone.

    Anyhoo, I will take any time Friday morning. God knows Steve doesn't care. He thinks it's women's work to meet the teacher. You may wonder why we even had a kid if he isn't going to participate. I ask myself that all the time.

    Let's have coffee sometime!

Jill

To: JDixon
From: AGordon
Date: 10/25
Subject: Parent/teacher conferences

Dear Jen,

I missed meeting you on curriculum night, but Don mentioned that he spoke with you. Did you really know each other in high school? Small world. I'm not sure if he has responded to this email, but I'm pretty sure we are good for any time after 12:30 on Friday. That's when we usually do the handoff.

Thanks,
Ali Gordon

Huh. It seems Don and his baby mama don't live together. He said they were co-parenting Lulu. I guess they're divorced.

To: JDixon
From: JJ Aikens
Date: 10/25
Subject: Parent/teacher conferences

Hi,

There is only one option for us and that's 12:30 on the 18th. Sorry. No flexibility whatsoever.

Thanks,
JJ

To: JDixon
From: Kim Fancy (Nancy's mom)
Date: 10/25
Subject: Parent/teacher conferences

Hi, Jen,

We have scheduled a trip back to Manhattan, so we have to go first on Thursday. We absolutely must make our flight in order to be at Lincoln Center for the ballet Thursday night.

Thank you,
Kim

To: JDixon
From: Asami Chang
Date: 10/25
Subject: Parent/teacher conferences

Jennifer,

We will take the first spot on Thursday—12:30. And I won't be buying you a coat for it, I can assure you. I have notified the head of the Parents' Association that you are soliciting bribes.

Asami

To: JDixon
From: Peetsa Tucci
Date: 10/25
Subject: Parent/teacher conferences

Hi Jen,

Thanks again for the play date. Zach had a great time. I think a remote-control helicopter is definitely on his Christmas list now!
    As for the conferences, we are around, so plug us in anywhere.
    See you for trick-or-treating.

Peetsa
xo

Peetsa's email makes me realize that I haven't heard from Miss Ward about having a Halloween party in the classroom. Max is crazy about dressing up and has been planning for weeks to wear his costume to school that day.

To: Miss Ward
From: JDixon
Date: 10/25
Subject: Halloween party???

Hi, Miss Ward,

I know you're busy, but I never heard from you about planning a Halloween party for the kids. Do you want me to pull something together?

Thanks,
Jennifer

Much to my surprise, her response is almost immediate.

To: JDixon
From: PWard
Date: 10/25
Subject: Halloween party???

Hi, Jenny,

I didn't see a request from you, but just so you know, I only have parties when I think the kids deserve them—not because Hallmark tells me it's a holiday.

> *By the way, when will you have my conference schedule ready?*
> *Keep up the good work!*

Peggy

Well what do you know. Miss Ward is able to come up with the one answer I would have never thought of.

I start tackling the conference schedule almost immediately. I knew that first slot on Thursday would be a popular one, because there's no school the next day: It's a great opportunity to take a long weekend somewhere. I have three people who insist that it is imperative they have it, so obviously none of them is getting it. I know, I'm a bitch. If any of them had asked for the spot instead of *demanded* it, it would have been theirs. As my mother always says, *ask* me to do anything. Don't *tell* me to do anything. As I type, I count the number of enemies I'm about to make. Ah, heavy is the head that wears the crown.

To: JDixon
From: NGrandish
Date: 10/27
Subject: Threats and bribes

Jen,

I've heard thru the grapevine that you are asking for a coat in exchange for a preferred conference time. Please don't do this. Go for something smaller, like jewelry or maybe a watch. The evidence is easier to hide.

Kisses,
Nina

To: Parents

From: JDixon

Date: 10/30

Subject: Parent/teacher conference schedule

Hi, folks,

If you've ever seen The Hunger Games, *you'll have an idea of what I went through trying to make everyone happy with these conference times.*

Here is how it shook out. If you don't like what you get, well, good luck finding someone who cares.

And remember, we have a half day on Thursday the 17th and no school on Friday the 18th. Please, please don't send your kids to school on Friday unless you want them to have an introduction to custodial services.

Over and out.

Jen

Conference Schedule:

Thursday, Nov. 17

12:30 Lewicki

1:00 Fancy

1:30 Aikens

2:00 Chang

2:30 Alexander

3:00 Brown

3:30 Kaplan

Friday, Nov. 18

8:00 Cobb

8:30 Dixon

9:00 Westman

> *9:30 Baton*
>
> *10:30 Tucci*
>
> *11:00 Elder*
>
> *11:30 Wolffe*
>
> *1:00 Gordon/Burgess*
>
> *1:30 Zalis*

I push Send knowing what a shit storm I have just delivered, and wait for the fallout. Of course Sasha Lewicki's out-of-office reply is the first to arrive, but it is followed very quickly by emails from Dr. Evil and Mini-Me.

To: JDixon

From: Kim Fancy

Date: 10/30

Subject: Conference schedule

Hi, Jen,

I'm sorry if I didn't make myself clear in my previous email. I simply must have the first conference time because we are flying to Manhattan! Please switch me with Sasha Lewicki.

Kim

To: JDixon
From: JJ Aikens
Date: 10/30
Subject: Conference schedule

Jen,

I'm really shocked by how you ignored all our requests, especially since you asked us to tell you what we wanted. I mean, Kim and I both asked for the first time slot, assuming you would give it to at least one of us. Kim has a flight to Manhattan. She has tickets at Lincoln Center. So you see how important it is that she get the first spot. I'm sure the Lewickis won't mind switching when you ask them.

Thank you,

JJ

To: Kim Fancy, JJ Aikens
From: JDixon
Date: 10/30
Subject: Conference schedule

Hi, Kim and JJ,

The schedule stands as is. If you would like to reach out to the Lewickis yourself, be my guest. They were the first to respond and I'm pretty clear on where I stand with prompt replies.

By the way, to my knowledge there are no airports in Manhattan. I hope someone didn't sell you a fake plane ticket!

Jennifer

To: Sasha Lewicki
From: JJ Aikens
Date: 10/30
Re: Conference schedule

Hi, Sasha,

How are you? My name is JJ Aikens and my daughter Kit is in class this year with your daughter, Nadine. I'm sorry we didn't get a chance to meet on curriculum night, but I'd love to get the girls together for a play date. JJ's usually playing with Nancy Fancy, but maybe we could set something up for November 20? Speaking of which, can I switch conference times with you on the 18th? I really need that first spot. Well, I don't, but Kim does (you know Kim Fancy, don't you? She moved here from Manhattan a couple of years ago). She needs to jump on a plane back to the city. We told the class mom, but she seems to just do things any way she wants. I don't think she's set a date for the class cocktail party yet, not to mention she didn't even bother to organize a class Halloween party!

 Anyway, let me know as soon as you can. And let's do coffee soon.

JJ

To: JJ Aikens
From: Sasha Lewicki
Date: 10/30
Subject: Conference schedule
I am out of the office until November 3.

Thank you,
Sasha

6

I'm not sure why I hate Halloween so much, but I really do. It might have something to do with my parents' lack of enthusiasm for "that heathen holiday," but who knows? Having kids means you have to jump on the bandwagon and pretend that dressing up in ridiculous outfits and going door to door begging strangers for candy is A-OK.

I blessed the day Vivs and Laura outgrew trick-or-treating, and I lived happily with the knowledge that I would never have to do it again. Yeah. That's what I get for making plans. Luckily, I live with the only person more in love with Halloween than a five-year-old boy. I've gone out with Ron and Max other years, but tonight they are flying solo. My only job is to give kids a hard time when they come to our house.

As I'm filling our trick candy bowl (the green skeleton hand comes down when you reach inside to get treats, mwa-ha-ha-ha!), the door-bell rings.

"Trick or treat, Mrs. Dixon!"

It's Zach T. and Peetsa. Zach T. is dressed as a mailman. Peetsa has a witch's hat on and a bottle of wine in her hand.

"Hey, guys! You look great, Zach. Let's see a trick."

He looks at me and frowns. Peetsa starts to laugh.

"Don't you know any tricks? I need to see a trick before I can give a treat," I say as I wink at her.

Zach thinks for a minute. "Well, I can burp the alphabet. Is that a trick?"

"Yeah, it is! Let's hear it."

As Zach burps away, I hug Peetsa and take the bottle of wine she offers.

"You read my mind," I whisper.

"T burp U burp V burp W burp X burp Y burp Z."

"Nicely done." I offer him the candy bowl. "Now can you go upstairs and see what's taking Max so long?"

"Sure!" He runs to the stairs.

"Oh, my God, do you make every kid do that?" Peetsa asks.

"Damn right. Nothing is free. They should learn that early in life."

I'm so glad Peetsa agreed to help me give out candy tonight. Buddy is doing home duty at their house and Ron is taking the boys out, so it's a perfect girls' night in. I head to the kitchen and pull out some wineglasses. As I go to open the bottle, I notice it has a screw top. I whistle.

"Whew! Hope you didn't break the bank with this one."

"Excuse me, but that's actually a really good bottle."

I wave the screw top at her.

"A lot of vineyards don't use cork anymore for some of their vintages. That, my friend, is a fine Australian Shiraz stolen from Buddy's wine closet."

"I love that you're so into wine."

Peetsa takes the glass from me.

"Well, Buddy's the real oenophile. I just reap the benefits. Cheers."

Just then I hear what sounds like thunder coming down the stairs, and a mailman, a ninja, and a football player appear before my eyes.

"Wow! You guys look awesome! Peetsa, this is my first husband, Ron."

Ron rolls his eyes. "She thinks that never gets old." He shakes hands with my new friend.

Peetsa laughs. "Well, it's pretty funny the first time you hear it."

Max strikes a pose.

"Ninja!" he yells.

"Show Mrs. Tucci your trick, Max."

"Mom, no one ever asks for a trick," Max whines.

"You never know," I say. "Come on, just show her."

Max grimaces but indulges me. He holds the sword sideways in both hands, brings it to knee level, and awkwardly jumps over it, through his arms. Peetsa and Ron clap. Zach hoots his approval.

"Love that!" exclaims Peetsa. "You will get so much more candy if you bust that move out at every house."

"Do it while Zach burps the alphabet!" I chime in.

"What trick should I do?" my husband murmurs as he kisses me on the cheek. He is decked out in a Kansas City Chiefs uniform.

"Maybe you could rough up the quarterback a little later." I give him a good pat on the butt.

"Deal." He smiles. "Okay guys, grab your bags and let's hit it. You girls have fun."

"Ninja!" Max yells as they head out the door.

✦ ✦ ✦

As Peetsa and I settle in to the two chairs I have moved close to the front door, I take my first sip of wine.

"Oh, wow. That *is* good."

"Mm-hmm." Peetsa washes down a bite of pizza with a big gulp. Just then the doorbell rings.

"Oh, God, here we go." I open the door and standing in front of me are three princesses a little older than Max.

"Yes?" I ask. "Can I help you?"

Silence.

"Trick or treat!" says the mother standing behind them. She's wearing a crown.

"What's your trick, Princess?" I ask with a big smile.

Nothing.

"They're shy," says the mom by way of explanation for their muteness.

"Hmmm. I really need a trick to give a treat."

Now they're all staring at me. The mother is giving me a look that says, "Really, you're going there?" I stand my ground. Then one of the little girls pipes up, "I can do a cartwheel."

"That is a great trick!" I encourage her. "Let's see it."

She puts down her crown-shaped candy bag, walks down the steps to our lawn, hikes up her dress, and does a perfect cartwheel. I clap and cheer and offer the candy bowl to all three girls.

"Bye, girls. Have a fun night." Just as I'm closing the door, I see the mother give me the finger.

Peetsa is doubled over laughing.

"Oh, my God! You are *horrible*. There should be a warning on your door."

Over the next hour, our conversation is interrupted about thirty times by the doorbell. After something like the sixteenth ring, I lose my enthusiasm for torture and just hand out the candy. Except when I open to see a group of teenagers just standing there holding bags. No costumes, no trick-or-treat. This is my pet peeve. I'm sorry, but door-to-door candy gathering is for children, not semi-adults looking for sugar.

"What's up?" I ask.

"Uh, trick or treat?" one of them tries.

"Great! What's your trick?"

"My what?"

"Your trick. The thing you do to get the treat."

"Uh, we just came to get candy. Do you got any?"

"Not for people who don't do a trick." I smile.

"Do you mean, like, magic or something?"

"Sure. Do you know any magic tricks?"

"Uh . . ."

"Dude, let's go," says another teen. "She's a bitch."

I look at the kid who just spoke. There's something . . .

"Robbie Pritchard? Is that you?"

"Oh, shit," they all say.

The Pritchards lived next door to my parents for years.

"Did you just call me a bitch?" I ask calmly.

At that, they all turn and run off the porch like a pack of scared dogs.

"I'll be calling your mother later," I yell after them.

Peetsa just shakes her head. "I see you bring the same enthusiasm to everything that you do to being our class mom."

"I know. I'm the worst."

"You're not the worst! I love your emails. I couldn't wait to meet you. But I'm not surprised you piss some people off."

"I didn't even want to do it, but Nina knew it was the only way I was going to . . . Wait, who's pissed off?"

Peetsa looks at her wineglass like it might have the answer.

"Umm . . . I don't know, I've just heard a few people talking."

I jump up.

"Who? What did they say? You *have* to tell me. I live for this stuff."

Peetsa laughs. "You really are crazy."

"I'm not! I've just been through this before, and I'm determined to get parents to lighten up."

"Anyone who is even remotely cool totally gets your humor. You know who the stick-up-the-asses are—Asami, JJ, Kim Fancy, Ravital Brown . . ."

"Zach B.'s mom?" I ask, a little hurt.

Peetsa nods. "But I think she just doesn't understand your sarcasm. She told me her husband has to explain all your emails to her."

"Huh. Well, maybe I can win her over. Who else?"

"That's all I know of. It's a small but vocal bunch."

"More wine?" I ask. I head to the kitchen, wondering how I can make an ESL person understand what snarky means.

"Sure, thanks. Hey, how's your daughter?"

"Which one?"

"The slutty one."

"Peetsa!" I scream in shock. "Please! We prefer 'loose' or 'sleazy.'"

We both crack up.

"She's doing fine. The nice thing about her generation is that they move on pretty quickly. Two days after her drama, some poor girl was snapped eating two hotdogs at once, so the spotlight is off Laura."

"I still can't believe you have two kids in college. Max must have been the shock of your life!"

I pour more wine for both of us and we head back to the chairs by the door.

"Not really. Ron wanted to have a kid."

"Didn't he already have two?" she asks, confused.

I inwardly cringe. This is the part I hate explaining to people.

The doorbell rings just as we sit down. Wow, sometimes you really are saved by the bell.

Peetsa jumps up.

"I've got it."

She opens the door and I hear two little voices sing, "Trick or treat."

"Do you have a trick to show me?" Peetsa asks them. I've taught her well.

Then a familiar voice says, "Hey, don't we go to the same school?"

I nearly spit my wine out. Suchafox is at my front door! I jump up from my chair and sprint to stand beside Peetsa.

"Hey, guys!" I say a little too loudly. Lulu is dressed like a zombie bride, the other little girl is a nurse, and Don is wearing a cowboy hat. He looks perfect, of course. The butterflies in my stomach start doing a happy dance.

"Jen! No way. Do you guys live here?"

"I do." Oh cripes, that giggle is back. "Peetsa is helping me out tonight. Do you guys know each other?"

"I definitely saw you at curriculum night," Peetsa says to Don. She has a goofy smile on her face. "I'm Peetsa, Zach T.'s mom."

"Peetsa?" Don asks, and once again I get a little glimpse into the hell that must be her world thanks to her unique name.

"Just like the food," I offer. "P., this is Don Burgess. We went to high school together. Isn't that crazy?" I giggle.

"Very," Peetsa affirms.

I turn to him. "Do you live in this neighborhood?"

"No, we live west of here, but Lulu wanted to trick-or-treat with Rachel. It's nuts. I don't see you for, like, thirty years and now I see you all the time."

"I know, right?" I giggle and offer the little girls the candy bowl.

"Wait!" says Peetsa. "What about the trick?" She turns to Don. "They're supposed to do a trick to get a treat."

"Really?" His look says it's the dumbest idea he's ever heard.

"Oh, P.!" *Giggle.* "Lighten up on the trick part, will you?" I smile at Don and shake my head like I don't know what the hell she's so uptight about. "Go ahead, girls."

I avoid Peetsa's glare as Lulu and Rachel dig into the candy bowl. They screech when the skeleton hand comes down to grab them and, after taking a handful of candy, they march down our front steps and onto the walkway. I glance toward Don and, for the briefest moment, I wonder what it would be like to kiss him. The thought is gone as quickly as it came, but I can't help feeling a little uncomfortable. Peetsa interrupts my wayward thoughts.

"So you guys were friends in high school?"

"Well, we knew each other, but we didn't really hang out," I answer quickly.

"But there was one pretty significant moment in the P.E. laundry room." He gives me a wry smile.

"Oh really?" She arches an eyebrow at me. "Tell me everything."

Don lets out a guffaw. "And this is where I leave you!" He starts down the stairs to where the little girls are waiting for him. "See you around."

I watch him walk away with what I'm sure is a ridiculous smile on my face. When I turn to go inside, Peetsa is staring at me.

"What?" I play dumb.

"That's my question. What the hell was that all about?"

"He's a father in our class." I shrug.

"Yeah, so is Buddy, but you don't act like *that* when he's around. What was that giggle?"

I lead her back into the house while I explain.

"I had a huge crush on him in high school."

"And apparently you still do." She imitates my annoying giggle.

"P.! Be nice. He's still so cute."

"He must have been really something in high school."

"He was such a fox."

Peetsa bursts out laughing.

"God, I haven't said that about anyone in years." We sit back down on our chairs. "So what happened in the P.E. laundry room?"

The doorbell rings again. I jump up to get it, thrilled to avoid Peetsa's question. *Maybe Suchafox forgot something!*

I'm only a bit disappointed to see it's not Don, but our sons standing there.

"Hey! How did it go?" I ask as they charge in with full bags of candy.

"Great! The Gibsons were giving out whole chocolate bars and we went twice. They didn't even notice." They start to dump their candy out on the living room floor.

Ron comes in, helmet in hand, looking shell-shocked.

"They ran the whole time. I didn't even let them have candy."

"Come have some wine, babe."

"No, thanks. I need a shower."

He heads upstairs and Peetsa gives Zach a ten-minute warning.

"Wheels up in ten, kiddo. Do your trading and put your stuff back in your bag."

"Okay!" Zach yells from six feet away.

Peetsa looks at me and frowns.

"What were we talking about?"

I grab the chance to change the subject.

"What do you really think of Miss Ward?"

"No, wait! P.E. laundry room . . ."

I wince. "Some other time, okay?"

She looks surprised. "Oh! Okay."

"So, Miss Ward, what do you think?"

She shrugs. "I don't know. Zach loves her, that's for sure."

"So does Max! I just get a really weird feeling from her."

"Well, you'd know. You spend the most time with her."

"That's just it. You'd think I would, because of the class mom thing. But honestly, I never see her and she told me at the beginning of the year that she doesn't want me bothering her with"—I make finger quotes—"class-related stuff."

Peetsa's eyes pop.

"She *said* that?"

"Better. She wrote it in an email. That's the only way she talks to me, and usually it's only to tell me to do something like organize the parent/teacher conferences."

"Is that normal? I've never been a class mom."

"There's really no normal. Every teacher is different. In the lower grades, they tend to want you helping out in the classroom as much as possible. But Miss Ward hasn't asked me once."

"Well, it's only been two months. But it was kind of weird that the kids didn't have a Halloween party. Did she say anything to you about that?"

I look at her over my wineglass.

"She said she doesn't celebrate *Hallmark* holidays."

Peetsa does a spit take.

"Oh, well, that makes sense," she says, wiping wine off her chin. "Who would want to celebrate that great *Hallmark* holiday, Halloween?"

"I'm just wondering, when *does* she give a party?"

"Arbor Day?" Peetsa snickers.

"Groundhog Day!" I chime in.

We laugh as Peetsa gets up.

"Zach, let's hit the road," she calls to her son. "Hey, thanks for tonight. This was fun."

"Best Halloween I've ever had," I say. And I actually mean it.

✦ ✦ ✦

In the bathroom, getting ready for bed, I mull over my lingering thought about kissing Don. I've never had a moment like that before, and it's making me uncomfortable on several levels. It was so out of left field. I mean, I adore my husband and we still have a pretty great sex life even after ten years. Since the day we met, I've never even thought of being with another man . . . unless you count my Bruce Springsteen fantasies. While I brush my teeth, I close my eyes and try to put it out of my mind. One thing's for certain, Ron Dixon is getting some tonight.

7

To: Parents
From: JDixon
Date: 11/18
Subject: Party time!

Hi, gang,

Long time no blah blah!

Big big news! Our children are going to have a compliment party ("You're cute"; "No, you're cute!"). Apparently they're encouraged to write down compliments to each other and put them in a jar. When the jar is full, voilà, a compliment party.

Miss Ward has chosen to let them make ice cream sundaes on the Wednesday before Thanksgiving (November 23) so she can send them off for the long weekend on a sugar high. I'll bring the ice cream, but we need the following toppings and supplies:

chocolate sauce
caramel sauce

sprinkles

gummy bears

plain M&Ms

whipped cream

marshmallow topping

spoons, bowls, and napkins

and of course the Batons will bring wine

Please remember, NO NUTS!!! (See, Shirleen? I didn't forget)

This is a wonderful opportunity for all of you to get into my good graces by volunteering early and often to bring something. As always, response times will be noted.

No, no. Don't thank me. It's my reward for being class mom.

Jen

✦ ✦ ✦

As I click Send, I look at my watch and realize I had better get my ass in gear if I'm going to be on time for my teacher conference with Miss Ward. I wouldn't miss this for the world. I have been shut down by her two separate times while trying to make casual conversation, so I can't imagine what having a real discussion about Max is going to be like.

I run upstairs to my bedroom and notice how out of breath I am. When are all my hard work and conditioning finally going to pay off? It's only five months until the mud run, and failure is not an option. I'd better talk to Garth about ramping up my cardio.

I throw open my closet door, pretending that I'm actually going to choose something other than my official mom uniform of Levi's jeans, white T-shirt, and gray (or black) sweater. I have twenty different combos of basically the same outfit, and that isn't going to change anytime soon. My only indulgence is a pair of black Prada short boots. I have had them for nine years and they probably receive better care than any of my kids. I only switch it up when I absolutely have to or when Ron makes a comment like "Didn't you wear that yesterday . . . and the day before?" He's actually the one who coined the phrase "mom uniform." He thought he was sending me a subtle message, but I took it as a compliment. I also have an evening mom uniform for special nights out. It's form-fitting black pants or pencil skirt, and a black button-down shirt. I have been mistaken for a waiter on more than one occasion. Once, we were at a fund-raiser at city hall, and Don Cheadle from *Ocean's Eleven* asked me to get him a refill.

Occasionally I will switch up the jeans-and-sweater look, but not today. Today I need all the comfort I can get. I never know which Miss Ward is going to show up, so I have to be at my most relaxed and nonjudgmental.

Ron is meeting me at the school, so I grab my purse and the car keys and head out the door.

Have I mentioned that I love my car? It is a totally tricked-out Honda Odyssey minivan, and let me tell you, I feel like the king of the road in it. Ron thought I was crazy for wanting the "I give up" car, as he calls it, but he'd never had kids before and didn't realize how vital automatic sliding back doors would be to our existence. He also didn't realize that I would be running Mom's taxi service for Max and his friends for the foreseeable future. Now he understands, and he even drives the minivan . . . sometimes . . . when he thinks no one will see him.

This is actually my third minivan, and by far my favorite. I've only had it for a couple of months, so Max and his friends haven't had time to crap it up yet. I'll try to keep the "no eating" rule as long as possible, but eventually I know I will have to let him have a snack while we are driving somewhere, and then it's all over. We traded in the last minivan without ever knowing what the hell that smell was, although I have a sneaking suspicion it was a combo of yogurt, urine, and the remnants of my first bottle of kombucha.

When I pull into the school parking lot, I see Ron waiting out front for me. I lock up the van and run to meet him. We are just on time.

As we walk down the hall to room 147, I try to remember who is scheduled to meet with Miss Ward before us. I know I considered putting Gordon/Burgess either before or after us just so I could get a glimpse of Suchafox, but the timing didn't work out.

When we arrive, Shirleen Cobb and her husband are coming out of the classroom, laughing, with Miss Ward right behind them. Everyone seems happy happy happy, which I take as a good sign. But when they see us, they stop laughing. Not a good sign for us.

Shirleen comes right over to me, as if we were in midconversation.

"Graydon cannot eat ice cream. It makes him terribly gassy even though he loves it, poor lamb. You need to think of a different party treat."

I glance sideways at Ron and smile. *Welcome to my world!*

"Shirleen, the ice cream party was not my idea. I'm just following orders. But I want you to know I thought of Graydon and am planning to bring Tofutti just for him."

Shirleen sizes me up and gives me a nod. "Good."

And off she stalks with her husband in tow.

"Always a pleasure," I murmur.

Ron leans into me. "You didn't introduce me."

"You're welcome."

Miss Ward beckons us into the classroom. She is wearing her hair pulled back into a tight bun, and her navy blue pantsuit is a flattering fit without being inappropriate. She is all business today.

"Hi, Jenny. And you must be Ron. Come on in and have a seat."

She motions us toward two children's chairs. Why do teachers do this? We are grownups with grown-up knees and grown-up butts. Would it be so hard to pull in a couple of adult-sized chairs for conference day?

As we navigate our way down into the chairs—holding on to each other for dear life—Miss Ward sternly consults a folder that says "Dixon, Max" in purple marker. When she looks up, she smiles.

"Well, what can I say? Max is a wonderful boy. He is kind and polite and really well liked by everyone in class."

Ron and I smile at each other. He takes my hand and squeezes it. My eyes get a bit teary.

"However"—Miss Ward consults her notes—"Max is the only child in the class who doesn't seem to enjoy P.E., although he loves recess. Any idea why that is?"

I look knowingly at Ron. He just shrugs.

"No idea," he says.

"Well, it's nothing to worry about. Just something I noticed." She smiles. "He is doing very well in math. Here is some of his recent work." She slides a few sheets of paper across the mini table and explains what the class has been learning. The papers have purple smiley faces at the top of them. I guess that's her equivalent of a grade. I'm tempted to ask what the kids who aren't doing well get at the top of their pages, but I decide I'd rather not know.

"Here is the book we're reading aloud right now." She hands over a book that I read when I was in first grade: *The Dragons of Blueland*, by Ruth Stiles Gannett.

"Hey, I remember this book," I say to no one in particular.

"Max is great when we are in listening mode, but when it comes to talking about the book, he never raises his hand. Any idea why that is?"

Ron looks up, surprised.

"Uh, okay. I mean, I read to him at night but . . ."

"Maybe stop after every page or so and ask him some questions or get his opinion on what you've just read."

I think about the books we are reading Max right now. Exactly what questions can you ask a child after reading *Hop on Pop*? Ron just nods in agreement—or defeat.

"I think Max just needs a confidence boost."

Confidence boost? He wears red pants, for God's sake. How much more confident can he be?

"That's pretty much all I have to say." Miss Ward stands. "Do you have any questions?"

Here's your hat, what's your hurry? I think, but do not say. Ron and I struggle to get out of the mini chairs.

"Uh, I'm sure I do, but I can't think of any right now," says Ron. I feel bad for him. He's not used to the crazy abruptness that is Miss Ward.

"Anything planned for the class that I should know about?" I ask.

"Jenny, *yes*! Thank you for reminding me. We are taking a class trip to the dump in two weeks and I'll need three parents to help chaperone."

"The *dump*?" I can't hide my incredulity.

"Well, it's really the Kansas City Recycling Center, but believe me when I tell you the kids get much more excited when I call it the dump."

I can't argue with her logic. I know Max loves going to the dump, but the real one. She is going to have a mutiny on the school bus when they pull up to a recycling plant.

"Okay. I'll send out an email and get some volunteers."

"I don't need to know the details, Jenny." Miss Ward ushers us to the door. As we are walking out, she inexplicably bursts into a peal of laughter. It actually makes both of us crack up, because it's so out of nowhere. Out in the hall, the Westmans look at us in surprise.

"Sounds like you guys had fun," Jackie says to me.

And that's when I remember the Cobbs walking out of the classroom before our meeting and laughing. Hmm . . . a little home-court intimidation. Crazy like a fox is our Miss Ward.

To: Parents

From: JDixon

Date: 11/15

Subject: Party time and trash talk

What is it, my birthday???

    You guys are awesome! I got all the volunteers I needed without having to send a follow-up begging email. My class parents are growing up so quickly!

Kudos to Sasha Lewicki's out-of-office reply for once again taking the top response time of 22 seconds, but hot on her heels was Jill Kaplan at 1:47. The rest of you lollygagged a bit, but hey, you got there in the end. Here's the lineup:

chocolate sauce—Kaplans
caramel sauce—Zalises
sprinkles (chocolate AND rainbow!)—Elders
gummy bears—Gordon/Burgess
plain M&Ms—Alexanders
whipped cream—Browns (guess we just learned a little more about the Browns, huh?)
marshmallow topping—Fancys
spoons, bowls, and napkins—Aikenses
cups—Eastmans
And the Batons will bring wine.

Expect some seriously sugared-up kiddos when you pick them up on Wednesday.

On another note, Miss Ward has planned a class trip to the Kansas City recycling center for Tuesday, November 22 (FYI, she's telling them they're going to the dump). We will need 3 parents to help chaperone the trip. So if you've had all your shots, don't be shy! Get those fingers tapping and volunteer.

GO TYPE NOW!

Jennifer

I mentally start to guess who will be among the brave and crazy enough to sign up. Of course, Sasha Lewicki's out-of-office reply is right on top of things.

To: JDixon

From: Sasha Lewicki

Date: 11/15

Subject: Party time and trash talk

I am out of the office until November 30.

Thank you,

Sasha

To: JDixon

From: Peetsa Tucci

Date: 11/15

Subject: Party time and trash talk

I'll go if you will.

xo

P.

I groan, although Peetsa is the one thing that would make a class trip to the dump tolerable.

To: JDixon

From: Ravital Brown

Date: 11/15

Subject: Party time and trash talk

This is not a joke, right? I am never sure. If it's not a joke, I will go. I mean, I don't like garbage, but I think Zach would like me to come.

Thank you,

Ravital

To: JDixon
From: Don Burgess
Date: 11/15
Subject: Party time and trash talk

Hi, Jen,

Not sure if I told you, but I'm the manager at the recycling center, so I can act as a chaperone. You and Peetsa should come. Our plant is pretty impressive.

Cheers,
Don

When Don said he worked in waste management, I didn't even think of the recycling center. Well, that seals it. I email Peetsa to tell her she's the lucky winner of a day of refuse. And while I'm at it, I assure myself that I was totally going to go anyway, even before I got the email from Suchafox.

8

"We're home!" Vivs and Laura scream in unison.

"What?" I exclaim. I drop the turkey I'm washing in the sink and run to hug my girls.

"I wasn't expecting you until the end of the day." I take them into my arms and squeeze my hardest. I can't believe they are both taller than me.

"Well, Vivs decided to ditch her last two classes, so we left at, like, ten." Laura can't help sounding like a tattletale.

"I didn't ditch." Viv scowls. "I was going to be the only one there. The teachers will probably thank me."

I'm about to make a crack about our hard-earned money when I realize something. "Hey, where's Raj?"

"He's not coming."

"What? Why?"

"Because he's an asshole, Mom," Vivs snaps, and walks upstairs, her long brown hair swinging behind her.

"Oh, God, what now?" I ask Laura.

She shrugs. "I have no idea. She wouldn't talk about it in the car. And she drove like a crazy person, Mommy! We got here in an hour."

I hug her. "How are *you*, my sweet girl?"

"I'm good!" She brightens. "I still love where I'm living. My roommates are so fun."

"And your classes? Ever get a chance to make it to any?"

"Occasionally." She smirks at me.

Laura has blossomed into such a beauty. Her oversized eyes and lips made her look a bit like a bug when she was younger, but she has finally grown into her face and has figured out how to tame her blond curls. She looks nothing like me or her sister.

"Where's Maximilian Swell?" she asks.

I smile at the nickname. Much improved over "Maxipad," which is the first one she gave him.

"He and Ron are out getting cranberries. Hey, can you grab an apron and start pulling bread apart for the stuffing?"

"Sure. Just let me go to the bathroom." Laura heads upstairs to the room she shares with Vivs when they're home. Two minutes later, both girls come down and put on aprons. I love that they just do this without a lot of nagging on my part. It reminds me of how strict I was when I raised them. They had set chores every day and were never allowed to be sitting down if I was still working. I've really slacked off with Max. Vivs gives me shit about it all the time.

As they pull apart two loaves of white bread, I go back to the turkey I had unceremoniously dumped in the sink. Vivs is taking her bad mood out on the bread and ripping it apart with gusto.

"Want to talk about it?" I ask.

"Talk about what?" She looks up, annoyed.

"Your bad mood."

"I'm not in a bad mood, Mom, I'm just preoccupied."

Unfortunately, Laura decides to jump in.

"Oh, and I'm just lucky to be alive, because you were"—she makes quotes with her hands, which are full of bread—" 'preoccupied' while you were driving."

"Oh, my God, you are such a baby." Vivs slams her hands down on the counter.

"Girls! What the hell? Is this how we're going to start Thanksgiving weekend? Laura, let it go about the driving. She got you here.

And you." I look directly at Vivs. "Either tell us what's going on, or snap out of it."

Vivs looks down.

"I'm sorry. It's just Raj did something so stupid and I'm really pissed at him."

She pauses, as if trying to decide something.

"He asked me to marry him."

"What?" screams Laura. "Are you kidding me? *That's* what you're upset about? A hot guy wants to marry you?"

"Shut up. You have no idea what you're talking about," Vivs shoots back.

Laura throws her hands up in the air.

"Somebody please give me a problem like that," she says to the air around her.

"Mom!" Vivs whines.

"Okay, stop. Jeez, you guys. You've only been home for half an hour."

I grab a towel to dry my hands and wish like hell it was time for a glass of wine. It's three o'clock somewhere, isn't it?

"So he proposed and you said . . ."

"No," Vivs answers quickly. "I said no. Of course I said no."

"Why would you say no?" Laura asks without an ounce of guile.

"Uh, because I'm not white trash living in the backwoods of Kentucky," Vivs says.

I look at Laura, who is still confused. I put my arm around her.

"Don't you think twenty-one is a little young to get married?" I ask her.

She looks at me thoughtfully.

"Not if you're in love. I would."

We both wait to see if she's kidding. She is not. This is definitely something to revisit later.

I turn to Vivs. "So, is your age the only reason you said no? I mean, do you love him?"

Vivs sits down at the kitchen table and takes a deep breath.

"I do. I mean, I think I do. How do you know?"

"Oh, God." I snort. "Don't ask me. It took me years to figure it out."

"Great, Mom. Thanks. Good talk." Vivs's voice is dripping sarcasm.

I roll my eyes at her. These are the mom moments that I love and dread all at the same time. I want to say the right thing, give her the right advice, but I'm not a hundred percent sure what that right advice is.

"Well, I think you have to look beyond the dizzy infatuation you have right now and think about who you want to share the best and worst times of your life with. The passion will fade—it has to, or you'd never get anything done." Vivs smiles at this. "But if you end up with your best friend, then you've made the right decision."

Vivs raises her eyebrows. "So Ron's your best friend?"

"Well, Nina really is, but Ron's definitely a close second, or maybe third. The point is, you want someone you can stand being around forty years from now."

"But how do you know that?" Vivs screams, exasperated.

"You know that when you get to know yourself better!" I raise my voice in frustration.

At this Norman Rockwell moment of holiday joy, Ron and Max walk in the back door to the kitchen.

"Uh, hi?" Ron asks with more than a little trepidation.

"Sissy!" Max jumps ahead of his dad and into Vivs's lap, giving her a big hug.

"Buddy!" Vivs squeezes him back.

"Hey, what about me, Maxilla?" Laura walks over and scoops up her little brother.

"I got a helicopter and I was a ninja for Halloween," Max chirps.

"Tell me something I don't know, brotha!" Laura puts him in a fireman's hold and takes him into the living room.

"Hi, Ron!" she calls over her shoulder.

"Hey, Laurs," Ron answers, still standing in the doorway holding a grocery bag. He closes the door and carefully walks to the counter, like he's casing a minefield. He kisses my head and bends to hug Vivs. "Anything I should know about?"

"Just girl talk." I give him my sweet smile.

"Ron, how did you know that Mom was the one?" Vivs blurts out.

Okay, girl *and* boy talk.

Ron looks leery but to his credit decides just to answer the question.

"How did I know? Umm . . . Well, I didn't at first."

I look up, surprised.

"No offense, honey, but you were a lot to take on. No man in his right mind wants to live with a woman who gives him so much shit all the time."

Shit? I think to myself. *He doesn't know what shit is! I'll give him . . . Oh.*

Ron continues. "But after a while I realized I was much happier taking shit from all three of you than I ever was with anyone else. So I knew."

"But he was forty-three at the time," I needlessly remind everyone in the room. "*And* he'd already had a full life with crazy Cindy."

Vivs ignores my babbling and looks directly at Ron.

"What if you had met Mom when you were twenty-one?"

I can tell Ron needs some context at this point, so I chime in.

"Raj asked Vivs to marry him. She said no and now he's not coming for Thanksgiving. There. You're all caught up."

"So, you're asking would I have married your mom if I'd met her thirty years ago?"

"Yes," Vivs says.

"Probably not, but I feel like that would have been a huge mistake. I can't imagine my life with anyone else. Can you imagine your life with anyone else?"

"Frankly, yes I can," Vivs answers, a little too quickly.

"Well, then," says Ron, starting to unpack the grocery bag, "you have your answer."

Vivs goes back to tearing up bread and I thank God for the millionth time that I married the right man.

✦ ✦ ✦

"What time are Nana and Poppy getting here?" Laura asks over breakfast on Thanksgiving morning. Ron has done his usual great job with bacon and eggs. He really doesn't cook at all, but he manages this one meal without too much mess.

"They're going to church this morning and then they'll be over," I say while chewing toast.

"They go to church a lot," Max observes.

"Okay, while I have you all here, this is how the day will play out." I go into drill sergeant mode. "Vivs, you have to make sure the turkey is stuffed and in the oven by noon."

"Check." Vivs gives me a salute.

"Ron, the potatoes and turnips have already been made, so all you need to do is put them in the microwave when I tell you to. Repeat, *when I tell you to.*"

"Jeez, a guy heats things up late one time and gets branded for life," Ron gripes.

I ignore him and move on. "Laura, you are on gravy-and-special-peas duty. You know the routine."

"Check," says Laura. "Make gravy, hide gravy from Nana, let Nana make gravy, then swap out Nana's gravy for mine. Easy."

"You say that now, but I think Nana's on to us. Watch her carefully."

"What's wrong with Nana's gravy?" Max asks. "I love it."

"You've never had it," Laura assures him. "You've only ever had my gravy."

"Lucky," Ron says, and gives him a solemn nod.

Let me just say that my mom has a good heart and no taste buds. Everything she makes has way too much seasoning. The problem's getting worse as she gets older. I feel so sorry for my dad. Thank God, he has terrible sinus issues, so I don't think he notices too much.

"And don't forget to dig out the gravy boat from hell," I remind Laura. "It's in the linen closet behind the old towels."

"Jeez, do we have to keep calling it that?" Ron sounds defeated.

"What else would you call it?" I ask him. It was a wedding gift from Ron's ex. She sent us a gravy boat shaped like a turkey, where the neck is the handle and the gravy comes out the ass. I insist on using it at least twice a year.

He shakes his head. "I was thinking just 'gravy boat.' but whatever."

"Max," I continue, "you are in charge of collecting leaves for the table. I want to see lots of different colors, okay?"

"Okay!" he says, clearly feeling very important.

"Okay," I repeat. "I will set the table and make sure the pies get put in the oven once the turkey is out. Any questions?"

I get a lot of blank stares.

"Right, then. Let's get to it. No TV until your work is done."

"I don't want to watch TV," Max says.

"I was talking to Daddy."

As everyone scatters to do their chores, I clean up the breakfast mess and then sit down to check my email. Amid the usual Pottery Barn, Shopbop, and Amazon notices is a note from none other than Miss Ward.

To: JDixon

from: PWard

Date: 11/25

Subject: I'm feeling thankful!

Dear Jenny,

As I sit here in my apartment on this beautiful Thanksgiving Day with a bottle of wine and all four Twilight movies to enjoy, I just want to thank you for your hard work and friendship so far this year. I really think we

---

make a great team! Having said that, I need you to be more on the ball with the field trips. We can't let what happened at the recycling center happen again. Agreed? Great.

    Have a nice dinner!

Peggy

✦ ✦ ✦

Ouch. I really can't believe she went there.

Peetsa and I chaperoned Tuesday's field trip and, as predicted *by me*, the kids had a mass meltdown when they figured out that they weren't going to the "real dump."

Thank goodness for Suchafox! He was waiting for us by the front door of the plant, and when he heard the sobbing from inside the bus he came onboard and took charge. Within five minutes, he managed to convince the kids how lucky they were to be here instead of the dump, citing the really bad smell and the giant rats. Luckily, the kids bought this hook, line, and sinker—especially when he said he would show them how to turn a plastic water bottle into a pair of jeans. Suddenly they couldn't wait to take the tour. Lulu looked so proud.

"P.E. laundry room," Peetsa mumbled to me as we walked the plant floor. I burst out laughing. Miss Ward gave us a stern look.

At the end of the tour, Don was as good as his word. We sat the kids down in a cafeteria-type room and showed them a video about plastic being made into fabric. Peetsa sat with her son and I noticed Miss Ward sneak out the side door with her cell phone as soon as the movie started. I settled myself in the back of the crowd and leaned back in my chair. That's when it happened.

Don came and sat beside me.

"Remember being so happy when we got to watch a movie in class?" he whispered.

Calm down, Jen.

"Yeah," I responded with my usual wit.

He rested his arms on his knees and leaned in so close I could see the light hairs on his ears.

"So . . ." He smiled.

"So . . ." I smiled back, trying to remember the last time I sat this near to a man who wasn't my husband.

"How do you think it's going?" he whispered.

"I think it's going great." I wondered whether we were talking about the same thing. I mean, I was sitting within inches of my high school crush. How much greater could it be?

"Do you think the kids liked the plant? Lulu was really nervous about everyone getting bored."

"No, they loved it. I loved it." I hoped my smile reassured him.

"Mom!" Max was standing in front of me.

"What?" I jumped away from Don. The movie was still playing and the kids were quietly watching. I focused on my son. "What's up?"

"Graydon's not here."

Don and I looked at each other and sprang up. Thirty minutes of panic ensued while we put out an APB on Graydon, who had taken it upon himself to look for the bathroom shortly after the movie started. He had left the recycling center and gone to the main building, where the offices were, after judging it the "safest bathroom option." Luckily, he didn't run into any peanut butter or airborne dust on his journey, or Shirleen would have had my hide. As it is, I think he got a rash from the soap in the bathroom.

I apologized to Miss Ward profusely and was classy enough not to point out that *she* was nowhere to be found for the first twenty minutes of Graydon's disappearance.

And now she throws it at me, on Thanksgiving? I think about a retaliatory email—something biting about drinking wine at ten o'clock in the morning and being a Twi-hard, but in the spirit of the day, I decide to take the high road. Instead, I text Don *Happy Thanksgiving* and thank him again for all his help with the kids on the field trip. And I am just a little bit thrilled when he texts me right back, *Any time!*

✦ ✦ ✦

"Ah, that was a fine meal, Mother." Ron pushes his chair back from the Thanksgiving table and pats his nonexistent belly. Sometimes he likes to pretend we're an old couple from the 1950s. It's one of those things that was cute the first five or six times but has since worn thin. I don't have the heart to tell him he needs some new material.

I have to say, dinner was delicious. Thanksgiving is one of those idiot-proof meals. Just make sure the turkey isn't overdone, and you're halfway there.

"You really outdid yourself, girlfriend," Nina calls from across the table. "Those peas were unbelievable."

Nina and Chyna always join us for holiday dinners, because we are the closest thing to family that they have in KC. Nina's parents both died in a horrible boating accident on vacation in the Bahamas. Nina was only eight years old and saw the whole thing from the beach. She went to live with her grandmother in Topeka after that. She doesn't talk about it much, but she did tell me that when her grandmother died, a lawyer handed her a check for $326,342 as some sort of compensation from the mega-resort where her parents were killed. Apparently, her grandmother had been holding on to it so Nina wouldn't "spend it on clothes or drugs," as the will put it. She was twenty-five and completely alone in the world. It was the perfect time for the dashing Sid to sweep her, and her money, off her feet.

"The secret is nutmeg," I tell her.

"And about a pound of butter," my mother chimes in. "Sweetheart, I swear you put in more and more every year. Your grandmother would be horrified."

"But not because of the taste," I counter. "Granny would be shocked because butter is expensive."

"That's true," my mom agrees. "My goodness, that woman was tight with a dollar. She'd make my father drive twenty miles away to save ten cents on paper towels."

Nina smiles. I can tell she enjoys the family banter, since she never really had any of her own.

"How is Garth doing?" my mother asks as she starts stacking all the dishes she can reach without getting up. Ron and my dad have wandered back to the television, and the girls and Max have gone to the basement to play Xbox.

"He's good. I really like him. He's such a nice guy."

"What's he doing today?"

I pause for a moment. "He didn't say."

"Well, you should have invited him for dinner today," my mom admonishes me.

"Mom, I barely know him! He barely knows *me*. It would have been weird to just randomly invite him to Thanksgiving."

My mom shakes her head. "I thought I taught you better than that, Jennifer Rose."

"You never taught me to invite strangers to dinner."

"He's not a stranger and he doesn't have any family in town."

"How do you know?"

"Because he told me. How much do you know about him?"

"Not much." I shrug. "We don't really talk."

"Well, maybe you should." My mother pushes her chair back and yells at a surprisingly loud volume: "Okay! Everyone is on cleanup crew except Jen and Nina." There are a lot of groans from the living room and basement.

"Come on. Many hands make light work."

Everyone drags themselves into the dining room.

"Do what Nana says or she'll make you say the rosary afterward," I warn everyone. Suddenly the pace picks up noticeably.

"Oh, we'll be saying the rosary anyway," my mother assures me. That elicits even more groans.

Nina and I grab the rest of the wine and our glasses and head into the living room.

"Your mama just gave you a spanking, my friend." Nina smirks.

"I know, right? What's her deal with Garth?"

Nina shrugs. "So how is my class mom doing?"

"Oh, you know, living the dream." I start to tell her about the drama surrounding scheduling the parent/teacher conferences.

"I don't know if Kim Fancy ever got that stupid time slot. I'm hoping Sasha Lewicki stuck with it."

"Who?" Nina asks from behind her wineglass.

"Sasha Lewicki. Her daughter is Nadine?"

"Never heard of her."

"Oh, my God. Does that mean I actually know someone you don't?" I'm sort of kidding, but not really. Nina makes it a point to know everyone because, as she says, "You never know where you'll find a good lead." As a freelance graphic designer, she is always looking for new clients. How she does it without pissing people off is beyond me.

"They must be new." She lowers her voice. "Still crushing on the old flame?"

"Trying not to. But it's kind of fun, you know?"

"Yes, ma'am, I do know." She laughs.

"Really?"

She nods. "There is a dad in Chyna's class who would be shocked to know the things I think about him."

"Stop it!" I never would have guessed.

She nods. "But he never looks twice at me. *You* need to be careful. Old flames like to reignite."

"He's not an old flame. *I* had a crush on *him*. It wasn't mutual."

"Uh-huh." She looks down at her belly and groans. "Why do I always overeat when I come here? Look at this shit!" She shows me a handful of stomach.

"Wanna try Garth? He comes to your house."

"Maybe in the new year. I've got another month of overeating to get through first."

To: Parents
From: JDixon
Date: 12/5
Subject: Miss Ward's class is having a bash!
To Be Sung to the Tune of "Santa Claus Is Coming to Town"

You better watch out. You better not cry.
You better not pout. I'm telling you why.
Miss Ward's class is having a bash!
I'm making a list of what we will eat.
10:30 in the morning is when we'll all meet.
Miss Ward's class is having a bash.
We'll need some bagels and cream cheese
Some fruit and doughnuts, too.
Some water, juice, tea, coffee,
And some bottles of Yoo-hoo hoo!
So, volunteer soon and don't you be late!
You don't want to make the list of people I hate.
Miss Ward's class is having a bash!

December 22, people. It is in the classroom right after the concert.

The lines are now open, so run, don't walk to your nearest computer and sign up to bring something.

Cheerio!

Jen

To: JDixon
From: SLewicki
Date: 12/5
Subject: Miss Ward's class is having a bash!

Hi,

I will be out of the office until December 8.

Thank you,
Sasha

To: JDixon
From: PTucci
Date: 12/5
Subject: Miss Ward's class is having a bash!

Hi, Jen,

We will bring bagels.

I'm surprised Miss Ward is letting you have a Christmas party. I thought she doesn't celebrate "Hallmark" holidays?

xo
P

To: PTucci
From: JDixon
Date: 12/5
Subject: Miss Ward's class is having a bash!

Hey, P,

Well, you would be correct about that. But if you read my email carefully, there is no mention of this being a Christmas party. It's just a party that takes place after the holiday concert. This was a big negotiating point with Miss Ward, believe me!

Are we still on for girls' night Wednesday?

xo
Jen

To: JDixon
From: SCobb
Date: 12/5
Subject: Miss Ward's class is having a bash!

Jen,

Not that you asked, but I will bring soy butter for Graydon's gluten-free bagel.

Shirleen

To: JDixon
From: DBurgess
Date 12/5
Subject: Miss Ward's class is having a bash!

Hey, Jen,

I'll cover doughnuts for you.

Cheers,
Don

To: JDixon
From: JWestman
Date: 12/5
Subject: Miss Ward's class is having a bash!
I'll bring cups.

Thanks,
Jackie

To: JDixon
From: KFancy
Date: 12/5
Subject: Miss Ward's class is having a bash

Hi, Jen,

Silly me, I thought this email was going to be about the parent cocktail party!
We will be happy to bring coffee to the party. Cream and sugar too, I'm guessing?

While I have you, let's look at December 1 as a good night for the adult party. I know it is only 12 days away, but I'm happy to host it. I just need you to send the invite.

It will be a great way for all of us to launch into the holiday season, don't you think?

Kim

"Suffering cats, that woman is persistent!"

"Who?" asks Ron. We are in bed doing what every red-blooded American couple does at night—watching TV and checking our email.

"Kim Fancy. She's been bugging me to have a class cocktail party since curriculum night."

Ron shrugs. "So?"

"So? What do you mean, 'so'?"

"So what's the big deal? It might be nice to hang out with other parents."

"We do. We hang out with Peetsa and Nina."

"No, *you* hang out with them." Ron mutes the TV. "Is it too much work for you?"

"No. She's going to host it. But she wants me to send out an email inviting people."

"And that's a problem because . . ."

I really hate when Ron gets like this. He's supposed to be on my side till death do us part. But sometimes he goes all logical on me instead.

"Because . . . I don't want to! It's *her* party. If it's a class event, then I feel like it should happen when I'm ready. Not because she wants it." As I'm saying this, I know it sounds ridiculous.

Ron just looks at me, then unmutes the TV.

As I watch *Law & Order: SVU* and brood, my phone buzzes. To my delight/surprise, it's a text from Don.

Hey there. I'm bringing doughnuts to the Christmas party. Is it okay if they have sprinkles? I'm not too familiar with food allergies and that Graydon's mom seems pretty strict.

I laugh.

"What?" Ron asks.

"Just one of my class parents asking a question."

He turns back to the TV, and I respond to Suchafox.

Neither am I, but I'm relatively sure that sugar is okay.

I hit Send, then start another message.

Hey, if there was a parent cocktail party before Christmas, would you and Ali go?

He replies immediately.

Can't speak for Ali, but I'd be there.

"Huh."

"What?" Ron asks again.

"Nothing," I mumble and start to type with purpose.

To: Parents

From: JDixon

Date: 12/5

Subject: And one for the grown-ups

Hi again,

Why should the kids have all the fun? Kim and David Fancy would like to invite the parents of Miss Ward's class to a cocktail party at their home on December 17 from 7 to 10 p.m. All you need to bring is your good cheer!

Address: 9314 West 146th Place in Overland Park. You can RSVP directly to the Fancys.

Hope everyone can make it!

Jen

To: JDixon
From: SLewicki
Date: 12/5
Subject: And one for the grown-ups

Hi,

I will be out of the office until December 8.

Thank you,
Sasha

✦ ✦ ✦

I have never been a big fan of organized "girls' nights." For years, every night was girls' night with Vivs and Laura. I was so busy with work and my daughters that I didn't have time for friends. Then Nina came along and she made it seem like a really good idea to go out and get drunk once in a while. So we have made it a bit of a tradition. Once a month or so, we go for margaritas at Luna Azteca. Usually it's just the two of us, but tonight I have invited Peetsa to join Nina and me. I figured it's a safe match because they already know each other.

I pull up to Peetsa's house in Ron's old blue Camry. I left the minivan for him so he can pick up Max and his friends from Scouts.

I don't even have to honk my horn. As soon as I pull in, she bolts out her front door and comes loping down the driveway. She practically rips the car door off getting in. I'm guessing she's trying to get away from the bitter cold night.

"Drive, drive, drive!" she gasps.

I throw it in reverse and do my best Mario Andretti out of there.

"What the hell?" I ask.

"Zach was in the bathroom. I had to get out before he figured out I was leaving."

"Won't he freak out when he sees you're gone?"

"No. It's the leaving that makes him crazy. Once I'm gone, it doesn't matter."

"Laura used to freak out whenever I left. Preschool was the worst."

"Max doesn't give you a hassle?" she asks, with more than a little envy in her voice.

I shake my head.

"As long as he can watch a little TV, he doesn't care who is watching him."

"Honest to God, I don't know what people did before TV. And I really don't get those anti-TV parents. I mean, good for you if you can amuse your kids *and* make dinner *and* fold laundry all at the same time. But I don't choose to make my life that hard, know what I mean?"

I laugh at her. I've never seen Peetsa so whipped up about something.

"What?" she asks.

"I've just never really thought about it." I shrug. "Who's so anti-TV?"

"Oh! Didn't I tell you? Miss Ward is. She emailed me the other day to tell me she thinks Zach watches too much TV."

"How the hell would she know?" The traffic light in front of us changes to red and I have to brake a little too hard. We both lean forward and then snap back into our seats.

"Apparently every morning at circle time she asks the kids to tell her what they did the night before. I guess Zach always says he watched TV. I mean, don't they all watch TV? Does Max?"

I don't know what to say. I'm definitely not *anti*-TV, but we do limit it to thirty minutes a night, mainly because Ron wants to spend time with Max when he gets home from the store. And when you factor in dinner, bath, and reading there isn't much time left. That's why more than half an hour is such a treat for him. But I don't say any of this. Instead I say:

"Of course! He loves TV." Which isn't a lie at all.

We pull up to Luna Azteca. It's freezing out so we hurry into the restaurant.

I see that the owner, Mr. Barrera, has gone with a tropical Santa motif for his Christmas decorations this year. Nothing says ho-ho-ho like Santa in red flowered shorts hanging ten on a light-up surfboard.

Nina is already sitting at a table and waves us over.

"There she is," I say to Peetsa, and we head to the table.

"Hey there!" I give Nina a hug.

"You guys know each other, right?"

They smile at each other.

"Yup." Nina nods. "We go way back."

And just like that, I feel uncomfortable. God, am I so petty and jealous that I can't have two people I adore have a history without me? What am I, in seventh grade? While I'm chewing on this, Nina says, "I started without you," motioning to the empty margarita glasses in front of her.

"Well then, we'd better catch up." Peetsa winks at me.

Just then the waiter appears with another drink for Nina.

"Two more for my friends, Jonathan," she says to the waiter, with a bit of a slur. "And keep 'em coming."

Hmm. Nina, drunk. Not like I haven't seen it before, but generally not before eight p.m.

"Hey, slow down there." I'm half joking and actually a little embarrassed. I don't want Peetsa to think my best friend is a lush.

"Let's get some guacamole, too, please," I yell to the waiter's back.

Nina definitely needs to get some food in her.

"So, what's up, girls? Anything new?" Nina asks, chewing her ice.

"Well, Max came home from school and told me Miss Ward has a great pair of legs. I'm trying to figure out which—"

"I found Sid," Nina blurts out.

"What?" I say, a little too loudly.

"Who's Sid?" Peetsa asks me.

"I didn't know you were still looking for him. What the hell, Neens?"

Nina avoids my glare. "I really wasn't, but I have a permanent Google search on his name, and this morning I got an alert."

"Who's Sid?" Peetsa asks again.

"You can do that?" I ask, impressed.

"Yes." Nina sounds annoyed. "Everyone can do that. He posted a picture on Facebook and it came up in the search." The ice chewing is getting more intense.

Peetsa slaps both hands down on the table.

"Who is Sid?" she asks for the third and sounds like final time.

"Sorry, P. Sid is Chyna's father."

Peetsa looks at Nina. "Your ex?"

"We were never married, but yeah, my ex. He took off just before Chyna was born." Nina throws back the rest of her margarita in one swallow.

At this magic moment, Jonathan returns.

"Here are your drinks, ladies!" he practically sings. "Guacamole is on the way. Do you want to hear the specials?" His smile fades as he reads the mood of the table. He wisely backs away. "Just call me when you're ready to order."

"He's fucking married," Nina spits out. "He's married. With kids." She puts her hands over her face.

"Oh, my God. Where is he living?" I have so many questions, but that's the first one that comes to my head.

"San Jose."

"California?"

"No, Pennsylvania."

Peetsa jumps in before I can make a snide remark back.

"Wait a sec. How long have you been looking for him? Twelve years?"

Nina and I both nod.

"Why wouldn't his Facebook page or something else have popped up before now?"

"He didn't have one," Nina answers between ice crunchings.

Jonathan our waiter slithers in and puts down the guacamole and a basket of tortilla chips. He raises his eyebrow to me, as if to say, "Order now?" I shake him off.

"He *just* got a Facebook page? A little late to the party, isn't he?" Peetsa looks incredulous.

"He was never the sharpest tool in the shed." I scoop up some guacamole and pop it in my mouth.

Nina gives me a sad look. "He really wasn't," she agrees. Her eyes start to water, but she lets out a laugh instead. "But, God, was he hot." She wipes her cheek.

"Well, I would hope so," says Peetsa. "I'd hate to think you fell for a guy who is both stupid *and* ugly."

This makes us all crack up.

"So, what's on his page?" I ask when we settle down.

"All he has right now is a picture of a three-year-old sitting beside a newborn baby and a lot of messages that say, " 'Welcome to Facebook!' "

"How do you know he's married?" asks Peetsa.

"It's in his status. It also says he works for some tech company." She turns to me in disbelief. "He's got a job! In high tech!" Her eyes well up again.

"What is he, the janitor?" I mumble. Nina starts to cry.

I'm not sure how long I'm going to be able to fake my sympathy. Sid is such a pant load, and seeing someone as dynamic as Nina fall to pieces over him makes me crazy.

"Hey, let's get Jonathan over here," I suggest. "If we're going to drown our sorrows, I need some food."

I wave to Jonathan, and Nina blows her nose with her napkin.

By the end of the night, Peetsa and Nina are three sheets to the wind; I have designated myself the driver since I nursed one margarita the whole evening.

After leaving Jonathan a very nice tip (I tend to tip well because I was a waitress in college and it's a pretty crappy job), we head out to the car. The freezing cold is like a slap in all our faces and I think helps to sober the girls up a little. I drop Nina first and watch from the car as she wobbles to her front door and figures out how to use her key.

"Wow," says Peetsa as we watch her stumble in. "Is she going to be all right?"

"I hope so. I don't envy the hangover she'll have tomorrow, but maybe she'll be a little less emotional about Sid."

"I've never seen this side of her." P. shakes her head.

"Everyone has their kryptonite." I shrug. "Nina's is Sid."

I back the car out of the driveway and head for Peetsa's house.

"What's yours?" she asks me.

"My kryptonite? Rock stars."

She laughs. "I would not have guessed that about you."

"Well, my friend, let me tell you a little story about Vivs's father."

10

Garth has me doing jumping jacks downstairs in Ron's Gym and Tan.

I've noticed that, since having Max, I don't do them with the same abandon I used to. Things just aren't as tight down there, if you know what I mean.

When I asked him to step up my cardio, I had visions of jogging on a treadmill. But this works, too, I guess. I definitely don't huff and puff when I run up the stairs anymore.

". . . ninety-eight, ninety-nine, one hundred. Good job, Jen! Nice form. Get some water."

"I have to cut it short today," I tell him between gasps and gulps of water. "We have a party to go to tonight, and I'm actually going to get a manicure."

"Oh, fun! I love holiday parties."

I smile at Garth. He's always so enthusiastic. When I tell him I need to get my car washed, he'll say, "Isn't a clean car just the best?" I wish I could rub some of his positive energy off on Nina. She has gone to the dark place since our night out. When I can get her on the phone, all she does is moan. I went to her house yesterday to bring her Chick-fil-A (her favorite) and she was a mess. She even asked me to take Chyna for the weekend, which I gladly did under the pretense that I needed a babysitter for both Friday and Saturday nights. It's half true: I'm going to leave Max with Chyna when we go to the Fancys' shindig tonight. I didn't really need her last night, but Ron and I took the opportunity to go see an early movie. It had real people and sex and swearing. I had forgotten movies like that existed.

I'm roused from my thoughts by Garth snapping his fingers in front of my face.

"Hello? Where did you go? I said get some water, not some shut-eye!"

"Sorry. Just thinking about tonight."

"Well, give me twenty push-ups and tell me all about it."

I drop to my knees on the mat and get into position.

"Oh, I think we can skip the girly push-ups."

I give him a frantic look.

"Come on. Let's try some real push-ups. Give me as many as you can."

I put myself into plank position and ease into it.

"One, two . . ."

"I'll count. You just work. So, where's the party?"

"At the home of some parents in Max's class."

Garth nods. "I'm guessing they're not friends."

"Why do you say that?"

"Well, if they were your friends you'd say the party is at a friend's house."

I don't know why I think this is so funny, but I can't stop laughing. Clearly, the endorphins are getting me high.

"Well, I hope you're wearing something sleeveless, giddy girl. Your arms are looking great."

"You know what? I think I will. What about you? Got a hot date tonight?"

Garth smiles. "I wish! I think my dating days are over."

I think about my mother's reprimand at Thanksgiving.

"Well, if you don't have any plans for Christmas, we'd love to have you for dinner. My parents will be here, too."

"Oh, that's so kind of you. Can I let you know?"

"Of course." I'm a little surprised that I didn't get a yes immediately, but whatever.

Garth extends his hand to me. "Okay, that's it for today. Have a great time tonight, hot mama."

"From your lips," I mutter.

✦ ✦ ✦

"So, what is this couple's name, again?" Ron asks as we are driving to the Fancys' neighborhood.

"Kim and David. Daughter is Nancy."

"And what does he do for a living?"

"No idea," I reply. "They're from New York, so something in finance maybe? Wow. Is that their house?" I point to the one at the end of the street. Sure enough, it matches the address I have written on a piece of paper in front of me.

"I'm guessing finance," Ron says.

The Fancy house is impressive. It takes up what looks like two standard-sized lots and has two driveways. That's a lot even for Overland Park.

I look down at what I'm wearing. I have abandoned the mom uniform for tonight and gone with a black sleeveless silk top, black skirt, and some ridiculous black heels that Laura made me buy when we were Black Friday shopping. I thought all black would help me blend in, but now I'm wondering if I should have worn my wedding dress. It's the *fanciest* thing I own.

"I've always wanted to see the inside of this house," Ron muses as we park on the street.

"You've seen it before?" I'm surprised.

"Cindy's parents live a block away. I used to take a lot of walks in the neighborhood to escape the insanity. I remember when they were just building this place."

"Who owned it back then?" I ask.

"Some AT&T bigwig." Ron shrugs.

"Oh, God," I sigh. "We should have brought a nicer bottle of wine."

✦ ✦ ✦

By the time we get up to the door, we have gained two more couples—Kim and Carol Alexander and the hunky dad with his loaded wife from curriculum night, Jean-Luc and Mary Jo Baton. I have no proof yet that he married her to get his green card, but I hope to by the end of the evening.

We all nod and smile hello; Kim rings the doorbell, which chimes out "We Three Kings."

A twenty-something man opens the door wearing a crisp white shirt with a black bow tie and black pants.

"Merry Christmas. Welcome. May I take your coats?" he asks without a trace of a smile.

We walk into a foyer that is almost as big as my living room. The ceilings have to be sixteen feet high. There are tasteful Christmas decorations decking the halls. You know the kind: white lights and tree boughs. No blow-up Santa for the Fancys. I feel like I've walked onto the set of a very classy holiday movie. Or a Pottery Barn photo shoot.

We unload our outer things on the unsmiling doorman and I look for a place to put the wine I have brought. I see a table laden with colorfully wrapped wine bottles, so I add ours to the pack with a sigh.

As we walk from the foyer into the living room, another guy in a bow tie offers us champagne and says, "Be sure to stop by the library to see the jewelry."

Ron grabs two glasses and hands me one.

"What jewelry?" he asks me.

"No idea," I say, and swallow my drink in one gulp.

"Slow down, slugger. It's a long night," Ron warns me with a smile.

"Champagne has no effect on me," I assure him. "I could drink twenty of these."

"I know for a fact that's not true." Ron hands me his champagne. "But I'm going to enable you just this once, because I know you don't really want to be here."

We walk into a gorgeously spread-out living room with a roaring fireplace at one end and lots of comfortable seating. In the middle of the room is a large wooden table overflowing with cheeses and breads and olives and vegetables, all placed around a beautiful wreath. Again, very catalogue-like.

The living room is crowded with people I know and some I don't, milling around taking in the general splendor of their surroundings. Yet another bow tie walks up to us with a large platter of shrimp.

"Shrimp? Have you visited the jewelry in the library?" He smiles and walks away.

"They must have some jewelry collection," Ron notes. "I'll bet they have security in there, too. Want to take a look?"

I nod, still chewing my shrimp.

As we wander toward what might or might not be the library, I scan the room for Peetsa and Buddy. Suddenly, I lock eyes with Dr. Evil. She looks incredibly skinny in a tight black dress with long sleeves and a high neck. Hanging from her ears are gorgeous drop earrings made of black pearls and diamonds. She is walking over to us with her husband, the dashing David, who looks every inch the master of the house in a burgundy velvet jacket and black pants.

"Jen. How great that you came. Thank you so much for organizing this party."

Is she kidding?

"Kim, this is my husband, Ron. Ron, Kim and David are our hosts."

The men shake hands and then David leans in to kiss me on the cheek. I'm not expecting it so it turns into an awkward kiss on the mouth.

"Oh, hi, um . . . We were just admiring your beautiful home."

"Amazing what a million dollars will get you out here in the sticks, isn't it?" She smiles with everything but her eyes.

David looks like Max does when being forced to say thank you. "Have you seen the jewelry yet?"

"No. We keep hearing about it, but we haven't made our way to the library yet." David nods and walks away. His attention has been drawn just over my shoulder. So has Dr. Evil's.

I turn to see what is so interesting and am just in time to take in the impressive sight of Miss Ward showing off her curves in a slinky red dress.

Wow. This is by far the hottest outfit I have ever seen her wear. The dress is knee length and tight, with triangle sections cut out around her waist and a V going down the back. Cindy Crawford in her heyday wouldn't have been able to pull this off. Her blond hair is long and loose around her shoulders.

"Jen, did you invite Peggy?" Dr. Evil asks me.

"No. I just sent the email to the class. Maybe one of the moms told her about it."

"Or one of the dads." Ron grins widely in Miss Ward's general direction.

Dr. Evil turns a polite death glare on him.

"Did *you* do it, Ron?"

Ron looks at me, and I can tell he's a little scared. His mouth says no, but only a weird squeak comes out. I feel bad for him, but I'm also secretly glad he is getting the full Fancy. I know he thinks I'm just exaggerating half the time, and of course I am, but it doesn't mean there isn't some truth in there. Just because they think you're crazy, it doesn't mean you're nuts. Put *that* on my gravestone.

I grab Ron's hand and steer him away from our hostess.

"Why would she care if Miss Ward is here?" Ron whispers.

"No idea." I finish another glass of champagne and look for the refill bow tie.

We mill through the living room for the next hour or so, talking to parents as we go. Asami Chang is all smiles for a change. Maybe she's enjoying the champagne, too. Ravital Brown runs up to me with her husband in tow.

"Jen, I want my husband to meet you. Rob, this is the woman who writes the crazy emails."

Rob shakes my hand.

"Wow, you really had my wife confused that first day. I had to talk her out of calling the principal." He smiles.

"But now I get it!" Ravital says triumphantly. "I know it's all a joke."

"Well, not all of it, I hope!" I laugh along with them.

I introduce them to Ron and they immediately start a conversation about their respective jobs. I tune them out and look around.

It's an impressive turnout. The Westmans are here, and I can't help but wonder if Jackie brought cups. I see the Elders, the Wolffes, and the Kaplans as I scan the room. I am curious whether Sasha Lewicki is here, but then, I wouldn't know even if she were standing right in front of me, since I have never seen her.

Everyone really cleans up nicely, especially Suchafox, whom I spy across the room. He has traded in his jeans for a black suit and tie. I'm surprised when I see him making his way over to me and giving me the old once-over. I feel myself blushing from head to toe.

"You look so pretty," he says, and kisses my cheek. Immediately I feel like I'm cheating on Ron. I don't want him to think anything is going on, but why would he? David Fancy kissed me on the lips, and my husband didn't even blink. My silly crush is giving me a guilty conscience.

"Hey, there. Where's Ali?" I ask, as though she's the one I really want to see.

He shrugs. "I guess she didn't come."

I grab my sixth glass of champagne from a roving bow tie and finally ask Don the question that has been burning in my mind since curriculum night.

"Are you guys not together?"

"Here you are!" Ron comes to stand beside me, with what can only be described as the worst timing ever.

"Hey there. I'm Ron Dixon." He sticks his hand out to shake Don's.

"Don Burgess. Nice to meet you." Killer smile.

"Oh, right, the high school crush!" Ron says, and my mind flashes to all the ways I'm going to murder him later. What would possess him to say that out loud?

"Really?" Don raises his eyebrows at me. "I had no idea."

"One of many." I assure him. I'm guessing I'm as red as Miss Ward's dress by now.

"Did you tell him about the P.E. laundry room?" Don jokes.

"What do you think?" I ask; then we both crack up. Not that anything hilarious happened in there, but I guess the champagne is kicking in.

"What happened in the P.E. laundry room?" Ron isn't laughing.

"Long story, sweetie. I'll tell you later."

"So, is your wife here?" Ron asks.

"We're not married, but no, Lulu's mom isn't here."

Ron nods. "I've been there. Divorce sucks."

"We were never married," Don offers up.

"Oh, sorry, man. I shouldn't have assumed."

"No worries. It's all good."

Wow. Thanks to my husband, I know more than I ever would have had the guts to find out on my own. Ron makes a great wingman.

While we're chatting, I start to notice people walking around with small gold shopping bags. Ooh! I love me a gift bag. I'm guessing whatever is in there is more expensive than the wine we brought. I see Peetsa with one.

"What'd you get?" I ask, with only a bit of a slur.

"A necklace." She sighs. "I think I'll give it to my mother. Did you buy something?"

"*Buy* something?" I ask.

"Some jewelry. They're selling it in the library."

"Who is 'they'?" I ask, making a beeline for the next room. Peetsa and Ron trail after me.

As I walk into the library, I can't believe my eyes. There are two large tables of jewelry—earrings, necklaces, bracelets, and rings all nicely displayed. JJ Aikens is behind the tables with another woman I don't know, and they are working diligently to keep the sales going.

I try to put the pieces together using my inebriated brain. Kim

Fancy pushes me to have a parents' cocktail party. She is eager to host it, but doesn't want to send out the invites. I send out the invites, which makes it look like I asked her to host it. We all get here, and she's pushing *jewelry*? I did *not* see this coming.

I walk up and stand beside Shirleen Cobb, who's trying on earrings.

"Those look pretty," I offer.

"Well, they should be for the price. Good lord." She takes them off and looks me up and down. "I thought this was a Christmas party, not a shakedown."

As she stomps away, I see JJ out of the corner of my eye.

"Hey, JJ. Where did all this stuff come from?"

"Oh, hi, Jen. Didn't think you were coming. This *stuff* is jewelry designed by Kim's friend Delia from Manhattan."

Someone hands me another glass of champagne. It's Ron.

"Say something nice," he whispers in my ear. I ignore him.

"How much are these earrings?" I hold up the pair Shirleen was so disgusted by. They are gold disk clip-ons.

"Those are two hundred and seventy-five dollars."

"Are they real gold?"

"Gold plated." She smiles. "Aren't they gorgeous? You would look great in those." She looks at Ron. "Are you Jen's husband? You should totally get her those for Christmas."

"Umm" is all Ron can think of to say.

"Really. You should. And you can even say you got them in Manhattan, because technically that's where they're from." JJ is working hard for what I'm sure is some sort of commission.

Just then we hear a loud crash from the other room. I hand JJ the earrings, and Ron and I hurry toward the noise. We are greeted by the sight of Nancy Fancy in her pajamas sitting on the floor with the Christmas wreath centerpiece and some cheese and bread around her. Kim Fancy glides over from the other side of the room.

"What happened?"

"I'm sorry, Mommy. I just wanted a piece of cheese."

Kim looks up at her guests with an embarrassed smile.

"Sorry, everyone. It seems Nancy still needs to learn how to *ask* for a snack."

There is some light laughter and then, out of nowhere, Miss Ward comes sprinting across the room like a streak of red paint.

"Oh, my goodness, sweetie, are you okay?" She kneels down beside the very embarrassed little girl.

"I'm okay," Nancy says in a tiny voice.

"Well, let me check you all over." Miss Ward starts to tickle Nancy, who starts to giggle.

"Thanks, Miss Ward," she says, and then gives her a hug.

"Awww," sings the Greek chorus of parents standing around.

Kim steps in, gives Miss Ward a strained smile, and helps Nancy get up. She whispers something in the little girl's ear that makes her nod and scoot out of the room.

"And that's our show for tonight," Kim says with a smile that once again doesn't reach her eyes.

I turn to Ron, who's staring at Miss Ward with a frown.

"What?"

"I might be crazy, but wasn't the V in the *back* of her dress?"

I look at Miss Ward, who is just getting herself off the floor and showing some impressive cleavage.

"Why, I believe you are correct, Mr. Observant."

Peetsa and Buddy join us as people get back to their conversations.

"Wasn't the V down the back of her dress earlier?" Buddy asks Ron.

"I said the same thing." Ron laughs, and they high-five.

"Really, guys?" I roll my eyes. "Buddy, close your eyes. What color are my pants?"

"Uh, black?" He blushes.

"I'm wearing a skirt."

"You have to admit it's kind of weird," Peetsa says. "Why would she turn her dress around?"

"Why does she do anything?" I'm frustrated and a little off balance from the champagne.

"Maybe someone took it off for her," Buddy mumbles to Ron and they high-five again. I take this as a sign that it's time to go home. I really want to take my pantyhose off.

"I'm going to pee and then we should get out of here before I say something I'm going to regret."

I'm not on the sturdiest of legs as I walk toward the foyer powder room, which I had noticed on the way in. I open the door and find Don Burgess zipping up his pants.

"Whoops, sorry." As I turn to back out, I trip on my heels and fall sideways toward Don. He grabs me with both arms.

"Wow, you're really falling for me," he jokes.

He stands me back upright, but doesn't let go. Either he doesn't think I can stand up on my own or he's enjoying this mini embrace as much as I am. For a moment we stand face to face and that urge to kiss him rears its ugly head again. But this time I feel the pull from him as well. The energy between us is heady—or maybe that's the Polo. Oh, my God, is this really going to happen?

"Everything okay?" Ron is standing looking at what I can imagine is a very compromising situation.

"You bet," Don answers quickly. "Jen tripped and I was just helping her steady herself."

He gives my arms a squeeze and lets me go. Ron walks right between us and takes my arm.

"Thanks, man, I've got her."

Don gives us a thumbs-up and walks back toward the foyer.

"Are you okay?" Ron's raised eyebrow tells me he's not pleased.

"I still have to pee," I admit. At the same time I take off my heels and hand them to him.

"Here, hold these so I don't fall again."

He takes the shoes, points me in the direction of the bathroom, and closes the door. I hike up my skirt, sit down, and take the whiz of a lifetime.

"Holy shit holy shit holy shit," I whisper to myself. *Did that really just happen?* I start to giggle. Suddenly I'm seventeen all over again and thrilled that Suchafox just spoke to me. This is too much for my inebriated brain to process. I flush, turn to the sink, and splash cold water on my face. One look in the mirror tells me that my water-proof mascara is actually *not*. I have two lovely black tears streaking down my cheeks.

"Crap." I grab one of the fancy towels and do my best to clean up my face. I really need to go home.

Heading out to the foyer, I see Ron, Peetsa, Buddy, and Don chatting with their coats on. Ron is holding mine plus my shoes.

"Feel better?" he asks, helping me into my coat.

I don't say anything, but I smile and put my arm through his. We say our good nights and I manage to escape without making eye contact with Don.

✦ ✦ ✦

I'm trying to find the words to describe how I feel. It's like someone has stuffed a wool sock in my mouth and pulled a rubber glove over my head. Ugh. Champagne hangovers are the *worst*. Why do I always forget that?

As I attempt to get up the courage to roll out of bed and relieve my bladder, the door bursts open and Ron and Max come charging in.

"Good afternoon, Mommy!" Ron sings at the top of his lungs.

Max jumps up to give me a crushing hug.

"Mom, you slept for so long! It's already lunchtime."

My stomach starts to turn at the thought of food. Ron hands me a giant cup of coffee.

"I put a little hair of the dog in there for you." He smiles and sits on the bed.

The thought of putting more alcohol into my system makes me want to throw up, but I give him a grateful smile.

"You put dog hair in Mom's coffee? Where did you get it from? Wait, *are we getting a dog*?" Max screams the last part, and my head nearly splits in two. Oh, my God, is this going to be a long day.

"No dog, sorry, champ. Let's let Mom get dressed and we can go pick up lunch, okay?" Ron starts to pull him off the bed.

"Dad says you're going to want Burger King for lunch, but I said no way because you always say we don't eat garbage."

"Well, today it looks like we will." I give Max the most enthusiastic smile I can muster.

There's nothing like a greasy burger when you have a hangover. That's pretty much all I took away from my four years at KU.

It isn't until I'm sitting on the toilet that the events of last night come crashing back to me. I hold my head in my hands and replay the scene outside the powder room. Boy, I am not the girl I used to be. The old Jen would have grabbed that man and kissed the shit out of him. But the girl who slept her way around Europe wasn't married, nor was she in love. And I really do love my husband. I don't *want* to be attracted to someone else. And yet, here I am.

I go back to my bed and call Nina. No answer, as usual. She's still in the dark place. I pause a moment, then dial Peetsa, but hang up before she answers. I've got to talk to someone about this, but I'm not sure how Peetsa will react. Damn it, Nina! Why can't you get your shit together so I can lose mine?

✦ ✦ ✦

We are chowing down on burgers and fries in the kitchen when I realize I'm feeling a bit better. Max can't believe his luck. He's actually having fast food and it isn't someone's birthday.

"Can we do this every Sunday?" he asks hopefully.

"Not a chance," Ron says, although I'm sure he would be okay with it if I weren't around to say no.

I glance over at my kitchen-counter office and play with the idea of checking my email. I'm wondering how much crap I'm going to get for last night's party turning into an episode of Home Shopping Network. Maybe none. I mean it's not like I invited everyone . . . Oh, wait. While I'm wondering who painted "Sucker" on me, I boot up my iMac with the twenty-seven-inch screen (go big or go home, baby!) and check my email.

Holy shit storm.

To: JDixon
From: AChang
Date: 12/13
Subject: Class-less party

Jen,

I can't say I'm surprised that you chose to turn a lovely class party into a jewelry sale. It's pretty much what we have all come to expect from you as class mom. I know some people enjoy your "wacky" emails and generally lax attitude toward the job, but last night was the last straw. Do you even realize that people felt obligated to buy that overpriced junk? I only hope the money is going to charity. But I have to say there will be no more charity for you. I plan to take this straight to Principal Jakowski first thing tomorrow.

Asami

Well, that was expected. I'll bet she was composing this in her head while smiling at me over her champagne glass.

To: JDixon
From: SCobb
Date: 12/13
Subject: Class party

Jennifer,

I'm surprised at you. What would make you think anyone wanted to go to a party so they could spend money? Such a tacky idea.

Shirleen

I'm surprised she didn't mention the fact that there were no gluten-free hors d'oeuvres.

To: JDixon
From: CAlexander
Date: 12/13
Subject: About last night . . .

Jen,

I'm glad you organized the party last night, but was selling the jewelry really necessary? Being asked to fork out money for some really crappy stuff kind of put a damper on the whole night.
    The lesbians are disappointed.

                                    Carol (and Kim)

Ouch. That one hurt. Now the cool moms think I'm a jerk. I scroll through the rest of the emails—ten in total—and pretty much get the same message from each of them. Then I get to the one from Kim Fancy, which is addressed to the whole class.

To: Parents
From: KFancy
Date: 12/13
Subject: Oh, what a night!

Hello, friends,

I hope everyone enjoyed themselves last night. It was certainly a pleasure to have you all to our home.

> *I want to send a special thanks to our class mom, Jen Dixon, for organizing such a unique and fun gathering. Good job, Jen! See everyone at the holiday concert!*
>
> *Love,*
>
> *Kim*

I'm contemplating how to respond to the class when one last email catches my eye and the Whopper I inhaled earlier does a flip-flop in my stomach.

> *To: JDixon*
> *From: DBurgess*
> *Date 12/13*
> *Subject: Last night*
>
> *Jen,*
>
> *Nice bumping into you in the bathroom! Let's have coffee sometime.*
>
> *Don*

For reasons I can't explain, I immediately grab for my cell phone and text Don instead of answering his email.

Thanks for catching me! So, do you mean coffee or, you know, COFFEE?

Only a few seconds go by before he texts me back.

Which answer gets me coffee?

I giggle. I'm not sure how to answer that one, so I don't.

11

To: Parents

From: AChang

Date: 01/05

Subject: I'm your new class mom

Happy New Year,

Most of you know me, but for those who don't, I'm Asami Chang and I will be taking over the duties of class mom from Jennifer Dixon.

It will be my pleasure to get our class back on track after a bumpy fall.

First of all, these emails will be content driven, not a forum for me to tell jokes and solicit bribes. Second, I welcome comments and input. I may be in charge, but you definitely have a say.

Below are things you need to know:

January 18 is picture day. Make sure your children's uniforms are clean and pressed. I'm concerned by the lack of emphasis most of you place on neatness. Please pay attention to this. I find a daily bath is very helpful. I've also noticed a lot of messy hair. I plan to stand beside the *photographer with a brush and I will be using it. I suggest a ponytail for the girls with long hair, or perhaps a braid. I'm happy to braid hair that day. I will assume if you send your daughter to school with her hair down, you want me to braid it.*

I'm organizing a class coffee meeting after pickup on January 12. We will meet at Homer's Coffee House at 8:30 a.m. Please be prompt.

Miss Ward informs me our children will be taking a field trip to the Quindaro Underground Railroad Museum on February 28. I will need one mother to go with me. Please don't volunteer if you already went on the recycling field trip. And be prepared to watch the kids closely and not socialize.

And now here are a few messages from the school administration . . .

I have to stop reading. My blood is boiling. I thought I was over being pissed off, but as I unclench my back teeth, I can see this clearly isn't the case.

How is it acceptable for Asami Chang to give grooming alerts and threaten kids with braids? All I ever did was try to make people lighten up.

Principal Jakowski's words are still burned into my brain. He had accosted me outside the gym just before the kids' holiday concert and basically fired me from being class mom.

"I'm sorry, Jen, but some of the parents feel you use the position to push your own agenda."

"What agenda? I don't have an agenda."

"Is it true you solicited bribes in return for better conference times?"

"That was a joke! Do you really think I'd let someone buy me a coat?"

"What about asking for Starbucks gift cards?" he asked.

"Oh, my God, I don't even remember doing that, but I'm sure I didn't mean it."

"And of course there is the jewelry incident at the class cocktail party."

"Why does everyone think that was my idea?"

"Mrs. Fancy said you asked her to throw the party. I mean, you did send out the invitations."

"She *wanted* to have the party," I explained. "I was just following orders."

"Well, according to her, you asked for the party on that specific date and her jewelry friend was booked to come to town for a visit. She felt she had to let her display her things as compensation for the party being held during her visit."

Clearly, this man will believe anything.

"I'm still having a hard time seeing how that's my fault."

"Yes, well, some of the parents have also complained that you make racist remarks in your emails."

"What?" I screamed. I couldn't believe what I was hearing. "That is not true!"

Principal Jakowski pulled out a piece of paper and handed it to me. It was one of my first emails to the class. I had been organizing the curriculum night class get-together. He had helpfully highlighted the offending phrase.

No hard feelings, Asami. I understand your people's lust for power.

I laughed before I could stop myself, and then put my hand over my mouth.

"Okay, I can see how that might look, but I was just trying to make light of the situation. I mean, the woman was trying to have me kicked out after one week on the job! Nina Grandish and I already talked about this."

Of course, Nina! She'd talk some sense into this guy. I suggested the principal call the head of the Parents' Association.

"I already have. I had to make three calls and text her twice before she called me back. She didn't seem interested in addressing the situation at all. In fact, she asked me to handle it. It seems she's been under the weather. Anyway, now I'm forced to get involved and I want you to know we take racism very seriously in this school."

At that very moment, I realized that I was fighting for a job I'd never wanted in the first place. Principal Jakowski was handing me a Get Out of Jail Free card and I was trying to get back in. Was I nuts?

"You want me to step down? Fine. Merry Christmas." I stomped into the gym just as the first group of kids was starting their performance.

As the sixth-grade class sang "Holly Jolly Christmas" (my God, that song is repetitive!) I stewed. They don't want me? *Fine*. Nina agrees with them? *Fine*. I'd fix her wagon. I'd fix all their wagons. Visions of prom night in the movie *Carrie* kept me busy while each class filed in and sang Christmas carols.

I really wished Ron had been able to make it to the concert. He would have talked me off the ledge. But he was in the middle of his Christmas savings bonanza down at the store. I'd promised him I would record the show on my phone.

So when Miss Ward took the stage to introduce the kindergarteners, I brought my focus back to the gym. Max had been very secretive about what the class was planning, so of course I pushed Record and braced myself. God bless that Miss Ward; she never disappoints.

The kids filed onto the stage in what are best described as tacky tourist costumes. Max was wearing a tropical shirt, a baseball cap, cargo shorts, and sandals with brown socks. Some of the kids wore cameras around their necks and zinc oxide on their noses. Naturally, they all looked adorable, but I couldn't imagine what Miss Ward had in store for us. She explained that they wanted to remind everyone that people celebrate Christmas all over the world, not just in places that have snow (because people *not* remembering that is one of the bigger problems we face in the world?) And then they sang . . . get ready for it . . . "Kokomo," by the Beach Boys! Not the Kodak moment I was imagining for my five-year-old son's first Christmas concert, but I laughed at the sheer cuteness of it. I shelved my mass murder plot, at least for a little while.

At the class party afterward, I was grateful to be surrounded by kids and parents the whole time, as it kept me from welling up about the shame spiral I was in. *Fired!* As class mom! How was I going to tell Max?

Out of the corner of my eye, I saw Don Burgess with Ali and Lulu, looking at the class's homemade snow globes. Part of me wanted to run to him and sob my broken heart out. Ron, while being my rock, would ultimately give me the "I'm the master of my own misery" speech. Somehow I knew Suchafox wouldn't do that. He'd take me in those solid arms and tell me the people who got me fired were all assholes. Or would he? I'll never know because, thank God, I didn't act on that impulse. But I did receive a text from him later that day.

Nice job on the holiday party. Sorry I didn't get a chance to talk to you. You seemed kind of down. Everything ok?

I didn't think my rage/humiliation was noticeable. I need a better game face.

Yeah, just the holiday blues, I guess. Thanks for noticing.

And not ten seconds later . . .

Well, I'm around if you want to talk.

Hmm . . . maybe *that's* what he meant by coffee. I thanked him and wished him a Merry Christmas. I was too bummed out to even attempt to be flirty.

I tried to do what Taylor Swift does and just *shake it off,* but between the class mom thing and my wayward thoughts about Don, a pall was cast over my whole holiday season. Christmas Day was a complete disaster. Nina and Chyna came, of course, along with my parents, the girls, Raj (back in favor for now), and, to everyone's surprise, Garth. I forgot that I had even asked him until he gave me his answer on Christmas Eve.

Nina still wasn't in great shape and I was in no mood to prop her up. I mean, she had basically thrown me under the bus. I thought it was gutsy of her to show up at all, but realized she probably did it for Chyna. She spent a lot of time by the Christmas tree, drinking wine. The only person she spoke to at any great length was Garth, although I couldn't imagine what they'd have to talk about.

It was nice to see Raj back in the mix. No ring on Vivs's finger, but no hostility between them, either. Apparently they were at an impasse.

And I guess I am, too. I log out of my email and sigh. Asami has won. The only thing left for me to do is get Max ready for picture day.

Oh, yes, that is exactly what I will do.

✦ ✦ ✦

As I plot my picture day revenge in my head, I run up to get changed for my first workout of the New Year. T minus four months until the mud run, and I know Garth is going to step it up.

My phone buzzes as I'm putting my T-shirt on. I figure it's Peetsa, but it's actually Don sending me a picture of a beautiful baby. What the . . . ? I type back to him.

What's up with the baby?

It's me. Cute, wasn't I?

Yes, you were. What the hell happened? You're hideous now.

Ha ha, puberty happened. We all can't be natural beauties like you.

I get goose bumps when I read this. I'm a natural beauty, am I?

Well, it's a curse, this beauty of mine. I spend all day fending off advances from strange men.

Hey, I'm not that strange.

I laugh out loud as I put the phone down to tie my shoe. It buzzes again almost immediately.

What are you up to? Can you meet for coffee?

There's that coffee offer again.

Sorry, I can't. I'm going to work out.

I could help you work out.

I'll bet you could, I think to myself, then snap back to reality. Why am I even encouraging this? Flirty texting is just a gateway to adultery. I know that's what Nina would tell me. But it's also harmless and kind of fun.

I'm sure you could, but I have a hot trainer waiting for me in my basement. Gotta go!

I push Send and turn off my phone in case I'm lured into any more sparring.

As I walk down to Ron's Gym and Tan, I note that Garth has finally taken my suggestion and let himself in. He's busy setting up some kind of obstacle course for me.

"Hey, Garth, happy New Year." I walk over and hug him.

"You too! What did you guys end up doing?"

"The only thing you can do when you have kids." I shrug. "You do fake midnight at nine o'clock and then head to Club White Sheets."

"Where is Club White Sheets? Is it that new place over on Grand?"

I start to laugh. "It's bed, Garth. Club White Sheets is bed."

He looks confused for a second, then bursts out laughing. His laugh makes me laugh ever harder and soon we're rolling on the floor.

Garth gains control first.

"Okay. Enough. While you're on the ground, why don't we start with twenty push-ups and fifty sit-ups, just to get warmed up?"

"Spoilsport." I scowl, but flip over and give him twenty perfect man push-ups. I surprise both of us.

"Nice, Jen. Wow! New year, new you."

"I can't believe I just did that," I pant.

I flip over and launch into my sit-ups with newfound confidence. By forty I'm hurting, but I make it to fifty before I collapse, panting.

"So much for the new me," I say.

"Don't be silly. You've come a long way, baby! I'm proud of you. Now, up off your caboose and let's get going."

✦ ✦ ✦

Garth manages to have me sweating like a pig by the end of the hour. As I'm walking him to the door, he casually asks about Nina.

"What about her?" I ask a little too briskly.

"Weeelll," Garth drawls. I think I might have scared him off.

"I had a really nice time talking to her and I'm wondering if she's mentioned me at all."

"Jesus, Garth, I don't know. I'll pass her a note in science class."

As soon as the words are out of my mouth, I feel bad. I can see the hurt look in his eyes.

"I'm sorry. I didn't mean that. I just haven't spoken to Nina since Christmas. She has been going through a bit of a rough patch thanks to her ex, and she hasn't been answering her phone."

Garth waves my comments aside.

"No worries. I was just wondering how she's doing. We had talked about her possibly designing a website for me."

"Well, she's really good at it, that's for sure. If she talked about it with you, I'm sure she's already coming up with ideas. It may take her some time to get out of her funk and get working, though."

"I get it," he says. But I wonder if he really does.

After Garth leaves, I check my phone and see it has blown up in the past hour, thanks to Asami's email. Everybody wants the 411 on my class mom demise. Peetsa, Ravi, and Kim Alexander all express their concern with a "WTF," and Shirleen Cobb is not at all happy about having to teach the new class mom all about Graydon's many needs. Only Suchafox sees a silver lining.

Maybe now you'll have time for coffee with me. ☺

I really need to make sure we're talking about the same type of coffee. But before that, I'd better figure out which one I want.

✦ ✦ ✦

I stroll up to the school the next day to wait for Max to come out, and I see what I have been dreading—all the mothers from my class standing around in little klatches, talking and drinking Starbucks. Normally I would be one of them with my grande skim chai latte, but because of my class mom shame, I have been avoiding this scene since the new year started. For the past couple of days, I have had Ron leave the store to do pickup, but today I decide to face the music.

As I walk toward the front of the school, I can't help but feel like everyone is talking about me. I know I'm just being paranoid. I walk up to Peetsa and Ravital Brown.

"Oh, my God, Jen, we were just talking about you. Where the hell have you been?"

"Did you write that email from Asami as a joke?" asks Ravi. "That was so funny. Best one yet."

I gave them both a hug. I've missed them.

"No, sadly—this time the joke's on me."

"So it's true?" Peetsa gasps. "One of Hunter's moms tried to tell me, but I wouldn't believe her."

"Well, believe it."

"Jeez. Are you okay?" she asks. "I can't believe you didn't tell me."

"You were away and I didn't want to bring you down over the holidays."

I tell them about my conversation with Principal Jakowski and they react exactly how I would expect my besties to react. Outraged! Infuriated! Bent on revenge! *Until* I mention the accusation of racism.

"I mean, come on, it was a joke!" I say, exasperated.

They look at me and then at each other and then at the ground.

"What am I missing?" I ask.

Ravi takes the bullet.

"Well, I have to admit when Asami asked me what I thought of the phrase 'your people's lust for power,' I said I thought it was a little off. I mean, now that I know you, I see you were being funny, but at the time I didn't know what to think." She looks at her shoes.

"Hey, we all love your emails," Peetsa adds, "but people are really sensitive about racism. I know you meant it as a joke, but maybe the class email isn't the best place for it."

I look at both of them and am about to say something when a swarm of kids runs out the front door. In the sea of winter jackets, Max is easy to spot in his leopard-print coat. He's carrying Zach B. on his back.

"Hey, Mom. Zach B. is riding me like I'm a horse."

"Well, you do look like an animal in that coat." I smile.

I look up at Peetsa and Ravi, who are hugging their boys.

"Ravi, I'm sorry if I offended you. Really. It was a thoughtless thing to write."

Ravital shakes her head.

"Trust me, I wasn't *that* offended."

"Oh, God, I'm really going to miss your emails," Peetsa moans.

"What, you don't like personal-hygiene tips in your class emails?" I ask. "I found that very helpful. A bath! Who would have thought?"

As we are walking to our cars, Peetsa asks me about Nina.

"You know, I haven't spoken to her since Christmas. She and Chyna came over for dinner, but she was still not herself."

"Wow, when she goes to the dark place she really pitches a tent." Peetsa shakes her head. "What did she say about the class mom stuff?"

"I haven't talked to her about it." I shrug. "Jakowski told her what he was planning and she said she didn't want to get involved."

"That's cold."

"I know, right?" Suddenly I feel vindicated. "I really think she could have put the kibosh on this whole thing if she had just taken her head out of her ass for five minutes."

Peetsa is shaking her head and laughing.

"Too harsh?" I ask.

She puts her thumb and finger up to show me an inch.

I buckle Max into his car seat and as I slide into the minivan I check my phone. I'm rewarded with a text from Don.

You look nice today. Very fit.

I immediately look up to see if he's watching me.

How the hell would you know?

I caught a glimpse as I was pulling up to get Lulu.

Oh. Well, thanks. What are you up to?

Taking Lulu to dance class. You?

Max has Scouts.

So . . . still no coffee?

Not today!

But there is the hope of someday?

Absolutely.

I put the phone in my purse and start the minivan. Texts from Don have become kind of a regular thing. I'm enjoying the sparring but can't help but feel that I'm doing something wrong, like picking my nose in public. Then *that* feeling gets me pissed off, because I'm just having fun and it feels good to have the attention of someone besides Ron and it doesn't mean anything and can't I just have a friend who is a guy, dammit? Welcome to the cocktail party in my head.

I pull out of the school's parking lot and decide to not think about it any more today.

✦ ✦ ✦

For the next couple of weeks my life goes back to its normal, dull housewifey routine, although without the class mom crap to annoy me I find I have a bit of spare time on my hands.

"Idle hands are the devil's workshop," I can hear my mother say. I never fully understood what that meant until I realize that I'm spending most of my spare time either flirty-texting with Don or concocting a plan to sabotage Asami's picture day efforts. My thoughts go from the benign (tell the kids not to smile, or else) to the macabre (light a fire in school so the sprinklers go off and soak everyone's hair. *Braid* that, *Asami*), but I don't want to do anything that will hurt or upset the kids, so my options are limited. I consider asking Don to be my accomplice, but realize I want to take either all the credit or all the blame, depending on how things go down.

Garth is pushing me harder than ever, and I have to say I'm pleased with the results. My usual post-holiday five pounds didn't materialize, so I'm looking and feeling better than I ever have.

"Any plans for the long weekend?" Garth asks as I'm finishing my final set of lunges across the basement floor.

"Nothing much. You?"

"Well, nothing yet, but I thought if you were up for it we could go to Wichita on Saturday. This charity I work with is having a scaled-down indoor mudder at Hartman Arena."

"An *indoor* mudder?" I take a swig of water. "They do that?"

"Actually, this is the first one."

"Sounds dirty and smelly."

"I'll be disappointed if it isn't," Garth assures me. "I think you need to get a look at what you'll be facing. You've only ever seen it on YouTube. I just want you to get a sense of the scale. What we're going to see still isn't a full mudder, but it's the best I can do in Kansas in February."

"It's not a bad idea. Can I bring Max?"

"Sure!" says Garth as he gives me a huge smile. "Aren't road trips just the best?"

✦ ✦ ✦

I'm standing with Peetsa and Ravi, waiting for the kids to get out of school. It's warm for January so we don't have our heads and faces covered as we usually do. I see Don Burgess standing with Kim or Carol Alexander, and I wave. Don holds up his phone and gives me a shrug. He's wondering why I haven't answered his text from this morning. I told him I was going to Wichita with my trainer this weekend and he's been bugging me for details.

Are you going to have coffee with him?

I take my phone out of my pocket and type a quick response.

I never disclose my coffee-drinking plans.

The girls and I are talking about our plans for Martin Luther King weekend. Peetsa tells us she and Buddy are packing up the kids and taking them skiing at Buddy's parents' place at Snow Creek. When I mention my big road trip to Wichita to observe the mudder, they are pretty impressed. Ravi says she doesn't have any plans so I ask if Zach B. wants to join us on our road trip. Selfishly, I know it will go better if Max has a buddy.

"He'd love to," she says, and then her face lights up. "Oh, my goodness, does that mean I'll have a Saturday to myself?"

"And a Friday night, if you'll let him sleep over."

Just then the bell rings and the kindergarteners start pouring out of the school. Normally they are a pretty wild bunch, but today I notice a lot of heads down and even a few kids crying. When I locate

Max's leopard coat, I can see that he looks very unhappy. When he sees me, his little face crumples and he holds out his arms.

"What is it, baby?" I get down on my knees to hug him. Peetsa and Ravi are doing the same thing with their kids. They both give me a "What the hell?" look.

"Max, sweetie, what happened?" I pull his head away to look him in the face.

"He's dead. We saw him."

"Who's dead?" I'm thinking the class fish.

"Martin Luther King. Someone shot him with a gun and they put him in a box just like Rufus." Rufus was our pet guinea pig. He died last year of natural causes and he's buried in a shoebox underneath the wild rhubarb that grows in the backyard.

"Oh, sweetie, I'm so sorry. Where did you see the picture?" I ask as I mentally compose a hate letter to Miss Ward.

"Mrs. Chang showed us."

"*What?*" Peetsa, Ravi, and I say all at once.

The boys cry louder.

I really want to go back into the school and find out what the hell happened, but I can't leave Max like this.

"Did he really die?" Max asks through his sobs. "He was so nice and helpful."

I can tell this is going to open up the death discussion again, and I'm just not up for it. Memories of Max dealing with Rufus's death come flooding back to me. He cried for days. Ron was at a loss, so he brought home a book that someone at his store recommended called *Something Is Wrong with Grandma*. It's supposed to help kids understand and deal with death, but all it did was convince Max that something was wrong with his grandma. It took him months to get over his fear that my mother was going to keel over any second.

"You know, he died a long time ago, and it was very sad. But he did so many amazing things in his life and when you think about it, he now has a whole day for people to remember how good he was."

"Where did they bury him?" Max asks me. I give Ravi and Peetsa a desperate look, because how the hell would I know?

Ravi comes to the rescue: "I think he's buried in Atlanta, right near where he grew up." That sounds about right. I give her a grateful smile.

Peetsa looks at all three boys.

"Did Mrs. Chang show you a picture of his grave?" she asks, trying to get a clearer idea of what they saw.

"No, it was a picture of him lying in a box with his eyes closed," Zach T. says. His eyes start to water.

Oh, good God. No wonder they're traumatized. Showing a picture of a dead body in a casket to five-year-olds. I turn to Max.

"Hey, can you sit with Mrs. Tucci in her car for a minute? I want to go talk to Miss Ward."

"Why don't I take all three of you to our place for hot chocolate?" Peetsa offers.

The boys nod and smile. Proof once again that chocolate solves just about all of life's problems.

"Want me to come with you?" Ravi asks me.

"Sure. P., we'll be over in a little while."

"Sounds good." Peetsa waves as she hustles the boys to her car.

Ravi and I head into the school and march right down to room 147.

"You can do the talking," she says as we reach the door.

"Count on it." I wink at her.

As we enter Miss Ward's colorful classroom, I can see we are not the first parents to arrive. Dr. Evil is leaning over the front of Miss Ward's desk and speaking in low but severe tones. As we walk in I hear Kim say, ". . . and I'm sick of it."

"Hi. Sorry to interrupt, but we have some really upset little boys on our hands." I look directly at Kim Fancy. "Was Nancy upset, too?"

"About what?" Kim's slight scowl tells me she's both annoyed and confused.

"Hi, Jen. Is this about the Martin Luther King presentation?" Miss Ward asks, as if she's asking how the weather is.

"Uh, yes. Max and his friends came out of school really freaked out from seeing a picture of a dead body."

"A what?" Kim and Miss Ward ask at once.

"Weren't you here for Asami's presentation?"

"No." Miss Ward actually looks contrite. "I, um, had some papers to grade, so I went to the teachers' lounge while she did it. When I got back, she told me she had already dismissed them."

"Seriously? You let a parent dismiss the kids?" I'm a little surprised. I'm also wondering what kind of papers a kindergarten teacher needs to grade.

"Well, I wouldn't normally, but she seemed to have things under control. You say she showed them a dead body? Whose?"

"Martin Luther King's," I say, exasperated. "He was in his coffin. Max is completely traumatized. He came running out of school crying."

Miss Ward and Kim look at each other. Kim shakes her head and walks out of the classroom. What the hell?

"Well, I will certainly talk to Asami about it and find out what happened," Miss Ward assures me. She pauses and smiles sardonically.

"Jenny, it's so funny to have *you* complaining about *her*. She complained about *you* constantly."

"Yes, it must be hilarious for you." I turn quickly and almost hit Ravi as I'm walking out. I totally forgot she was with me.

As we head down the hall, Ravi seems to read my thoughts. "I can't believe she left the class alone with a parent. Is that normal?"

"Depends on whose world you live in." I sigh.

12

Saturday morning at 7:50 sharp, Garth arrives at my house, his usual ten minutes early. I'm just clearing breakfast away for Max and Zach B. They are bleary-eyed from their sleepover and I predict a car nap in the not too distant future.

"Hey, Garth. Want some coffee for the road?"

"No, thanks. Brought my own." He holds up a Starbucks cup. I immediately think of Don and laugh to myself.

"What's your poison?"

"Grande triple-shot latte with extra foam." He smiles and cheers me.

"Well, that will put some punch in your pumpkin." I cheers him back with my mug. "We'll be ready in five."

I'm halfway up the stairs when I yell over my shoulder.

"Okay, boys, lock and load. Wheels up in five. Bring a couple of pillows. Let's move it, monkeys!"

I hear Zach B. say, "Your mom talks weird."

I check my phone and find a text from Don:

Have fun in Wichita.

I smile. This is the weirdest relationship I have ever had. We text all the time and know everything about each other's lives, but we never meet up for that much-talked-about coffee.

We decide to take my bitchin' minivan so we have room to stretch out and the boys can watch a movie. Don't judge me. I wish I were the type of mom who has endless ideas for car games and the energy to play them, but I am not. What I do have is an endless supply of DVDs that I pull out for any car ride longer than forty-five minutes, because that is Max's breaking point.

The boys snuggle up to their pillows in their car seats as we take off and about ten minutes into *The Lego Movie*, they are passed out.

"So what is the charity you work with?" I ask Garth as I steer the van onto I-35 South. The weekend morning traffic is light.

"The Wounded Warrior Project."

"You know, my mom volunteers for them. She hosts a Proud Supporter event every year with her church group."

"I know. That's where I met her." Garth seems to smile at the memory.

"Were you helping out at the pancake breakfast or something?" I sneak a look at him.

"Something like that."

"Wait, are you a vet?"

He nods. "I did two tours in Afghanistan."

"When?" I say a little too loudly. Shit! I check the rearview to make sure the boys are still sleeping.

"Oh, 2004 to 2006."

"Were you in combat?"

"Well, I wasn't there for the weather."

"Did you get hurt?"

He shrugs.

"I took some shrapnel in my left side. I got off easy compared to some of my friends."

"Holy shit! I can't believe I didn't know this about you. Why didn't you tell me?"

"It never came up."

We both stare at the windshield, watching miles of highway slip beneath us before I speak again.

"Do you mind talking about it?"

He chuckles.

"No, not at all. What do you want to know?"

I think about that for a minute and self-edit the inappropriate questions that race to the tip of my tongue.

"Um, what do you guys miss most when you were over there?"

"It's different for everyone," he muses. "Everyone misses home in one way or another. Could be your family, your bed, wearing jeans, normal food. For me, it was Campbell's tomato soup."

"What?" I start to laugh. "Tomato soup?"

Garth nods. "Don't ask me why, but the whole time I was away I craved tomato soup. When I came back, I couldn't get enough of it."

I shake my head. "Too funny. I wonder what I would miss."

"Whatever it is, I guarantee it won't be what you'd expect it to be."

As we are passing Emporia, which is just about halfway, I ask Garth if he needs a bathroom break.

"That would be great," he says.

I pull off the highway and head to the first gas station I see. While Garth finds the restroom, I fill the tank. Of course, the lack of car movement makes the boys wake up, and they ask to go to the bathroom, too. And get a snack. And get water. And start the movie again. By the time I take a pee break and we're back on the road, a half hour has passed.

"What time does this thing start?" I ask, glancing at the clock on the dashboard.

"Noon. We're good for time." Garth reclines his seat a bit and gets comfortable. "So, have you talked to Nina?" he asks as casually as he can.

"Nope."

His disapproving stare almost gives my cheek a tan. My shoulders sag.

"I know I need to. I hate not talking to her."

"So what's the problem? Pick up the phone."

"I will. It's just way past time and I don't even know what to say to her."

"Well, neither of you has been a particularly good friend at this point, so maybe start with 'I'm sorry.'"

I start to argue, but don't have the heart. He's right. Nina and I have never before gone this long without talking.

"I'll call her when we get home later."

"You'll feel better," Garth says and shuts his eyes. "Mind if I take a catnap?"

"Go for it. I'll probably sleep on the way back."

"Guess that means I'm driving, then." Garth smiles to himself. Before long, he's out.

✦ ✦ ✦

As we pull into the parking lot of Hartman Arena, I can already see it's a big event. We park nowhere near the entrance and have to hike to the doors. The boys are practically bouncing out of their shoes. Neither has ever been to Wichita.

Inside, Garth is greeted like he's a regular at these events. Everyone waves or says hello or pats him on the back.

"Wow, I feel like I'm with the most popular boy in school," I say to him.

He rolls his eyes. "Not quite. But if you go anywhere often enough, people are going to get to know you."

We stop at a cluster of tables with a huge Wounded Warrior banner hanging above them. A clean-cut, good-looking older man gives us a big smile over the crowd around him.

"Garth, man, how are you?"

"I'm great, Jack. How are you doing?"

"I'm good." He looks at the boys and me.

"I'm Jack."

"Hi, I'm Jen." I go to shake his hand and see that his right arm is gone. He offers his left hand and I'm a bit thrown. I rebound from the awkwardness with my usual grace and style.

"Oh, sorry, uh, hi." I change my handshake position to a wave. "This is my son, Max, and his friend Zach."

The boys are staring with their eyes and mouths wide open.

"Where's your arm?" asks my chip off the old block.

"I lost it," Jack says solemnly.

"Where did you lose it?" Max is almost whispering.

Jack puts his one hand on his hip.

"Well, if I knew that, don't you think I'd go get it?"

Max starts to giggle and then so does Zach B.

Garth steps in.

"Sorry, where are my manners? Jen, Jack and I served together in Afghanistan."

"Nice to meet you." I give him a grateful look.

"You, too. How do you know this jarhead?"

I turn to look at Garth and raise my eyebrow.

" 'Jarhead.' I like that."

Garth gives me a fake scowl.

"I've been training Jen for the Kansas City Mud Run in April."

"Well, you're in good hands. He is one tough mudder himself. Are you signed up for today?"

"Nope," I say. "We're just spectators and supporters of the cause."

"Well, you better get in there. It's about to start. Garth, why don't you guys sit in our section?" Jack offers.

"Great, thanks." Garth steers me toward the arena. "Come on, guys, let's get some seats."

✦ ✦ ✦

The indoor mud run is really impressive. The course takes up the entire floor of Hartman Arena, which is the size of a professional hockey rink.

Every inch has been carefully designated for a different obstacle, and I'd be lying if I said the sight didn't scare the crap out of me.

"This is so cool!" Max screams over the loud music pumping through the arena speakers. He and Zach B. are taking it all in with huge grins on their faces. I grab their hands and lead them up into the stands. We take our seats by a handful of people who, judging by the number of missing body parts, are veterans, and their families. It's then that I finally get a good look at the course. Before I start to freak out, Garth is talking me through it step by step.

"So, it starts with a run up to the top of the arena and back down again. Then you climb a rope over a ten-foot wall, followed by a long crawl through the mud over there that has barbed wire stretched across the top." He points to the other side of the building.

"After that, you have to carry a huge log about five hundred yards with a group of people, then run up that thing that looks like a half-pipe wall. You need to get a lot of speed for that. You'll want to quit halfway up, but good momentum should take you to the top. Climb over it, then jump into the freezing-cold water."

I wince. I don't even like lukewarm showers.

"Get out of the water and go over to the wall with the pegs. Grab two rings and hook them onto the pegs to get yourself across the moat. That's probably the toughest part. You need a lot of upper-body strength. After that, it's pretty smooth sailing. Normally, you'd have to jump through fire just before the ice bath, but the fire department wouldn't give them an indoor permit, so it's just running up and down a few dirt mounds before you cross the finish line."

My heart is thumping like a jackrabbit's, my mouth is dry, and I'm relatively certain I have soiled myself. I can't speak.

Garth starts to laugh.

"Hey, what's up? You could do this. You could totally do this."

"In what universe can I jump through fire?"

"Well, it's not really something we can practice, but you will find that in the heat of the moment—no pun intended—your adrenaline will carry you anywhere you need to go."

He puts his arm across my shoulders and gives me a hug.

"You will do this, I promise."

I look at Max, who is watching the arena floor and chomping on a hot dog—courtesy of Jack, who has just joined us—and suddenly it is very clear to me.

I will do this.

✦ ✦ ✦

On the way home, I let Garth take the wheel and I nap. I have a terrible dream that I'm competing in the mudder but I only have one arm. I wake with a sudden jerk as I let go of the ring I'm holding on to on the pegboard.

"Holy crap!"

Garth looks at me. "Did you have a mud-mare?"

"I think I did," I say, rubbing my eyes. I check out the backseat; the boys are watching yet another movie. Max has hit his screen time for the month, that's for sure. "Is that normal?"

"Oh, yeah, especially while you're training. What was it about?"

"I was competing, but I only had one arm. When I got to the pegboard I had to let go, because I couldn't move the ring to the next peg." I shake my head. "That was brutal."

"You should see the guys do it who actually only have one arm. Insane upper-body strength." There is a lot of admiration in Garth's voice. I'm thinking I've only scratched the surface of my trainer's surprising emotional depth.

✦ ✦ ✦

When we get home, after dropping an exhausted Zach B. off, my prince of a husband takes charge of Max, which gives me time to wash the day off my body. After my shower, I wrap a towel around my head, grab my robe, and head to my side of the bed. This is it. I'm calling Nina until she picks up.

I've settled in for a long session of redialing, but she picks up on the first ring.

"Hi." She is whispering.

"Hi. Why are you whispering?" I'm whispering, too, for no reason.

"Chyna just fell asleep on the couch. She was at a gymnastics tournament today and she's beat." I can tell Nina is moving into another room so she can talk.

"How did she do?" I ask. This is so weird.

"Third place overall for her age group. First place on the beam."

"Wow, that's great. Tell her I said way to go."

"I will."

And . . . silence. I take a deep breath.

"Look, Neens . . ."

"Hang on. Before you say anything, let me tell you how bad I feel about the way I've been acting. I'm really sorry. After I found Sid, I basically took a nosedive into depressed oblivion and I've just resurfaced."

"Oh, Neens, I'm sorry, too. I just didn't know what to do for you. And then when you didn't help with my class mom situation, I just got really pissed."

"Your what?"

"It's nothing. Just that thing with Asami and Jakowski, you know . . ."

"What are you talking about? What happened?"

"Holy shit, you really don't know?"

I briefly tell her all the gory details of my class mom downfall and how Principal Jakowski had apparently called and consulted her, but she told him she wasn't interested in handling it and he should.

There is silence at the other end of the call. I think we've been cut off.

"Hello?"

"I'm here," Nina says, but she sounds like her mind is elsewhere. "I don't remember him even calling. Shit, this is worse than being blackout drunk."

I laugh, but it comes out as a half laugh, half sob. Sort of like a hiccup.

Nina laughs. "What the hell was that?"

"I'm just so happy to be talking to you." I sniffle.

"Yeah, well, I'm out of the bell jar so tell me everything."

I give her the rundown on my ouster as class mom and also update her on Vivs and Laura. Suddenly something occurs to me.

"So, what ever happened with Sid? You seem kind of over it."

"Oh, I'm way over it. What an asshat."

"Tell me something I don't know."

"Yeah, yeah, I know. It took me a while, but believe me, I'm here now. He actually hit on me."

"You *saw* him?"

"No, on Facebook. Hang on, I'll send it to you." I hear some shuffling and Nina's voice at a distance saying, "Girl, you are not going to believe it."

My phone buzzes as Nina says more clearly. "Okay, I just copied the IMs and sent them to you."

"Hang on." I look at my phone and push Messages. I see what Nina has sent.

"Holy shit, how long is this?"

"Long. Just scroll. The first part is just us catching up and him explaining why he left. Not apologizing, mind you, just *explaining* that he freaked out and realized he wasn't ready for a kid. That he thought it would be better for me if he left because he knew he wasn't going to be able to help me."

"Wait." I'm scrolling and trying to listen to her at the same time. "He's talking about not wanting to meet Chyna . . ."

"Oh, yeah. He doesn't want to upset her life or his new kids' lives. They aren't even his kids! He married a pregnant widow."

"Eww," I say involuntarily, wondering just how desperate a woman would have to be to allow Sid into her kids' lives.

"I know. Even I can see the eww in it now."

I keep scrolling, trying to skim all the bullshit about his new life and new job at the high-tech company, which I find out is more of a low-tech company that makes the hydraulic mechanisms for office chairs, or "computer chairs," as the company calls them. Explains the name of the company, Compu-lift. Apparently, Sid is a "tester," which means he sits on his ass all day making sure the chairs go up and down.

"Huh. Sure that job isn't too much for him?" I say into the phone.

Nina laughs. "Get to the good part."

I keep scrolling and find where he talks about how tough marriage is.

"How the hell would he know? If that baby is a newborn he can't be married more than a few months."

"Seven."

"Oh, my God. Who is this poor woman he married?"

"According to Sid, her dad owns the company where he works. He told me they're grooming him to take over."

I snort. "So he married the boss's daughter. Good to know he uses his brain for something more than testing chairs."

"What part are you at now?" Nina asks.

"Um . . . you're asking if he will come to see Chyna."

"Okay, read from there. This is when he makes the jump from scumbag to douchebag."

I don't want to tell her that jump was made years ago, so I just read.

Sid: I just think it would really mess Chyna up for me to walk into her life out of nowhere.

Nina: I'm sure she'd be happier finally getting to meet her father.

Sid: Doesn't she have a father? Like one of the guys you hooked up with after me.

Nina: I never hooked up with anyone else.

Sid: Yeah, right.

Nina: I was a heartbroken single mother of a baby. I didn't want to be with anyone.

Sid: Even after all these years?

Nina: I've been busy.

Sid: Busy missing me?

Nina: Busy raising a child, working, and volunteering at school. I don't have time for that shit.

Sid: You had time for it with me.

Nina: Oh, please.

Sid: Remember the weekend we rented that cottage?

Nina: No.

Sid: Come on. We didn't wear clothes the whole weekend. That's the shit I remember. The shit I miss. I've been thinking about it a lot lately.

I stop reading.

"Gross!"

"What part?" says Nina's disembodied voice.

"He's reminding you of that weekend you rented the cottage."

"The one that cost me a thousand dollars. How fucking stupid is he to bring that up?"

"I'm assuming that's a rhetorical question."

"Hardy-har. Keep reading."

I return to the IM stream.

Nina: But not enough to come back.

Sid: Do you want me to come back?

Nina: For a long time I did.

Sid: What about now?

Nina: Now? Why would you come back now? You have a new family.

Sid: I could come for a visit.

Nina: I thought you didn't want to meet Chyna.

Sid: I could come back and see you.

Nina: Why would you do that?

Sid: I don't know. Just see what's up.

Nina: What do you mean?

Sid: You seem lonely, baby. Maybe I could cheer you up a bit.

"Oh my God!" I scream at my phone.

"Can you believe him? I was like, where the hell did that come from?"

"I hope you shut him down."

"Not well enough. I just said no, thanks, and haven't answered any of his messages since."

"When was the last time you heard from him?"

"Today. He sends me messages almost every day."

"What do they say?"

Nina sighs. "It's a lot of 'What did I do, baby? Are you mad at me? I still want to come for a visit' and shit like that. I should just block him, but I'm sort of enjoying torturing him a bit."

"You aren't torturing him enough!"

"But I really don't want any contact with him. I think ignoring him is good enough."

I'm not convinced, but it's not my battle.

"My turn," Nina says. "Whatever happened with your fantasy man? What was his name, again?"

"Don." I smile. Finally I can talk to someone about this!

I tell her all about how fun he is to flirty-text with and read her some of my favorites.

"And in this one he asks me . . . Nina? Are you still there?"

I hear breathing on the other end of the line, and then Nina practically takes my head off.

"Jen, you need to shut this shit down immediately!"

"What? Are you serious?"

"Yeah, I'm serious."

"Neens, they don't mean anything. They're totally harmless."

"Oh, really? Do you show them to Ron? Are you and he getting a good old laugh about all those coffee double entendres?"

"No. But I would show them to him. They're just funny."

"So you wouldn't mind if Ron had a little banter going on with an old girlfriend of his?"

"Jesus, he wasn't my boyfriend," I mutter. But I give her question some thought. Would I mind if I saw a stream like this on Ron's phone?

"I see what you're saying, and I get how it looks, but I know what my feelings are and I have no intention of cheating on Ron."

Even I can hear how lame I sound, but all Nina says is "Yeah, well, it's always fun until someone loses a husband. Just be careful."

I really don't want to fight with her, so I promise that I will.

We make plans for lunch the next day and, after a lot of "I love you"s and "I'm sorry"s, we hang up. I feel better than I have in weeks.

13

To: Miss Ward's Class
From: AChang
Date: 01/17
Subject: Picture Day

Hello, Parents,

It has come to my attention that some of the children did not react well to my PowerPoint presentation on the life and death of Martin Luther King. In hindsight, showing him dead in a coffin may have been too much.

Just a quick reminder that tomorrow is picture day. I know that a long weekend can sometimes make people forget. I hope you have already ironed your child's uniform. I want us to be the cleanest class at William Taft. A bath tonight would really help with that.

I will be there tomorrow to make sure your children are neat and smiling.

Regards,
Asami

To: PWard
From: JDixon
Date: 01/17
Subject: Picture Day

Hi, Miss Ward,

Do you need any help wrangling the kids tomorrow when they're getting their pictures taken? I'd be happy to help.

Thanks,
Jen

To: JDixon
From: PWard
Date: 01/17
Subject: Picture Day

Jen,

Sorry, but that's a question for the class mom. You can reach out to her.

Thanks,
Peggy

Damn. I was hoping to avoid that. Ugh. This is going to hurt.

To: AChang
From: JDixon
Date: 01/17
Subject: Picture Day

Hi, Asami,

Happy New Year. Hope you are enjoying your new job. Your first email
was very informative.

    I was just wondering if you need any help wrangling the kids
tomorrow while they are getting their pictures taken. I would be happy
to keep an eye on them in the hallway before they go in, or bring a
snack.

    Let me know.

Jen

To: JDixon
From: AChang
Date: 01/17
Subject: Picture Day

Jen,

Well, I certainly didn't expect to hear from you. I really don't think I will
need help, but if you are having trouble disengaging from your power
seat and you want to come in for a bit, I guess it would be fine. Please
bring the children a snack.

Asami

A snack, yes! I shut my laptop and turn my chair to look at my kitchen. I got me some baking to do.

✦ ✦ ✦

Never say never. This is my new motto. I said I would never have another kid after Laura, and lo and behold I did. I said I would never read *Fifty Shades of Grey*, but after seeing Nina's reaction to it, I did. And I said I would never again make my mother's Sticky Chewy Five Napkin Brownies, but here I am putting the second batch into the oven.

These babies are killer. The recipe calls for, among other things, nine eggs, two cups of sugar, a whole pound of butter, toffee, chocolate chips, and whipping cream. Totally unhealthy, but they taste like heaven and my kids love them. The only downside is they are a leeetle messy to eat. If I'm being honest, you need a lot more than five napkins to keep yourself together. A container of Wet Ones is more like it.

Asami asked for a snack, and a snack she will get. Yes, that's right. I'm going to give a bunch of five- and six-year-olds the equivalent of a mud pie to eat before they get photographed. I'm *that* small and petty. Our new class mom should never have reminded me to bathe my child.

✦ ✦ ✦

On picture day, I sally forth to school around ten a.m., armed with the Sticky Chewy Five Napkin Brownies, a roll of paper towels, and, of course, a gluten- and nut-free snack for Graydon.

I head to room 147, where I see that Asami has all her hair-styling equipment lined up on a tray and ready for action.

The children are seated at their tables, listening with rapt attention as Miss Ward explains the best way to smile for a picture.

"When they ask you to smile, try to think of a funny joke. That way, when you smile it will be with your whole face and not just your mouth."

She then proceeds to show the kids what a just-a-mouth smile looks like. She looks ridiculous, but the kids love it. They are laughing and doing it to each other.

"Okay, settle down. Now, who knows a joke, so I can show you a smile with my whole face?"

Sixteen hands shoot up, including Max's, and I can't help but wonder what jokes he knows. There is a chorus of "Me, please, me please, oh *me please*!" as Miss Ward takes her time deciding.

"Zach T. What have you got?"

Zach T. beams with excitement as he stands up.

"Knock, knock."

"Who's there?" "Europe."

"Europe who?"

"No, you're a poo!" Zach yells out, and the class explodes with laughter as Miss Ward's face bursts into a bright smile. Even Asami is laughing.

"Good one, Zach. Put a marble in the compliment jar."

As Zach proudly steps up I hear my universal name being called.

"Mom!" Max runs up and hugs me like he didn't just see me an hour and a half ago. I love it. Way too soon, he will find it embarrassing when I come to his classroom, but for now it's still a treat.

"Hi, buddy." I give him a big squeeze. He still smells of last night's bath and I take an extra whiff before I let him go.

"Jennifer, I'm glad you're finally here" is all the greeting I get from Asami. "The photographer is set up two doors down the hall. The children will get their individual shots done and when they're all finished, the photographer will take the group shot. I will be with the photographer and you will be with the class, sending the kids to me one at a time. Got that?"

"And good morning to you, Asami!" I reply.

"Did you bring a snack?"

I hold up my shopping bag.

"What are those for?" she asks, pointing to the paper towels.

"Just in case the kids get messy." I hope to God she doesn't ask me what I brought. "I even have something special for Graydon," I add by way of distracting her.

But it isn't necessary. She just nods to me and picks up her hair supplies. As she heads out the door, she has one parting instruction.

"Don't give them their snack until they come back from getting their picture taken."

"Got it!" I say, a bit too enthusiastically.

Miss Ward has been watching the whole exchange. She raises her eyebrows at me.

"Wow, Dixon goes to China, huh?"

Why is that okay for her to say, but my "your people" comment is still offensive? Seriously, where's the line? Do they keep moving it?

"Okay, class, Max's mom is going to let you know when it's your turn to get your picture taken. The rest of the time, we will be practicing our letters. I want everyone to get out your workbooks and start working on capital 'M's."

There is a brief commotion as the kids get their books from their cubbies; then they all settle down. I have to say, I still think Miss Ward is crazy, but damn if she doesn't run a tight ship. She walks over and hands me a piece of paper.

"Here's a class list. May as well go in alphabetical order." She heads to the door.

"Class, Max's mom is in charge. Please listen to her."

"Wait, where are you going?" I ask and I can hear a little panic in my voice. I don't want to be left alone with sixteen kids. I can barely handle my one.

"Just to the bathroom. I'll be right back." As she walks out, I see she's carrying her cell phone. Who does she need to call right now?

I consult the list and revel in the irony that it is the one I typed up for her at the beginning of the school year. When I look up, sixteen pairs of eyes are gazing at me, gauging my level of commitment to keeping order.

"Okay, Kit, you're up first. The rest of you, back to your letters."

Kit Aikens jumps up like she has just won bingo and skips out the door. Damn those lucky kids with "A" last names, always first for everything. I eye the rest of the group to let them know I'm not going to take any nonsense, and they all get back to work..

I take this opportunity to head to the long table at the back of the classroom and take out my weapon of mass destruction—the Sticky Chewy Five Napkin Brownies. Oh, they smell divine. I have a small twinge of guilt as I look at how nice all the kids look today, but when Kit Aikens walks back into the room with tears in her eyes and her beautiful blond curls tamed into a braid, I realize I'm on the side of right.

"Hey, Kit, come on back here. You can have a brownie while you work." I look at the list. "Hunter, you're up next."

Hunter dashes out the door with the reckless abandon that only a six-year-old can supply. Kit joins me at the back table.

"Do you like brownies?" I ask with a smile. I feel like I'm pushing drugs.

She nods and takes one hungrily. I hand her a paper towel. "You might need one of these."

When Hunter returns, his hair all combed back and spit-shined, I send Nick Baton out and invite Hunter back for a snack.

It's all going as planned until a severely braided Nancy Fancy gets back from her photo shoot with Miss Ward in tow. By this time eight of the sixteen kids are covered in chocolate. It's smeared on their faces, in their hair, on their clothes. Miss Ward walks in and just stares, her mouth gaping. I decide to just keep it moving.

"Nancy, come on back and have a snack. Lulu, it's your turn to go next door."

As Lulu walks out, Miss Ward is still standing in the doorway, taking in the splendor of my work in progress. She waits a good minute before she slowly walks to the back of the room, grabs a brownie with her perfectly manicured hands, and stuffs it in her mouth.

"Good brownies, Jenny." She walks back to her desk, licking her fingers.

I'm a little shocked. I never thought I'd have an ally in Miss Ward. Maybe Asami is getting on her nerves, too.

By the time Isabel Zalis comes back for her brownie, the class looks pretty comical. All the girls' hair has been put into some sort of braid, and all the boys have had their hair wet-combed out of their face. They have all done a stellar job with the brownies. Even poor Suni Chang, who did her best to stay neat, ended up with brownie on her nose. It looks as though someone has filled a room with 1930s-style gangsters and Pippi Longstockings and splattered mud all over them. The one exception is, of course, Graydon Cobb, whose hair is too short to grease back and who didn't have a brownie. Weirdly, it works. This is going to be one cute class photo.

To: Miss Ward's Class
From AChang
Subject: Class photos
Date: Jan. 19

Dear Kindergarten Parents,

I take full responsibility for yesterday's class picture fiasco. I assure you that under my watch the children were spic-and-span and their individual photos will look very sharp. However, because of a certain parent's unfortunate choice of snack, the class picture turned into a dog's breakfast. I have been assured, by the photographer, that it is "quite cute," especially since Miss Ward covered herself in chocolate to blend in with the class. We will see. Perhaps we can all pitch in and hire the photographer to come and reshoot the class picture.
    Onward.

                                                                Asami Chang

To: AChang
From: SLewicki
Subject: Class photos
Date: Jan. 19

Hi,

I will be out of the office until January 31.

Thanks,
Sasha

To: AChang
From: SCobb
Subject: Class photos
Date: Jan. 19

Asami,

What snack? Was Graydon given chocolate? Do I have to give you his list of allergies again?

Shirleen

To: AChang
From: AGordon
Subject: Class photos
Date: Jan. 19

Asami,

I believe I can speak for most of the mothers of girls when I say the snack was the least offensive thing that happened yesterday. When I picked

Lulu up, she was very upset that you braided her hair even though
we had just washed and blown it out for picture day. She told me all the
girls felt the same way. What were you thinking? When you sent us the
emails about bathing our children and telling us you would be standing
by to do hair, I thought you were kidding. I would agree to put in money
for a reshoot, but only so we could get rid of the braids.

Ali

14

I'm a good daughter. At least, that's what I tell myself as I cross the bridge into Kansas City, Kansas, to find organic prunes for my mother. There is only one grocery store within a twenty-mile radius that carries the kind she likes. Apparently they act as a laxative for my dad, who, according to my mother, "can't get the train out of the tunnel." She is more than capable of driving to get them herself, but honest to God, I don't think she wants to spend the gas money. She's getting more like my grandmother every day.

It's actually a splendid day for a little road trip. It's mid-February—the thirteenth, to be exact. It's still cold, but the roads are dry and the sun is shining.

God, I love my KCK—that's Kansas City, Kansas, for those of you *not* from the Wheat State. It's where I grew up and what I know best. I remember when I was a kid my dad would take me and my friends up to Sauer Castle at night and scare the crap out of us with goofy stories that seemed so scary at the time. He'd talk about a guy with a crazy cat who lived in the castle and wasn't allowed out; then he'd pretend to see the guy in the window. We would all scream and laugh at the same time.

But now we live in Overland Park, Kansas, essentially a suburb of Kansas City, *Missouri*, which is generally known as Kansas City.

The two KCs are spitting distance from each other, but sometimes I feel like a traitor for moving across the bridge.

Max is spending the day at the store with Ron, so I have a little extra time on my hands. Plus the place with the magic prunes is right beside this really cool coffee shop, called Grab a Java, that I love and hardly ever get a chance to go to. It's the kind of place where bearded lumber-sexuals and their female counterparts hang out. I feel hip just walking in there. It was the first place I ever ate avocado toast. I consider texting Don to see if he wants to meet me there, you know, for coffee, but ever since my conversation with Nina I have been trying not to instigate anything. Now I'm just a reactor.

I'm feeling pretty good about myself these days. The fallout from Brownie-gate was almost nonexistent. My sabotage efforts, though not in vain, turned out to be unnecessary. Asami took almost all the heat because of the hair debacle. And once again, as predicted by *me*, the chocolate-smudged class photo was absolutely adorable.

Physically, I'm feeling great. I'm at peak performance level for a woman of my age and commitment to exercise. That's what Garth tells me, anyway. I've cut back on my wine since January and plan to stay semidry until after the mud run. It's not like I have a drinking problem, but I am trying to eat and drink clean to help make my body a more efficient machine. My only indulgence is one cup of coffee a day, which is why I'm humming Katy Perry's "Roar" when I pull into the parking lot of Rupert's Fine Foods. I can already smell the Grab a Java brewing.

After picking up a shitload of prunes, some Ezekiel bread, coconut water, and kale, I head next door craving the double breve I'm going to revel in. As I'm walking, some yelling down the street grabs my attention. I look toward the sound and about fifty yards away are two women, a blonde and a brunette, standing beside a black SUV yelling at each other. The blonde is dressed all in black and the other seems to have a white jacket on.

I'm not much of a rubbernecker, but for some reason I'm intrigued. The words aren't clear, but both women seem to be giving as good as they get. Then, much to my surprise, the brunette hauls off and slaps the blonde across the face and boy it's a resounding smack. What can I say? We grow our women tough here in KCK!

I walk into Grab a Java and head to the counter, wondering under what circumstances I would slap another woman. Asami comes to mind.

Grab a Java is its usual groovy self. Today's barista is a nymphlike little pixie with cropped jet-black hair and a stud in her lip. The chalkboard sign tells me her name is Jack. Of course it is. No girl who looks like that is ever named Susan.

"Hey." I nod. She nods back. Very hip.

"Double breve, please."

She nods again. I look around the tiny shop. It has a rustic charm. Metal and wood tables are scattered around the room, as are barrels filled (not really) with coffee beans. The walls are black chalkboard and present the menu of drinks and food—limited but good. Did I mention the avocado toast? All kinds of quips are also scattered around the room; my favorite is "Dear Karma, I have a list of people you missed." It's surprisingly quiet for a Saturday—only three people hunched over their computers with their headphones on, a guy writing music notes on a piece of paper, and an older man reading the paper with a dog sitting at his feet.

"Double breve." Jack speaks her first words to me. "Four twenty-five."

I pay and toss the change into a jar labeled "Tipping—Not Just for Cows." Normally I would stay and savor my coffee—being here is like a little vacation—but my mother is probably waiting to stew up the prunes for my dad, so I jump back into the Odyssey and pull onto the street. First, though, I take a selfie in front of Grab a Java and text it to Don. So much for being the reactor.

I notice the battling women are still standing by the side of the road. I take a peek as I go by and lock eyes with Kim Fancy. Five things go through my mind immediately.

1. Hey! There's Dr. Evil.
2. I wonder if she knows about Grab a Java.

3. Who is she with?

4. Huh, I wonder what they were arguing about?

And finally,

5. Holy shit! One of them bitch-slapped the other.

I'm way past them by the time that final thought enters my mind.
I try to remember who slapped who. They were both on the street,
but I'm pretty sure the one in white did the smacking so that would
be Dr. Evil. Well, no surprise there.

As I'm crossing back into KCMO, my cell phone rings. It's Nina.
I put it on speaker.

"You are not going to believe what I just saw!"

"What's going on? Where are you? I need to talk to you."

"I'm driving home. Want to meet me?"

"Sure, but I'm hungry, so can we meet at the place with the signs?"

"I can be there in, like, ten minutes."

"Well, slow your ass down, 'cause I won't be there for twenty."

"K. See you there."

I laugh and slap the steering wheel. The caffeine is clearly kicking in.

✦ ✦ ✦

The place with the signs is Nina's and my favorite little diner. It's
actually called Stu's Diner, but that name just doesn't do it justice.
Not only are there overstuffed red leather booths and an old-school
jukebox that doesn't play anything released after 1977, but also the
walls of the restaurant are covered in funny signs that the owner (not
named Stu, oddly enough) has collected from across the country. If
he couldn't steal the actual sign, he would take a picture and repli-
cate it when he got home. Over the years, customers have sent him
pictures of signs for him to hang as well. You can go there twenty
times in a year and always find something new to read. Oh, and they
happen to have the best apple pie in three counties.

The tiny place is packed, but as I walk in I spy a free table in the corner under a sign that says:

UNATTENDED CHILDREN WILL BE GIVEN
ESPRESSO AND A FREE PUPPY.

I commandeer the corner and wave to Stephanie, the waitress on duty.

I don't know how long she has been working here, but she reminds me of the character Flo from the old sitcom *Alice*. Flo was a tall thin drink of water with a head of relentlessly bright red hair done up in a bouffant. She had a sassy southern accent and was always telling her boss to "kiss my grits" as she smacked her gum. Steph doesn't have a southern accent, but the rest rings pretty true.

"Be with you in a jif, hon!" she yells to me across the diner. Not one person lifts their head in surprise. Everybody knows Steph.

I take out my phone and check my messages. An IM from Nina saying she is "five away," a picture from Ron showing Max doing the flexed arm hang at the store, and a text from Don asking if he can join me. I realize that he thinks I'm still at Grab a Java. I IM Nina *Here,* send Ron a kiss and a hug, and text Don *Sorry, no. I was just giving you a coffee update*, to which I get an immediate sad-face reply. When I check my email, wouldn't you know there's one from Kim Fancy.

To: JDixon
From: KFancy
Subject: Was that you?
Date: February 9

Hi, Jen,

Was that you driving through KCK this morning? You should have stopped. Peggy and I were just meeting for a cup of coffee at that weird *little place beside the grocery store. We were discussing the spring carnival.*

See you soon.

Kim

I stare at my phone. Holy shit! I can't believe it. She slapped *Miss Ward*? What the hell?

Nina makes her entrance at this opportune moment. I wave enthusiastically at her. I'm practically jumping out of my chair.

"Hey, girl—" Nina starts.

"Shut up and sit down! You are not going to believe the gossip I have for you!"

"What?" Nina looks momentarily confused.

"Okay, so I'm over in KCK getting my mom some things at the organic grocery store she loves."

"The one by Grab a Java?" Nina asks unnecessarily.

"Yes."

"Did you stop in for a breve?"

"Neens, stop interrupting."

"Sorry," she grumbles. "I need coffee."

"Anyway as I'm going into Grab a—"

"What's up, girls?" Steph's voice makes me jump. "Apple pie's almost gone, if that's what you came in for."

"I'll have coffee and scrambled egg whites and wheat toast, no butter," Nina orders.

Steph nods and looks at me.

"I'll take the pie."

She nods again. As she is walking away, she points to the wall.

"Did ya see the new one?"

We both look at where she's pointing. It's a large piece of plywood with orange letters:

PLEASE DON'T THROW CIGARETTE BUTTS ON
THE FLOOR. THE COCKROACHES
ARE GETTING CANCER.

Nina laughs. "Nice one, Steph!"

"Came in from Tucson," she yells from behind the counter.

Nina looks back at me. "Okay, so you went shopping . . ."

I lean in.

"No. I went to the organic grocery store across the river to get my mom some prunes."

"Uh huh. Prunes." Nina seems distracted. I see Steph coming with her coffee, so I sit back and wait.

"Here you go, honey. Pie and toast will be up in a minute." She looks at me. "Ice cream or Cool Whip?"

"Neither, thanks."

I turn back to Nina. She is savoring her first sip with her eyes closed.

"Oh, my God, do I need this. You won't believe what I did last night. I—"

"Whoa, whoa, whoa. Me first. I have to tell you what I just saw."

"Seriously? I called you," Nina reminds me.

I sigh in frustration.

"Okay, I'll say mine and you say yours and we'll decide whose is better. Me first. I saw Kim Fancy slap Miss Ward across the face!"

Nina's eyes widen. "Oh, man, that *is* good."

"What's yours?" I ask, pretty confident that I have won.

"I had sex with Garth last night."

I look at her evenly. "You totally win."

Nina nods knowingly and takes a huge gulp of her coffee.

"Holy shit! How? When? Why?" I have more questions than I know what to do with.

Nina is about to answer when Steph descends upon us with eggs and toast and pie. She also puts the check down.

"More coffee, hon?" she asks.

Nina nods gratefully.

"Okay. Spill it."

She sighs. "It was our third date."

"*Third date*? He never said a word." I'm shaking my head. It always amazes me how men can keep a secret. You ask them not to say anything, and they actually don't. We women could learn a thing or two from that.

"We didn't want to freak you out, so we decided to keep it on the down low for a while."

"Okay, whatever. How did it start? Did you start his website?"

She looks at me with surprise. "You heard about that?"

I nod. "Garth mentioned it, but didn't tell me any of this."

"Well, we sort of connected at your Christmas dinner. I was still in my Sid funk, and he was just really nice to talk to, you know?"

I smile. I certainly do know.

Steph swoops in with a refill and is gone.

"So after that, he would call once in a while to check in, and we just started having these great phone conversations, first about his website and then about everything else. I told him all about Sid and my parents and grandmother—about how I raised Chyna by myself. He told me about being in Afghanistan—girl, he saw some serious shit over there. He told me about his breakdown at the gym and how he still goes to therapy for post-traumatic stress."

I can't believe my ears. How does she know more about Garth than I do?

"He *told* you all that?" I ask.

"Well, I asked him about it. We've been talking a lot."

"Talked yourselves right into bed," I say, with a bit too much snark.

Nina raises her beautifully arched eyebrow at me.

"Sorry. I just can't believe I didn't know any of this. Wait, did you have *phone* sex?"

Nina snorts coffee out of her nose and starts to giggle.

"No. Oh, my God, no. Only you would ask that. No, we were talking one evening and realized we had both skipped dinner, so we decided to meet at Garozzo's. We had a great time together. Did you know he doesn't drink alcohol or eat pasta?"

"No, but I'm not surprised. He's in great shape."

"I hear that!" Nina says, and I think she's blushing. I sit back in my chair, trying to process all this new information. The tectonic plates of my world have had a true rattling this morning.

"By the time we had our second date, it felt like our twentieth," Nina feels the need to add.

"Uh-huh. Are you trying to rationalize your sluttiness to me or to you?"

"To you." Nina doesn't bat an eye. "I'm all good with my sluttiness."

"Are you charging him for your, um, services?"

"Yes!" She smirks. "But I'm giving him the special friends discount."

My phone buzzes and I sneak a glance at it. Don has texted me an emoji of a turd drinking coffee. I turn my phone face down.

Nina's crystal blue eyes are staring at me. "Something important?"

"Nope. So, was Chyna home?" I deftly pivot.

"No, thank God. That's why I wanted to meet you. When did you tell the girls about Ron?"

I scoop the last of the scrumptious apple pie into my mouth and scowl. The girls' first time meeting Ron is not one of my favorite memories.

We had been dating for about a month before I even told him I had kids. I wish I had taken a picture of the look on his face. Here he thought he was dating this hot (his word, not mine), single thirty-something who had never been married and who seemed relatively normal. After pleasuring him in the front seat of his car one night, I casually mentioned that I was harboring two small fugitives in my home. He took it relatively well. At least, he didn't run screaming in the other direction.

It was another month before I let him meet them. Shrinks these days will tell you to wait a year, but that wisdom wasn't available to me, so I went with my gut. (Actually, I'm sure it was available some-where, but I'm generally lazy when it comes to researching stuff like that.)

I invited Ron to dinner one Saturday when my parents were away on a spiritual retreat or, as I like to call it, a booty call with the Lord. There was no way I was going to bombard him with two kids *and* Kay and Ray.

The girls knew that I had been going on dates with someone, but they also thought I was taking a pottery class at the local Our Name Is Mud. It was the only way I could get out more than twice a week. Ron and I were at that euphoric beginning of a relationship where we couldn't keep our hands off each other, and we were having *a lot* of car sex. When I told the girls I was going to introduce them to the man I was dating, they reacted like the polar opposites they are. Vivs rolled her eyes and said, "Well, this should be good." Where does her sarcasm come from? Laura started jumping up and down, beyond excited, asking if he was going to be our new dad. I thought she was joking, so in my infinite wisdom I told her yes, he absolutely was, as long as they didn't blow it for me. But guess what? She wasn't joking, and she didn't think I was, either.

Ron arrived promptly at six with gift bags for the girls, who were ten and twelve at the time. I could tell he was nervous, and not just because he had pit stains the size of pizzas under the arms of his gray polo shirt. He was very jittery and kept looking around the kitchen as if someone was going to jump him. I kissed him, handed him a beer, and told him to relax.

"They're just little girls," I assured him with as much conviction as I could muster. I really wasn't sure how the evening was going to play out. Good thing I didn't have high expectations, because it ended up an unmitigated disaster.

The first to appear was Laura. She was wearing her prettiest dress and had tried to put her hair in a bun, without much success.

"Sweetie, I'd like you to meet my friend Ron. Ron, this is Laura, my little one."

"Hi, Laura. So nice to meet you." Ron stuck out his hand for a formal greeting, which Laura bypassed in favor of a huge hug.

"Welcome to our family," she said sincerely.

I guess I should have seen that coming.

"Thank you." Ron looked a little confused, but to his credit he went with it. "It's so nice to meet you, Laura. I love your hair."

Laura looked surprised and pleased. "Really? I just did it all by myself."

"Well, I helped," was how Vivs announced she had arrived in the kitchen. She had chosen to wear all black, which included the expression on her face.

"Ron, this is Vivs. Vivs, this is my friend Ron."

Ron just smiled this time, but it was Vivs who formally put her hand out. Ron shook it.

"My grandpa says you can learn a lot about a man by his hand-shake," Vivs informed him. "Yours is wet." She wiped her palm on her black pants.

"Oh. Sorry about that," Ron mumbled.

"Vivs!" Laura frowned at her sister. "Maybe he just washed his hands."

"Who's hungry?" I jumped in before it all went south.

"I am!" Ron said, a little too enthusiastically. "How about you guys?" He looked toward the girls. Laura nodded like a bobblehead. Vivs ignored him and turned to me.

"What are we having?"

"Lasagna."

She made a face like it was the worst thing I could be serving, even though it was one of her favorites. I gave her my stone-cold stare.

"Cut it out," I said quietly.

Ron picked up the bags he had dropped by the door.

"Hey, I brought you guys something."

He handed the girls identical lime-green gift bags tied with pink ribbon.

Laura stepped forward and took the bag shyly.

"Thank you so much. I love it."

"You haven't even looked at it yet." Vivs rolled her eyes and held out her hand to take her bag from Ron.

"Thank you."

"It's hard to buy for people you've never met, so if you don't like it you can exchange it," he assured them. I gave him a "You're doing great" smile.

The girls simultaneously opened their bags to find matching pink Gap sweatshirts and a large Hershey kiss. The perfect gift for Laura and the absolute last thing my newly goth devil child would want.

Laura gave an overexaggerated gasp. "Oh, pink is my favorite color! Thank you so much." She immediately put the sweatshirt on and gave Ron another hug. Meanwhile, Vivs and I were in an evil stare-down. Her big brown eyes registered contempt, and my eyes said, "I dare you to say anything but thank you."

I laugh when I think about it now, but at the time I was convinced that I would never see Ron again. But he showed up the next night just before dinner with a black Gap sweatshirt for Vivs. That didn't win her over completely, but it was a glimpse into the thaw of what was certainly the brief ice age of her tween years.

I look up and see Nina waiting for an answer.

"I guess it was about two months. We had a rough start with the girls, remember? Vivs and that goth phase?"

"Oh, my God, the one she couldn't quite commit to?" Nina and I crack up at the memory of Vivs acting all dark and dangerous until a Backstreet Boys song came on the radio. Then she would forget herself and start singing her head off. When our laughter turns to sighs, I look directly at Nina.

"Are you sure about this?"

"About what? Garth?"

"About Garth, Chyna, everything. I feel like you just got out of the Dumpster. Are you ready to jump back into something? I mean, you barely know him."

"Are you kidding me? Do you know how long it's been since I've had sex? I know I was hung up on Sid, but shit, no one is more ready than me."

"Well, I'm glad for you, but I think you should wait to introduce him to Chyna."

Nina nods and finishes her eggs.

"Now, tell me"—she licks her lips—"who bitch-slapped who?"

✦ ✦ ✦

That evening, as I'm making Max's favorite dinner, skillet tacos, I ponder the events of my day. As if the one-two punch of what I saw in KCK and Nina's news wasn't enough, I'd still had an entire day of errands to tackle. I got the minivan washed, took a load of stuff to the dry cleaners, replaced the battery in Ron's favorite watch, talked to our local kids' gym about Max's sixth-birthday party next month, and spent a half hour on the phone with Peetsa analyzing the Dr. Evil/Miss Ward smackdown. Her theory? That Miss Ward has been making eyes at the dashing David Fancy, and Dr. Evil was just protecting her territory. I have to say, it has some legs. If Miss Ward flirted with Ron, I'd definitely be scaring her straight with a few choice words, but physical violence? Not unless she slept with him. But in that case, I'd be saving most of my rage for Ron.

I sigh as I take a sip of cooking wine, so named because it's the wine I drink while I'm cooking. I look at the clock and realize the boys should be home any minute. Skillet tacos are ready and Chyna is on her way over to babysit. Ron and I are going out to celebrate Valentine's Day. It isn't until tomorrow, but Ron likes to take me out for what he calls Scoundrel's Night. Apparently it's the night before Valentine's, when men take their mistresses to dinner. He thinks it's sexy, and who am I to argue? It's also a lot cheaper, and you aren't locked into one of those stupid theme menus that every restaurant seems to think is necessary on February 14.

I grab my wine and sit down at the kitchen-counter office to check my emails. Hmm . . . Overstock.com is having a Valentine's Day sale. Nothing says "I love you" like discount furniture. There is a note from my mom thanking me again for the prunes, which apparently did the trick for my dad. There is an email from Laura with the itinerary for our family ski trip to Utah in March, and, to my great surprise and horror, I see an email from Asami Chang. I take a deep breath and click on it.

To: JDixon
From: AChang
Subject: A question . . .
Date: February 13

Hello, Jen,

When you were class mom, did you ever hear from Sasha Lewicki, aside from her out-of-office reply?

Asami

I have to laugh. I want to tell her Sasha and I are best friends and see each other every weekend. But I don't, because I'm trying to turn over a new leaf and embrace the Asami. I'm also slightly curious about why she's asking, so my reply is friendly and open.

To: AChang
From: JDixon
Subject: A question . . .
Date: February 13

Hi, Asami,

No, I never did, but she sent sushi to the curriculum night party, so I know she exists. LOL!

Jen

I know, I know: weak joke when you have to put LOL at the end, but since there is no definitive proof that Asami has a sense of humor, I thought I'd spell it out for her. Her reply is almost instantaneous.

To: JDixon
From: AChang
Subject: A question . . .
Date: February 13

Jen,

I don't think she does.

Asami

I blink three times and stare at the screen. What the hell does *that* mean? Sasha Lewicki doesn't exist? I'm working through this thought when the Dixon men come tramping through the door. They spent the morning at the store and the afternoon attempting to ice-skate at the indoor rink. Ron wanted to take Max to the frozen pond, but I suggested that if it was too cold he wouldn't like it and the whole experience would be over before it even started. If Ron took him to the indoor rink and plied him with hot chocolate, he would definitely be more cooperative.

"Mom!" Max yells needlessly.

"Hey! How was your day?" I ask as I pull off his leopard-print jacket, orange hat, and soaking-wet striped mittens. I notice that he has a black scarf tied over his lime-green pants. It looks like a skirt.

"It was awesome! I made it all the way around once by myself." Max's cheeks are rosy and his eyes are shining. My heart bursts with love for this little munchkin. I look to Ron for confirmation and he nods.

"Next stop, hockey." He grins.

"Or I could do what that guy was doing in the middle of the ice—remember, Dad?"

Max starts to spin around in the middle of the kitchen.

"Figure skating," Ron mouths to me, and I have to look away so I won't laugh at the disappointment on his face.

"Looks cool. Now go wash your hands. Dinner's ready. Skillet tacos just for you."

"Ninja!" Max yells, and runs to the bathroom off the kitchen.

"How was your day, babe?" Ron gives me a quick kiss on the lips and heads to the fridge.

It's such a simple question, but with so many possible answers. I decide to keep it brief.

"Well, let's see. My best friend slept with my trainer."

Ron registers only mild interest. Why don't men ever react the way you want them to?

"Really? I didn't know they were a thing." His head is in the fridge so I can barely hear him.

"I just found out myself. I'm a little freaked out."

Ron turns around with one of Max's Danimals in his hand.

"Why?"

"I think Garth might be a player."

"A player?" Ron cracks up. "I don't think so." He downs the Danimals in one gulp.

"Why not?"

He keeps laughing.

"Well, to be a player you've got to have game. And that man just does not have it. I mean, he's a nice guy, but there's no way he's playing Nina."

"I hope you're right. I don't think she could take another heartbreak."

"What heartbreak? They slept together once."

"Sometimes once is all it takes for a woman to fall in love. A man, too, by the way."

Ron looks at me skeptically. "Did you fall in love the first time we had sex?"

"Well, no. But it was three sweaty minutes in the back of your car. All we did was burst the dam of lust that had built up. The first time we made love in a bed, I was pretty swept away."

"So location has something to do with falling in love."

"Oh, my God. Are you even listening to me?"

Just then, the back door opens and Chyna walks in. At the same time Max returns with clean hands and an empty stomach, so I know that our discussion is over. Ron turns and heads into the living room and I'm relieved, because clearly I am arguing myself into a corner and making no sense to anyone.

"Chyna! Sweetie. How are you?" I give her a hug.

She smiles and hugs me back nice and tight.

"I'm good."

She looks so much like her mom that I often wonder if she has even one drop of Sid's DNA.

"How's your mom?" I ask as I fill a plate for Max and place it in front of him.

"Really good. She's been in such a great mood lately."

"I've noticed that, too. Hey, can you sit with Max while he eats? I have to get ready."

"Sure thing. Hey, Max, whatcha eating?" She sits down beside him.

"Skillet tacos." Max answers with his mouth full, of course. "Want some?"

"Yeah, I do!" Chyna knows she can help herself to anything in our house. We have an open-fridge policy.

While they eat, I dash upstairs and find Ron in the shower. I head into the bedroom and check my phone. Two texts from Don. One is a selfie outside the Starbucks near school and the other says:

Do you have time for a Valentine's Day coffee tomorrow?

I actually do have time tomorrow, but I hold off texting him back. Not sure where the line is these days, but I think that would definitely be crossing it.

✦ ✦ ✦

J. Gilbert's is the best steakhouse in Overland Park. Their dry-aged steaks are phenomenal and the restaurant has a comfortable old-school feel with its mahogany furniture and crisp white table linens. There isn't one waiter under the age of fifty, and they are formal to the point of being rude.

But the waiters are worth tolerating because J. Gilbert's happens to serve the most delicious onion rings I have ever tasted. They are pretzel-coated and served with three dipping sauces that are so good I don't know which one to have first. Ron knows it's my favorite fancy place, so he surprises me once in a while. Tonight it genuinely is a surprise, because we were just here for New Year's Eve.

"Twice in two months? Are you cheating on me?" I narrow my eyes at him over my menu.

"Actually, New Year's was kind of a bust, if you remember, so I thought we deserved a do-over." Ron gives my hand a squeeze across the table.

He's being kinder than I deserve. I was still in my class mom funk on New Year's Eve and I was determined not to have a good time.

Mission accomplished, by the way. Not only did I have a shitty time, I was able to suck the fun away from everyone at our table, which was filled with Ron's favorite customers and their spouses. It's one of my superpowers, along with growing a person in my stomach and peeling labels off beer bottles intact. It was definitely not my finest moment as the wife of a successful sports-store owner, but in the moment I felt more than justified in forcing my pity party on everyone.

So on the most romantic of holidays (ahem), I'm thrilled to embrace this do-over night with the love of my life and an excellent bottle of '94 Turley Zinfandel (clearly I'm taking a little break from that clean eating and drinking). We order dinner, then sit back and enjoy our first few sips of wine. What a perfect night.

Just as I am getting my first hint of a buzz on, my eyes are pulled across the room to a couple being seated on the other side of the restaurant. Both tall and thin, him with short salt-and-pepper hair and her with long brown hair flowing down her back.

Well, well, well, if it isn't the dashing David and Kim Fancy, celebrating Scoundrel's Night at the same place we are. My mind starts to click through the events of this morning—the bitch slap and all—and I try to piece together why these two would be out for a romantic dinner.

"Jen!"

"What?" Ron's voice snaps me out of my reverie.

"What are you staring at?" He looks annoyed.

"Sorry, babe, I just noticed the Fancys sitting across the room and wondered what they're doing here."

Ron shrugs.

"Same as us, probably."

I doubt it, but say nothing. Instead, I ask him to tell me all about his ice-capades with Max this afternoon.

"Man, he really loved it. Good call on the indoor rink, by the way." He raises his glass to me in salute.

"Did he really go around the rink by himself?"

"I was right behind him, but yes, he did." I can tell Ron is proud. "It didn't take him long at all to find his legs. Now, if I can just get a stick in his hands . . ."

I give him an encouraging smile while he unfolds his long-term plan to get Max to the NHL. As I take a sip of my insanely delicious wine (seriously, if you can ever find a bottle, you will not be disappointed) I glance back over to the Fancy table. They are sitting across from each other, but are both leaning in. Kim seems to be doing a lot of talking while the dashing David just nods and listens. Is she reprimanding him for his affair? Is she telling him that she smacked his mistress around? That he better not dare step out on her again or there will be hell to pay? Damn, I wish my lip-reading skills were better. Or, you know, existent. The waiter, walking to our table, interrupts my view.

"Petite filet for the lady and porterhouse for you, sir. Enjoy." He turns on his heel and walks away just as a second waiter arrives with our side dishes and of course, my onion rings. We dig in.

Dinner is so good I forget about the Fancys across the room. Ron regales me with tales from the trenches of retail and has me howling over an incident with a woman who wanted to return a tennis racket because she said it didn't improve her game.

"How long had she been using it?"

"About a year." Ron shakes his head. "The grip was worn down and everything. She threatened to call the Better Business Bureau if I didn't give her a refund."

"So what did you do?"

"I told her this wasn't Costco and that there was no proof she had even bought the racket at our store, but I'd be happy to sell her a new one with a forty percent discount."

"That was generous."

"What are you going to do? Even a bad customer is still a customer."

I drain my wineglass and sigh contentedly.

"Thank you, my darling, for this do-over dinner. I love you so very much."

Ron grins. "Now, that's the booze talking, but you are so very welcome."

As we stand to leave, I look around to see that we are just about the last table in the restaurant. I love when that happens. You get into a cocoon of conversation and the entire world disappears around you.

Ron heads to the bathroom and I check my phone. There's a text from Don.

???

I get a tight feeling in my stomach. How could I even think about having coffee with another man after such an amazing evening with my husband? He doesn't deserve that. I text back immediately.

Nope. Sorry. Very busy day.

I put the phone back in my purse as Ron joins me.

"Everything okay at home?" he asks, assuming I was checking in on Max. Jesus, strike two. I really need to get my head out of my ass.

I nod to him and can only hope I'm right.

✦ ✦ ✦

Ron has a tight hold on me as we walk through the parking lot. Half a bottle of wine is a lot for me, and I'm a little unsteady. A car pulls up beside us.

"We meet again." Kim Fancy's voice floats from inside a silver Mercedes. "We saw you guys in the restaurant, but you seemed so deep in conversation that we didn't want to disturb you."

"We're celebrating Scoundrel's Night," I say with a slight slur. "How 'bout you?"

I hear a snort from the dashing David, who is behind the wheel.

"Nice," he says to Ron appreciatively.

"I don't get it." Kim sounds annoyed.

Ron decides to explain.

"We're celebrating Valentine's a day early. Same with you guys?"

Kim Fancy lets out a very un-Fancy-like guffaw.

"God, no. Tomorrow I expect to be going somewhere much nicer than *this* place."

And once again I'm reminded why I don't like Kim Fancy.

15

To: Miss Ward's Class
From: AChang
Date: 2/20
Subject: Class trip

Hello, parents,

I'm sorry to interrupt your week-long celebration of Mr. Lincoln's birthday, but I have not yet heard from any of you regarding chaperoning the class trip to the Underground Railroad Museum on February 28. I have, however, heard from many of you about the absence of a Valentine's party in the classroom. Miss Ward, who does not like to celebrate Valentine's Day, was not in favor of a party. I'm sure you parents were more disappointed than the children.

Anyway, I would like to know who is volunteering for the class trip. Even if you have been on a previous class trip, you can volunteer again.

Thank you,
Asami

I'm finding Asami's class mom emails more and more intriguing. She obviously caught shit for not having a Valentine's Day party. I knew it was never going to happen, given Miss Ward's aversion to "Hallmark holidays." But seeing her beg for volunteers (oh yes, I would say opening it up to me and Peetsa is her way of begging) is interesting. I think Asami is learning the hard way that (creds to the great Erma Bombeck) the grass is always greener over the septic tank. She will get no more grief from me. She is clearly getting enough from everyone else. Looks like karma found its target after all.

✦ ✦ ✦

I can barely look at Garth as we work out on Monday. I know, and he knows I know, and neither of us has said anything. It's very distracting, picturing Garth naked and sweaty on top of Nina. I blanch for the fiftieth time in the past hour and try to keep my focus on the task at hand, which is using all my body weight to try and push Garth over.

"Come on Jen, *push*! Push me like you hate me!"

That's it. I double over laughing. I can't help myself.

"Is that how you sweet-talked Nina?" I'm panting and laughing at the same time.

Garth gives me a pensive look. "Why, yes, it was, but I said it with a growl. It's pretty sexy when I growl."

I stand up and hug him—for the first time, I think. "I'm guessing it must be."

I grab a towel from the nearby dirty laundry basket and wipe off my face and arms.

"I'm really happy for you guys. It's a big move for Nina."

"For me, too," Garth says, and his sincerity makes me want to know more.

"When was the last time you had a girlfriend?"

"A girlfriend? Probably ten years."

"That's quite a dry spell." Have I mentioned I enjoy stating the obvious?

Garth laughs. "That's putting it mildly. But it wasn't exactly dry. I kept company with some very nice ladies over the years."

I guess that's his polite way of saying he slept around, which doesn't sit well with me at all.

"I hope that's not what Nina is."

I can see the surprise register on his face.

"I don't know what she is yet. But I know I like her very much and I'm pretty sure she likes me."

I chew my cheek and debate whether I should say more or shut up. Sadly, saying more wins out.

"Well, you should know that she hasn't 'kept company' "—I make air quotes—"with anyone since Sid left, so, whatever your feelings are, please keep that in mind."

And then I see it in his eyes. I have managed to piss off the nicest guy in the world.

He takes a deep breath.

"Jen, I know Nina is your best friend, but I think you should just keep out of it, at least until *we* figure it out." He turns and starts putting equipment away.

Over his shoulder, he mumbles, "I think we're done for the day."

I really don't like the way this is playing out.

"Garth, wait." I'm not sure what I want to say, but I don't want to leave it like this. I need to lighten things up.

"I'll kick your ass if you hurt her." I smirk.

He smiles and shrugs. "And what happens if she hurts me?"

Since that hasn't even occurred to me, I don't have a ready answer, so I say the first thing that pops in my head.

"Then she'll be the one getting the ass kicking."

✦ ✦ ✦

Garth and I head upstairs and say good-bye. I walk to the kitchen for some water and do a double take when I see Vivs sitting at the table playing cards with Max.

"Aren't you supposed to be in New York?" I know she and Raj had planned a romantic getaway to the Big Apple. Well, actually New

Jersey, where Raj has an uncle who lives in Teaneck. But they had plans to hang out in the Village with some friends.

"Don't ask," Vivs sing-songs. She slaps a card down and yells, "Uno!"

Max jumps up from his chair "No, Sissy! Not gonna happen." And he slams down a multicolored card. "I'm changing it to red! Take that, sucka!"

"Whoa! Excuse me, what did you say?" I seriously can't believe that just came out of Max's mouth.

"I said, 'Take that, sucka,'" he repeats, with a little less enthusiasm. "Graydon says it all the time."

"Well, just because Graydon says it doesn't mean you can. It's just not a nice thing to say to someone." I consider calling Shirleen to share this little nugget about her perfect son. Maybe later. I turn to Vivs. "How did you get here?"

"I drove with Laura."

"She's here too?" I can't remember the last time the girls were home for Presidents' Week.

Vivs puts down her final card. "Red Maxazillion!" she yells, and then whispers, "Take that, sucka."

Max giggles and starts gathering up the cards. I give Vivs a disapproving scowl.

"So where's Laura, upstairs?"

"She's at Town Hall helping this guy set up for his show tonight." Vivs tosses this at me as though I should already know. I'm so not in the mood for this.

"What guy? What show? You girls think you tell me things, but you don't. And why aren't you in New York?"

Vivs sighs and gives me her "I'm barely tolerating you" look.

"I'm not in New York because Raj blew me off to help work on the plans for the new addition to the library at school and Laura has been dating this bass player and his band is playing Town Hall tonight. There, all caught up." She turns back to Max to start another game of Uno.

There is so much mind-splintering information in that one

sentence that it takes my almost-fifty-year-old brain a few seconds to process it all. I pick the most shocking thing to attack first.

"Laura is dating a *musician*?" Oh, my God. Where did I go wrong?

"She only started seeing him about a week ago. He's nice. The band sucks, though."

"How come she can say 'sucks,' but I can't say 'sucka'?" Max jumps in.

"Max, can you go play with your helicopter while I talk to Sissy, please." It's a command more than a request.

"But we just started a new game."

"We can play later, bud. I'm here till Saturday."

Max seems satisfied with this promise and runs up to his room.

Now that I'm alone with Vivs, I grab a bottle of water and a yogurt from the fridge and join her at the table.

"Okay," I sigh, "from the beginning, please. What is Raj doing?"

Vivs sighs and shuffles the Uno cards with vigor.

"He got asked to work on the plans for the new library at school. So he bailed on New York."

"Isn't it a big deal for him to be asked to do that?"

"Yeah, but we've been planning this trip since Christmas. He chose work over me. That's just not a good sign for our future."

I nearly burst out laughing. For someone so smart, Vivs can be so obtuse, not to mention self-absorbed.

"Sweetie, he didn't pick work over you. He picked a once-in-a-lifetime opportunity over a trip that can happen pretty much any time. Surely to God you see that."

Vivs finishes shuffling and puts the cards back in the box.

"I guess I do. I mean, I do. I'm just bummed. And I made him feel guilty about it, so now I feel worse. Am I the biggest bitch on the planet?"

Not the *biggest*, I think but do not say.

"Not even close." I stand and walk around to her side of the table to give her a hug.

"Just make sure you apologize to him. I mean, it's pretty huge, what he's doing."

She nods. "Maybe I'll make him some cookies. Or you know he loves the Five Napkin Brownies."

I decide to change the subject before I get roped into making them.

"So tell me about Laura's new guy."

She shrugs. "I really don't know that much. His name is Travis, he's a creative writing major, he's my age, and he plays in this band that's pretty popular on campus, although I don't know why. Their music is so average. The lead singer is this hot Asian guy. I'm surprised she didn't go after him."

I can't imagine Laura "going after" anyone.

"What's the name of the band?"

"Sucker Punch."

"Eww." I can't stop my reaction.

"I know, stupid name, stupid songs. I don't know what people like about them. But Travis seems okay. I promised Laurs I'd go with her to see them tonight. I'm dreading it."

"How bad can they be? They have a gig at Town Hall," I offer.

"Yeah. On a *Monday*."

She has a point.

"Wanna come?"

"Seriously?" I can't believe my daughter is asking me to hang out at a concert.

"Sure, why not? You can tell me if he's any good on bass."

Bass players were never my specialty, but the thought of going to hear a rock band is mildly pleasing. I haven't revisited the shame of my youth since Max was born. I wonder if I can convince Ron to go.

"Maybe. Let me talk to Ron and see if I can get a babysitter."

I pick up my phone and notice a text from Don.

Hey, is everything okay? I didn't mean to freak you out by asking to go for coffee on Valentine's Day.

Truth be told I wasn't freaked out, but it was a bit of a wake-up call for me. I had made a promise to myself that night that I would dial down the flirt.

You didn't. I'm just crazy busy.

Well, my offer for coffee stands.
Good!

Back in reactor mode where I belong, I start to make plans for tonight.

✦ ✦ ✦

I secure Chyna to babysit, and reach out to see if anyone else wants to join us for dinner and a "show." That's how I present it, anyway. The Tuccis are in, and it only takes a little begging to convince Nina that she and Garth should give their binge-watching of some series on Netflix a rest and come out to have fun. I feel like I need to see Garth and Nina together to get a sense of what's really going on. I have a sneaking suspicion that I'm the only one creating drama in their relationship.

As I'm cleaning up the lunch dishes, Laura comes in the back door and rushes to give me a hug.

"Mom!"

"Hey, sweetie. Such a nice surprise that you guys are home." I hug her back.

"I know! It was kind of a last-minute decision."

"I heard." I give her an expectant look.

"Did Vivs tell you about Travis?" She is blushing.

"Yes. He sounds really cool. Can't wait to hear him play."

"Wait, are you *coming* tonight?" I can't tell if she is excited or horrified.

"Yes! Vivs invited me and I invited Peeta and Buddy and Nina and Garth."

"Oh, my *God*, Mom! Are you kidding me?" Yup, horrified.

"No, it'll be fun!"

"Not for me! I don't want Travis to have to meet all of you." She's whining now.

"Don't be silly. He doesn't even have to know we're there."

"Oh, yeah, right. I'm going to kill her. *Vivs*!" she suddenly screams at the top of her lungs.

"Laura! Stop yelling. We're going to come and see Sucker Punch play"—try saying *that* with a straight face—"and have a fun night out. If you don't want us to meet Travis, fine. We'll meet him another time. But we're coming. I haven't seen a live band in ages."

Laura is still sporting a pout, but she doesn't say anything else except "Fine," and stomps up the back stairs, no doubt to lay her wrath at Vivs's doorstep. Better Vivs than me. I need to find a place for all of us to eat before the concert.

✦ ✦ ✦

After dinner at our local Bonefish Grill—picked because of its proximity to Town Hall—we all stroll over to the venue. I have been eyeing Nina and Garth all night and I've come to the conclusion that I will learn nothing from watching them. They don't give anything away except the idea that they are a very happy couple.

We all get in line to buy tickets and discover that, believe it or not, Sucker Punch is *not* the headliner. That distinction goes to an all-girl Led Zeppelin cover band called Lez Zeppelin. Sucker Punch is one of two opening acts.

Ron has his arm around me as we walk through the door, give the tattooed gentleman $40, and get our hands stamped. *Our hands stamped!* It's been too many years since I've had the telltale sign of a night out imprinted on the back of my hand. I can't help feeling a bit giddy.

We stop by the mandatory coat check and entrust our garments to a painted lady whose T-shirt says "Call Me Maybe." She doesn't give us a ticket in return, and I can't help but wonder if I'll ever see my black sheepskin jacket again.

Town Hall is exactly what it sounds like—an all-purpose venue used for everything from Christian revivals to Zumba classes. It is a very large rectangular room with a stage at one end and a balcony that runs along the other three sides. It has the feel of a school gymnasium but without the smell of utility balls. You can pretty much hold any event here, but you cannot serve alcohol. It's a municipal rule that has been challenged many times over the years but has yet to be changed.

The joint is packed with the unwashed youth of KC. Okay, they probably aren't unwashed so much as trying to look that way. I don't really get the whole ripped-jeans, holes-in-the-T-shirt, bedhead look that seems to be so popular, but then again, I'm sure my mom didn't get the slutty-biker-chick look that I sported as a teen.

There are no seats, of course, so we all just stand around waiting for something to happen. Soon enough, a group of kids, dressed pretty much like their audience, ambles onto the stage with guitars and start plugging into the amplifiers. There is some ungodly noise as they get tuned up and I realize my heart is racing. Man, does this bring me back. I turn to Ron with what I'm sure is the goofiest smile I've ever displayed.

He raises an eyebrow. "What?"

"Nothing. I'm just . . . it's fun to be here, that's all."

He smiles and nods like he's humoring a mental patient. I look down the line at the rest of our crew, but don't see anyone quite as excited as I am. Peetsa is plugging her ears, and Buddy is yelling something in Garth's ear. I notice Vivs has joined us and is talking to Nina. I walk over to them.

"Is this Sucker Punch?" I yell.

"No. Next band. This is Grope. High school kids."

Just then Grope's lead singer steps up to the mic.

"Good evening, Kansas City!" he screams, and immediately gets feedback from the monitors.

"Whoa. Sorry about that. Uh, we're Grope and we're here to get you rockin'. One two three four . . ."

And it begins. Grope starts rattling out a song about going to hell. It's actually not too bad, considering how young they are. I look to my right and see my friends nodding their heads to the beat. Okay. Not a disaster. Grope's second song is a ballad—a sensitive song about a bitch who did him wrong. The melody is good, but these guys really need help with their lyrics. "I was trashed so I crashed at her hash-pad." *What?*

They get the crowd going with their third and final song—a pretty decent cover of "London Calling," by the Clash. Always leave 'em wanting more, Grope. Well done.

After a quick changeover, Sucker Punch hits the stage. Four guys—all adorable—take their places with much more panache than Grope. Vivs is right, the lead singer is a very good-looking Asian boy/man. He's obviously in his twenties, but has a young look. He reminds me of John Cho, the guy from *Harold and Kumar*.

I look at the bass player and see a thin blond guy with a very cute smile and a great ass. I know it's not something I should be noticing about my daughter's boyfriend, but I do still have a pulse, and may I say he is wearing his skintight khakis very well.

The lead singer introduces the band, then says, "Let's hear it one more time for Grope."

The audience gives a generous round of applause and then Sucker Punch kicks off their set with a slow song that eventually builds to a frantic beat. I don't love the song, but I can tell these guys are talented musicians. Travis is totally in tune with the drummer and doesn't grandstand like the Grope bass player did. I can already tell he's a nice guy. I feel my hand being squeezed and I see Laura has joined us in the audience.

"What do you think?" she screams in my ear, so loudly that I feel reverb.

"They are awesome!" I scream back. She looks relieved.

We listen to all three of their songs together. Laura knows every word, and my heart aches just a bit. I remember being that girl.

When Sucker Punch finishes their set, the crowd shows its appreciation by asking for an encore. I'm a little surprised. I mean, they weren't *that* good, and Lez Zeppelin's fans have been waiting patiently through two boy bands.

Laura is beaming.

"Travis is going to be so happy. They're not allowed to play another song, but he was hoping people would want one."

Peetsa, Buddy, and Ron join Laura and me to give their two cents.

"This is so fun!" Peetsa enthuses. She is still yelling, even though the music has stopped.

"Great bands!" Buddy adds. I don't believe either of them.

"Where is everyone else?" I realize half our party is MIA.

"They all went to watch from the balcony," Peetsa explains.

"Mom, do you want to come and meet the band?" Laura asks. I'm floored. I didn't think she even wanted me here. I guess I've passed some unspoken test.

"You mean go backstage? You don't have to ask me twice!"

Laura winces. Whoops. Not cool, I guess.

"I mean, sure," I rebound. "You guys wanna come?" I ask the Tuccis.

"I think we'll hang here and catch the Led Zeppelin band thing," Buddy says, and Peetsa nods her agreement. I give them a knowing smile and follow Laura to the door beside the stage.

Town Hall isn't exactly Wembley Stadium, but backstage still has the slightly seedy electric undercurrent of exclusivity. I'm in my wheelhouse. The only things missing are beefy security guards, a bevy of skanks, and a pass around my neck. And alcohol. But whatever, I'm here and I'm feeling great.

Laura leads me through a common area with sofas to a hallway by the back door where Sucker Punch is packing up their instruments. Laura runs to Travis and throws herself at him. Good lord! I guess I never taught her the art of playing hard to get. Actually, I never practiced that art, either.

When they come up for air, she is rapturous.

"You were amazing! You sounded so good."

Travis seems pleased.

"Did you see when I gave you our sign?"

She beams and starts making out with him again.

I realize I should stop staring at them. I turn and see the rest of the band just packing up their stuff and joking around. The lead singer is wiping off his guitar. Up close, he really doesn't look that much like John Cho, but he reminds me of someone.

"You guys were great," I offer him.

He gives me a puzzled look.

"Uh, thanks. Are you with Lez Zeppelin?"

"Me? No." I start to giggle like an idiot. "No, Laura's my daughter." I point to the makeout session.

"Oh, cool. She's cool."

I'm about to say something stupid like "Just like her mom" when I hear a voice that makes the hairs on the back of my neck stand up like quills on a porcupine.

"Jeen!"

We both turn and see Asami Chang walking toward us. Immediately three things pop into my head:

1. What the hell is she doing here?
2. She looks good in those leather pants.
3. Why did she call me Jeen?

"Hey, Auntie!" The lead singer scoots around me and gives Asami a hug.

Auntie?

"You were wonderful!" Asami is gushing and fussing over the man/boy, who I now understand to be her nephew and named Jeen. I realize she hasn't even noticed me. Time to put a buzz kill on her night.

"Asami? Hi!"

They look over at me.

"Is this your friend, Auntie? I was just talking to her."

The look on Asami's face is pretty comical as she tries to fit all the pieces together.

"Jen. What are you doing here?" I can't tell if she's shocked or pissed off.

"Here to see the band, just like you." I walk toward her.

And then something completely unexpected and magical happens: Asami smiles. It's a genuine "I'm happy the stick is finally out of my ass" smile. It changes her face completely.

"Weren't they wonderful? Did you meet Jeen? Jeen, this is Mrs. Dixon."

"Just Jen." I smile and shake his hand.

"Jeen is my nephew," she explains needlessly. She turns to him. "I like this band of yours!"

"Thanks." Jeen smiles. I can tell he's happy to have her approval.

"So different from the string quartet!"

He laughs. "Yeah. Can't get much more different."

Just then the grinding beat of "Whole Lotta Love" starts up, signaling that the headliners have taken the stage. I can't hear lyrics, just the muted bass and drumbeats.

I feel like I'm having a bit of an out-of-body experience. Asami has a nephew who left a string quartet to play in a rock band called Sucker Punch *and she's okay with it*. Who is this woman?

"Has your father heard you play yet?"

I don't get to hear the answer to this question, because Laura suddenly appears in front of my face.

"Mom!"

"What? Sorry. I ran into a friend."

"Come meet Travis!"

With difficulty, I turn away from the Asami show and walk toward the object of my daughter's unbridled desire.

Travis is hunched over his bass case. As we walk up, he straightens, hitches up his pants, and runs a hand through his hair. He's nervous. Good.

"Mom, this is Travis."

I put on my best mom smile and stick out my hand.

"Hi, Travis. You guys really rocked it tonight."

"Thanks, Mrs. Dixon. Nice to meet you."

His handshake is warm and firm, and he looks directly in my eyes. *Not bad, Travis. You've been raised well.*

"How many shows have you guys done together?" I ask.

"This is our third since Jeen came on board. We're still working out the kinks."

"Not at all. I thought you guys were pretty tight."

Travis just smiles. I'm sure he's thinking, *How the hell would you know, old lady?* To which I'm thinking: *Well, I'll tell you how I know, buddy boy. Ever heard of a little band called INXS?*

"Mom, what were you talking to Jeen about?" Laura interrupts the cocktail party in my head.

"What? Oh, nothing. I know his aunt." I look back over and see Asami talking to Jeen and the drummer. Man, peel an onion and you get a lot of layers.

Travis and the band finish packing up their equipment to the slow thumping beat of Lez Zeppelin playing what I think is "All of My Love." I can't help feeling like I'm missing the best band of the night. I go over to where Laura is standing.

"Do you need a ride home, sweetie?"

She blushes, which I take to mean either no or "I don't know yet." Travis answers for her.

"I think we're going to hang for a while." He puts his arm around her.

I've seen enough PDA to last me a while.

"Okay. Have fun, guys. Travis, it was nice to meet you. I'm sure I'll see you again."

"I hope so." He shakes my hand again. Call me lame, but that stuff goes a long way with me.

As I'm heading to find the rest of my posse, Asami catches up with me.

"Your nephew is very talented," I tell her. "And he looks so much like you!"

"Thank you. He is a classically trained cellist, but we always knew he wouldn't stick with it. This really suits him."

I nod, and as we walk toward the front of the house, the music gets louder.

"Are you going to watch the band?" she asks.

"Not sure. I have to find my group. Is your husband here?"

She looks down. "No. I came by myself to see Jeen."

"Well, I'm here with the Tuccis and Nina Grandish. You can hang with us if you like." I can't believe the words coming out of my mouth. Someone should check the weather in hell.

"That would be really nice, thanks." I think we're both surprised that she has accepted my offer.

I whip out my cell and text Ron to ask where he is.

He responds pretty quickly: *Up in the balcony to your right.* I look up and see him waving at me. Nina and Garth are with him, but there's no sign of the Tuccis.

I lean over to Asami and yell, "Come on. They're upstairs."

By the time we navigate the crowd and the questionably up-to-code stairway, Peetsa and Buddy are with the rest of the group. I'm getting a lot of funny looks as we join them.

"Look who I bumped into backstage," I yell just as the band wraps up "The Rain Song."

There are nods and smiles all around, but it is quite possibly one of the most awkward moments of my life, and that's saying something.

We all watch Lez Zeppelin for a while. These girls are amazing. Even if you don't happen to enjoy the musical stylings of Robert Plant and Jimmy Page, you can't help but appreciate what talented musicians these women are. The crowd is going wild, and even my little nerd group is grooving.

As they wind down the show with "Stairway to Heaven," Asami leans in and asks if I would be able to chaperone the class trip next week.

"Didn't you get any volunteers?"

She shakes her head. "Not one."

I actually feel sorry for her.

"Well, it's hard sometimes. Just keep at them. I had to do a lot of begging."

"Being class mom is a lot tougher than I thought."

"Miss Ward doesn't help much, either."

Asami's eyes widen.

"I know! I can never tell what she wants."

"Don't beat yourself up about it. She's a tricky one."

I'm getting tired of yelling, and my throat is really dry. I turn to the group and suggest we head out before the stampede toward the door starts. They agree and we all maneuver our way down the deathtrap-like stairs, surprisingly get the correct coats from Miss Call Me Maybe, and go out into the cold, clear February night. As Ron strides away to get our car, Peetsa comes up and gives me a hug.

"We're heading home." She then adds in a whisper: "I want a full report in the morning." I give her an extra squeeze.

"We are, too," Nina says from the comfort of Garth's arms.

"Thanks, you guys, for coming. I know it meant a lot to Laura. Neens, I'll call you in the morning. Garth, see you Thursday." I blow them both kisses.

I notice Asami is still lingering, so I offer her a ride home.

"No, thanks. I have my car. I just wanted one more minute with you."

"What's up? I'll chaperone the trip if you want me to." I'm starting to shiver.

"Thank you, that would be great." She pulls her collar up around her neck to stay warm. "But I just wanted to apologize to you for pushing you out as class mom. You didn't deserve it."

Wow, an apology from Asami. I'm floored. I see Ron pull up in the car, so I only have a minute.

"Well, I kind of did after the 'your people' comment. I really was just trying to be funny, but I know it was inappropriate and I'm sorry I hurt your feelings.."

"I accept your apology." She nods and turns to walk away. "Good night, Jen."

"Good night, Asami."

And that, children, is the story of how two mortal enemies found peace. And to think it all started with a sucker punch.

16

To: Miss Ward's Class
From: JDixon
Date: 3/5
Subject: I'm back, babies!

Dear Parents,

Big, big news from room 147! Asami Chang and I have decided being
your class parent is a two-mom job, so we will be splitting duties. Asami
will handle the detail-oriented stuff that, let's face it, I stink at, and I will
be in charge of communicating with all of you. So if you're allergic to
snark, you better stop reading now.

First, shame on all of you for not volunteering for the fabulous trip
to the Quindaro Underground Railroad Museum. Asami is too nice to say
anything, but I have put a black mark beside each of your names. The
kids all had such a wonderful time after the initial disappointment when
they found out there wasn't an actual train ride involved.

Moving forward, there are a lot of opportunities for you to get back
in my good graces. First up, the William Taft Annual Book Fair! It's

happening March 10. The Parents' Association needs 3 volunteers from each class to make sure no brawls start over who gets the last copy of Captain Underpants.

More breaking news from room 147! Just after spring break, we will be having an Easter/Passover party! According to Miss Ward, these are not, repeat not Hallmark holidays and are therefore worthy of celebration. We will be decorating eggs and Jill Kaplan has volunteered to show the kiddos how to make charoset, which is a very yummy Seder treat. So, to that end, here's a list of what we'll need. Remember, there is no shame in offering to bring more than one thing.

3 dozen hard-boiled eggs
stickers
small chocolate eggs
a live rabbit (not really, just making sure you're still paying attention)
apples
cinnamon
grape juice
fruit for Graydon
water
cups (already got you signed up, Jackie)
wet wipes
We will provide the PAAS egg-dyeing kits.
Thank you for your cooperation. Response times will be noted and demerits will be given.
Don't thank me, I'm just glad to be back.
Jen (and Asami in spirit)

I feel good as I click Send. I've missed having my little rant sessions to the class. I'm sure there will be a lot of surprised responses to the news that Asami and I are co–house parenting.

It was actually her idea. A few days after the concert at Town Hall, she called and asked if I could meet her for coffee. I was a little unsure because, let's face it, it's one thing to have a cease-fire with someone, but quite another to all of a sudden become girlfriends.

But I was needlessly concerned. As we sat down with our lattes on one of the couches at the Starbucks right by the school, Asami, true to form, came right out with it.

"Jen, I don't expect we will ever be friends, but I think we would make a good team."

"A good team of what?" I really wasn't sure where she was going with this.

"Class mothers. You have your strengths and I have mine. Together we could get the job done really well, don't you think?"

I looked at her skeptically. Was this Asami's idea of humor?

"Do you mean *this year*? Be class mothers together this year?"

"Yes, exactly. You can write your silly letters and get people to participate, and I will make sure everything else runs smoothly."

I ignored the implication that things didn't run smoothly under my regime and gave Asami's idea some real thought. I didn't take long to realize it was a pretty good one, and it actually appealed to me.

"Sure, why not?"

"Honestly, I don't get your jokes, but people seem to really enjoy the wit in your emails."

I smiled at the backhanded compliment and raised my cup to her.

"Here's to strange bedfellows."

"Indeed." Asami raised her cup, too.

So here I am, back in the saddle with half the workload and permission to write ridiculous emails. I feel like I should go buy a lottery ticket and keep the lucky train rolling. But I can't, because I have to start doing the heavy lifting for Max's birthday party this weekend. So I grab my keys and sprint to the minivan to avoid the freezing rain we are being treated to.

We are having his party at a place called Emerald City Gym. It's one of those great play-zone places that have all kinds of fun things for the kids to do. The staff sets up and cleans up, so all we have to do is show up. I can't help but think it must be the worst job ever to wrangle kids at one of these birthday parties. I'm planning on tipping well.

Max has invited all the boys in his class, because "girls are gross" according to Graydon Cobb, who has apparently become the oracle of Miss Ward's kindergarten class. Whatever pearls come out of his mouth are repeated at dinner tables throughout the greater Kansas City area, including mine.

"Jingle bells, Batman smells, Robin laid an egg," Max cheerfully sang one evening. "Graydon made that up. He's so funny."

I guess we can add plagiarism to Graydon's list of talents.

Party City is my first stop this morning to pick up goody-bag crap. If I ruled the world, there would be no such thing as a goody bag. There would be an implied contract between the inviter and the invitee: I give you food and cake and some kind of activity, and you bring me a present. Why do I have to then give *you* a present? Isn't that what the party is?

When Vivs and Laura were small, you just gave candy at the end of the party—probably in a clear plastic bag with a ribbon . . . maybe. These days the gift bag is just that, a gift, and it's supposed to be something that is in theme with the rest of the party. The pressure is crippling, I tell you.

Max's theme this year is ninja warriors, so as I walk the aisles of the store I keep that in mind. Little did I know that the ninjas have a whole aisle to themselves. Banzai! This party is practically going to plan itself. I pick up ninja masks and figurines and fake swords for the gift bags, along with two ninja piñatas, plus cups, tablecloths, plates, and napkins.

After I pay and load my bags in the back of the minivan, I check my phone for emails and messages and I am surprised to see ten replies to the class email I sent out an hour ago. As usual, Sasha Lewicki's out-of-office reply leads the pack. Is that woman ever in the office? I guess she's at home taking care of her sick daughter. At least, I hope she is. Thank goodness every other reply is from an actual human.

To: JDixon

From SCobb

Date: 3/5

Subject: I'm back, babies!

Jennifer,

I just googled charoset and it has nuts in it! Are you trying to kill my son? I will bring fruit for Graydon.

Shirleen

To: SCobb

From JDixon

Date: 3/5

Subject: I'm back, babies!

Shirleen,

Please, this is not my first trip to the rodeo. The charoset recipe Jill is using has no nuts.

Jen

To: JDixon

From CAlexander

Date: 3/5

Subject: I'm back, babies!

Welcome back, Jen!

You can put all the eggs in our basket (get it?).
  Also, Kim can do the book fair. What time should she be there?

         Thanks,
         Carol

To: JDixon

From RBrown

Date: 3/5

Subject: I'm back,babies!

Jen,

I hope this isn't a joke and you are really back. I'm so excited!
  We can bring eggs for everyone. Also Zach is really excited about
Max's party on Saturday.
  See you then!

         Ravi

> *To: JDixon*
>
> *From DBurgess*
>
> *Date: 3/5*
>
> *Re: I'm back, babies!*
>
> *Hey, Jen,*
>
> *Way to go, getting your old job back. You'll have to fill me in. You know, a man could die of thirst trying to get a cup of coffee out of you. Just sayin' . . .*
>
> *BTW, Lulu will bring in eggs for everyone.*
>
> *Cheers,*
>
> *Don*

Poor Don—he must be so confused. After a five-month bout of flirty texting, I have pulled way back. He still texts about once a week, trying to meet up, but I'm either make-believe busy or actually busy—truthfully, more the latter than the former. I may never know what he really meant by "coffee," but I'm okay with that.

> *To: JDixon*
>
> *From JJ Aikens*
>
> *Date: 3/5*
>
> *Subject: I'm back, babies!*
>
> *Jen,*
>
> *Well, this is quite a turn of events. I guess I should say welcome back, but I think you know it would be insincere. So I'll just say we will bring eggs for everyone to decorate.*
>
> *JJ*

Oh, mother of God. Am I being punked? I scroll through the other emails to find that yup, everyone wants to bring eggs. What are the chances? I definitely need to think of a better system. I peck out an email on my phone.

To: Miss Ward's Class
From: JDixon
Date: 3/5
Subject: Egg-cellent response!

Me again,

Thanks for the great and may I say timely responses! Shirleen, your charming email came in second place after Sasha Lewicki's out-of-office reply, with a winning time of 58 seconds. Well done.

It may surprise you to know that just about everyone offered to bring eggs. I guess the yolk's on me! Since we don't need 10 dozen eggs, I'm going to assign some of you other things to bring. See the list below, and thanks again for getting back to me so quickly.

Eggs—Alexanders, Burgess/Gordon (two dozen each, please— hard-boiled)
Stickers—Aikens Family
Cups—Westmans
Apples—Browns
Grape juice—Kaplans
Water—Changs
Fruit—Cobbs
Cinnamon—Zalises
Wet wipes—Wolffes
And the Batons will bring wine.

> *Please bring all supplies on the morning of April 4 when you drop your kids off. I know, I know, it's a month away. I'll send a reminder email a few days before.*
>
> *As for the book fair, thanks to Kim Alexander and Peetsa Tucci for volunteering. Is there anyone else dying to straighten up books for 3 hours? No? Okay. Guess it's on me, then.*
>
> *Jen*

✦ ✦ ✦

After I drop the party supplies at Emerald City Gym, I stop by the Upper Crust bakery to give them the good news that I will need a ninja cake that feeds twenty. Not a Teenage Mutant Ninja Turtles cake, a real ninja cake. I think I have a 50/50 chance of actually getting the right cake.

My cell phone rings as I run to the minivan. The rain has stopped, but the temperature is now below freezing so I nearly wipe out on the icy tarmac as I yank open the car door. I sit down and grab my cell from my purse.

"Hello," I say, a bit too loudly.

"Jen, it's Asami. Do you have time to meet me for coffee?"

"Anything wrong?"

"No, I just want to talk to you about something."

"Is it about the class email? Because if you don't want to bring water, I can bring it."

"No, water is fine. Do you have time to meet or not?"

Now, that's the Asami I know and love. I look at the clock on my dashboard and calculate how much I still have left to do before I pick up Max.

"How about two o'clock at Starbucks by school?" I can't imagine why she needs to see me, but whatever it is can't take more than half an hour.

"See you there." She hangs up before I can say anything.

✦ ✦ ✦

Asami is already waiting when I walk in at two o'clock on the dot, secretly patting myself on the back for once again stuffing ten pounds of potatoes into a five-pound bag.

After I grab a chai latte, I join her on the couch. She has certainly made a brave choice of headgear on this cold, wet day. She is sporting a green hunter's hat with eyes on the front and a lid that looks like a duckbill.

"So what's up?" I take a sip and ease my coat off.

As usual, Asami comes right to the point. She leans toward me with purpose.

"I think I told you once that I believe there is no such person as Sasha Lewicki, and now I'm more convinced than ever."

Really? This is what I had to rush here for? I never pegged Asami for the conspiracy-theory type.

"How can you even think that? I mean, I know I've never met her, but I heard that Miss Ward goes to her house, like, three times a week and tutors Nadine."

"According to whom?" Asami raises a very defined eyebrow at me.

"Uh, I can't remember who told me. Why?"

"Because I went to the address listed in her school file, and guess what? No one lives there. It's one of those old abandoned row houses off Mission Street near the Walmart."

I really don't know what to say. Do I want to ask how she got access to the Lewickis' school file in the first place?

"Maybe they moved. Or maybe it's a misprint. There could be a lot of explanations." I can't believe I'm the voice of reason in this conversation.

"Maybe, but then I Googled Sasha Lewicki, and guess what? All I found was some doctor who works at Kaiser Permanente in California and a girl at Boston College who puts inappropriate pictures of herself on Instagram." She pauses for what I guess is effect or drama, then says, "There is no Sasha Lewicki in Kansas City."

I want to say *"So what?"* but I can see that Asami is really whipped up about this. I take a long sip of chai in the hopes of finding some answers for her.

"So what's your endgame here, Asami? What exactly are you trying to do?"

"I'm trying to prove that these people are made up."

"By who? And for what reason?" I can't keep the irritation out of my voice.

"Well, *that's* what we need to find out." Asami sits back for the first time during our conversation and crosses her arms.

I'm still not convinced there is anything to give a royal rip about, but I take a few breaths to absorb her information. Okay, we have a kid in class that no one has ever seen; a mother who only answers emails with an out-of-office autoreply, but manages to contribute to class parties; and there is a wrong address in the school records. If she is made up, someone has taken the time to plan this ruse admirably.

"Have you talked to Miss Ward? Asked her about it?"

"Of course I have." Asami seems insulted. "She brushed me off by saying she couldn't talk about another student."

I remember having a similar experience when I casually asked Miss Ward about Nadine at the beginning of the year. At the time, I wasn't fishing; I was just making conversation. I look at my watch. We have about ten minutes.

"Okay, let's say Nadine and Sasha are made up. So what? It doesn't affect the class dynamic at all. Why do you care?"

"It just bothers me. It's like a loose end that is just . . . dangling there." Asami waves her hand in front of my face. "Plus I can't stop feeling like someone is having a good laugh at our expense, and I do not like to be laughed at."

If you don't like to be laughed at, you should seriously rethink your hat choices, I think.

"Okay, so what would you like *me* to do?"

"I want you to help me get to the bottom of this. See if we can force this person to show herself."

"Right. And how am I supposed to do that?"

"I was hoping you'd have an idea. You've got that slick, cagey mind."

I chew my lip and consider the backhanded compliment my co-class parent just launched at me. God, she is hard to take seriously with that hat on. I start to put my coat on, and she does the same.

"Let me think about it," I say as we walk to the door. "My slick, cagey mind needs time to brew."

We run to our respective cars in a lame attempt to hold on to the warmth from Starbucks, and drive the quarter mile to school. We park and get out and Asami joins me as I walk to where we wait for the kids. As we approach, I can imagine Peetsa and Ravi checking me out with my new bestie, but to my surprise I find them locked in conversation with none other than Shirleen Cobb.

"Hey, girls, what's up?" I say by way of inserting myself into the exchange.

"Jennifer, I'm glad you're here. Does Graydon say inappropriate things to Max?" Shirleen asks.

"Inappropriate?" I look to Ravi and Peetsa for any clue as to what we have walked into.

"Yes, inappropriate. Surely you, of all people, know what that means."

And I thought I was the snarky one.

"Well, to be honest, he did tell Max not to invite girls to his birthday party because they're gross."

Judging by the openmouthed stares I'm receiving, this is the wrong answer. When will I ever learn that the only thing you say to other parents is how wonderful their child is? Even if they ask you for the truth, they really don't want it.

"I don't see anything inappropriate about that. In fact, it is extremely age *appropriate*."

"And that's why I never said anything to you about it." I look around the circle. "Why are we talking about this?"

I feel like Peetsa is about to say something, but Shirleen jumps in.

"As a matter of fact, Zach told my son that his mother said that

Graydon says too many inappropriate things and he shouldn't listen to him."

"Which Zach?" Asami and I say at the same time.

"That's what I'm trying to find out." She turns to Peetsa and Ravi. "But I don't seem to be getting anywhere."

"It must have been Zach E., Shirleen," Peetsa says, in her most appeasing voice. I'm impressed by her ability to throw Trudy Elder under the bus without even blinking. "I certainly hear all about Graydon from my Zach, but I would never say anything like that to him."

Ravi nods solemnly, but doesn't say anything.

"Well, I guess I should go have a word with Trudy." Shirleen turns to leave our weird little circle of friends, but then pauses for a final comment.

"I sure hope you girls will always come to me if there's a problem with Graydon."

With that, she stalks away.

"Because clearly you are open to the criticism," I say when I know she's out of earshot.

My besties laugh. So does Asami.

Just then the bell rings and our cuties come trudging out looking the way most kids do by this time of winter—exhausted and disheveled. I spot Max's leopard-print jacket in the crowd and wave to him. He has accessorized today with a headband that has brown felt antlers on top. He is walking arm in arm with Zach T., and they both look upset.

"Hey, sweetie." I give him a quick hug. "Are you okay?"

"I'm fine." His voice tells me he's anything but.

I look to Peetsa to see if she has any idea what they're so glum about. She shrugs and takes Zach's bag from him.

"See you guys tomorrow," she says.

"Don't forget to ask your mom!" Zach yells to Max as he walks away, holding his mother's hand.

"Ask me what?" I look down at him.

"You know it's five days till my birthday, right?"

"Five days till your birthday party," I correct him as we walk to the car, "a week till your birthday."

"Did you get the cake yet?" he asks, handing me his backpack.

"Well, I ordered it. We won't pick it up until Saturday."

As I buckle him into his booster seat, he lets out a very big sigh for a little boy. I buckle myself in and turn on the car. I check my phone before I pull out and see I have a text from Don.

You're having a party without me?

I guess word is out about Max's shindig.

We are. Six-year-old boys only. Girls are gross.

What about 48-year-old boys?

They're gross, too.

LOL

I shake my head and put my phone in my purse.

"How was school today?" I ask over my shoulder.

"Good."

"What did you do?"

"Nothing."

"Who did you play with?"

"I don't know." He suddenly looks at me as though he has just realized I'm there. "Hey, Mom, can we invite Jack to my party?"

"Jack?" I frown. "Who is Jack?"

"You know, Garth's friend from when we went to Wichita that day."

"Why would you want to invite Jack, sweetie? We barely know him."

"Mom, *please* can you ask him? Please?"

"Well, I'll need to know why first."

Max frowns. "Graydon doesn't believe we know a guy with one arm. He called me and Zach B. liars."

"He did?" I start planning my phone call to concerned parent Shirleen Cobb.

Max nods. I look in the rearview mirror and see him squeeze his eyes shut tight. I can tell he's upset.

"Did that make you sad?"

He nods and looks out the window.

"Did you cry, buddy?"

He lets out a long dramatic sigh. "I did for a minute. And then I manned up."

I suppress a smile, knowing that last part is courtesy of his dad.

"So can we ask him, Mom? I want to show Graydon I'm not lying."

This is what I find hard about parenting. The petty, small, vindictive part of me wants to say, "Hell, yes, we'll get him there and teach Graydon Cobb a lesson or two about calling people liars." But the rational adult side of me knows my son needs to learn to rise above this crap. Plus it sounds like he was doing some pretty serious bragging about meeting a man with a handicap. I'm not too happy about that.

✦ ✦ ✦

I tell Garth the whole story over jumping jacks on Thursday morning.

"Honest to God, just when I think I've heard it all from that kid," I puff.

Garth chuckles. "You know, Jack is such a nice guy, I'm sure if I asked him he would stop by. Shut this kid Graydon up."

I stop jumping and try to catch my breath.

"Please don't. But I'd love it if *you* would stop by."

"Really?" He seems surprised.

"Of course. You're practically family now. Plus, I'm dying to see you eat a piece of cake."

Garth laughs.

"I will if it's chocolate. I can't stay away from that."

"I noticed." I smirk. "Come with Nina. It'll be fun."

"Okay, thanks for the invite. I'll talk to her. Now let's work your legs a little more."

We get back to business and soon I'm a sweaty mess. Garth tells me that he's going to move our workouts outside as soon as the snow melts. I'm a little nervous to leave the comforts of Ron's Gym and Tan, but I think it will be nice to change the scenery up a bit.

17

Saturday morning, I jump out of bed like the woman on a mission that I am—for today, anyway. Max's birthday party starts at eleven, and I have a ton to do. I glance at the rumpled sheets on the other side of the bed and see that Ron is already up and at 'em as well. I'm impressed. I grab the To Do list I scribbled in the middle of the night when I couldn't sleep. Most of it is illegible but I can get the gist of it.

—*Remind my parents where the party is, again*
—*Put gift bags in the car*
—*Pick up cake*
—*Pick up balloons*
—*Decorate party room*

Normally I would farm some of this out to Vivs and Laura, but they are barely going to make it to the party. They are driving up from school with Raj and Travis and not leaving until ten this morning, because apparently Travis "needs his sleep." Yes, Travis is still in the picture. I'm thinking this might be love for my little girl. Never mind that the great Steve Perry of Journey says, "Lovin' a music man ain't always what it's supposed to be," Laura is smitten and she's going to roll the dice with Travis. God, I envy her. She has no idea what it's like to get your heart broken.

I quickly shower, don the mom uniform, and trot down to the kitchen for a much-needed cup of joe. No sign of Ron, but I find a note taped to the Keurig telling me he has gone running. I pop a pod into the machine and grab the milk. It's ridiculous how much I need this first cup.

As I'm savoring my maiden sip of the day, Max comes into the kitchen, rubbing his eyes. He walks over for a hug.

"Good morning, sweetie pie." I give him a big squeeze. "Happy birthday-party day."

His eyes spring open so quickly it's comical. "It's my party today?" He starts to jump up and down, doing his happy dance, which looks a little like the way Martin Short dances as Ed Grimley. "Can we go now?"

I can't help but laugh as it is only 8:30 in the morning.

"Well, we've got a few things to do before we go. First, breakfast. You want to have a lot of energy for the gym. How about an egg in the hole?"

"Okay." He sounds a bit disappointed. I know he's dying to get the party started. Just then Ron comes in the back door, looking like the Unabomber with sunglasses and his hood up.

"Man, is it chilly out there!" He stomps around for a bit, then shrugs his running jacket off.

"Dad, are you ready for the party?" Max asks.

"Absolutely, buddy. Just give me ten seconds."

"Coffee?" I hold up my mug.

"Please." He kisses me, then takes a huge chug from his water bottle.

I throw a pod in for him, then start on Max's breakfast.

"I have a few errands to run before the party. Can you get Max ready and bring him to Emerald City around ten forty-five?"

"No problem. Want me to bring anything?"

"I think I've got it all. Just make sure the guest of honor is there."

"Who's the guest of honor?" Max asks. He has an orange juice mustache.

"You, silly." I place the egg in a hole in front of him and he digs in with gusto.

The kitchen-counter office beckons me, so I have a seat and fire up the iMac to check my emails and send one to Asami.

To: JDixon
From: KHoward
Date: 03/10
Subject: Max's party

Hello, darling,

Can you remind me where Max's party is again? I keep forgetting the name of it. Also send me the address so I can put it in the Garmin.

Love,
Your Mother

To: JDixon
From: SCobb
Date 3/10
Subject: Today

Jennifer,

I'm just writing to make sure this party will be a safe environment for Graydon. Have they done a sweep for nuts and dust? Or should I send him with his mask?

Shirleen

I roll my eyes. I'd feel sorrier for that child if he wasn't so much like his mother. I send my mom the address, tell Shirleen that a mask is always a good idea (that'll teach Graydon to call my son a liar), and then send Asami the news she has been waiting for.

To: AChang
From: JDixon
Date: 3/10
Subject: Operation Who Is She?

Hi, Asami,

I think I've figured out a way to smoke out Sasha. Let's meet at Starbucks before pickup on Monday.

Jen

I close the laptop and look at my watch. Yeesh! Nine fifteen already. I'd better get my ass in gear. I run up the stairs two at a time ('cause that's how I roll these days) and holler to Ron, who's in the shower.

"I'm heading out. Remember, get Max dressed and over to Emerald City by ten forty-five."

"You got it!" he yells back. I can smell his musky shampoo from the hallway.

I charge back down the stairs and grab my keys from the hook by the kitchen door.

"I'm on my way, buddy. Dad's going to bring you to the party."

"Where are you going?" Max looks up from Ron's iPad.

"I'm going to set up for the most awesome ninja party ever." I give him a kiss on the head. "See you in a while."

"Ninja!"

✦ ✦ ✦

I have to give myself snaps. Max's party is a bona fide hit. Seven boys from his class and three from his Cub Scout Troop all arrive in various forms of ninja dress and start running around Emerald City like it's on fire. I told everyone it's a drop-off party, but there are always mothers who want to stay. Today it seems everyone wants to hang out, so I'm treated to time with Peetsa, Ravi, Hunter's two moms, Shirleen, Trudy Elder, Jackie Westman, and, to my delight, Jean-Luc Baton, whom I have not seen since curriculum night. Still gorgeous, I'm happy to report. I have to say that as much as I love my husband and happen to think he's the bee's knees, nothing can put a spring in your step quite like a good-looking man in your midst. Jean-Luc is the only dad here besides Ron, so they're huddled in a corner, talking about work no doubt. The moms are sitting sipping coffee and looking happy to be doing nothing for a minute.

The party room looks great, thanks to my decorations and the ministrations of Brandon and Kayla, my Emerald City ambassadors. They were able to make magic with my Party City purchases and the black, green, and gold balloons I picked up this morning.

A flurry at the door catches my eye: my girls have arrived with their beaux. Does anyone say "beau" anymore? I picked it up when I was ten and reading *Anne of Green Gables* and it stuck with me.

"Mom, sorry we're late. Seventy was a parking lot getting into the city." Laura gives me a quick hug.

"That's okay, baby. You haven't missed much." I look past her and wave to Vivs and Raj. "Where's Travis?"

"Parking the car. Where should I put these?" She holds up a couple of presents wrapped in ninja paper.

"Over in the corner. Do me a favor and circulate with your sister—introduce yourselves to people. I have to go talk to my guy about the food."

As if on cue, Brandon walks in.

"I think the boys are getting hungry. Should I bring the food out in about ten minutes?"

"Perfect. Thanks."

"Would you like something besides pizza for them?" He nods toward the mothers.

Since I hadn't been expecting eight moms, I hadn't made any arrangements for them.

"Um . . . how about a couple of large Caesar salads with chicken?"

Brandon nods and heads off to the kitchen.

I walk toward Vivs and Raj and give them both a welcome hug.

"Thanks for driving in for this, you guys."

"Like I'd miss Maxi's birthday party!" Vivs snorts.

"Are grown-ups allowed to play out there, too?" Raj wonders.

"Why? You want to go play, little boy?" Vivs teases him.

He blushes. "Well, it looks like fun."

"I think you can, Raj, just take your shoes off and watch out for rug rats." I smile.

"Oh, rats don't bother me. When I was a kid, I spent every summer in India." He heads off, yelling for Travis to join him.

Vivs and I look at each other and burst out laughing. The moment is cut short when Max comes running into the party room. I see Ron has convinced him to wear plain old jeans and a T-shirt to his party. I'm thinking that might be why he storms over to me crying angry tears.

"I hate this party!" he yells. "Why did we have to have it here?"

"What on earth are you talking about?" I get down on one knee and hold his arms.

"I want another party somewhere else." He's sobbing now, and has a bubble of snot coming out of his nose. I look up and notice the whole room has gone quiet. I so love an audience when I'm having a bad moment with my kid. I give Peetsa a pleading look, and she nods.

"Does anyone need to use the bathroom?" She sounds like she's asking a group of preschoolers. Most of the moms get up with her, but Trudy and Shirleen stay put. I turn back to Max.

"Max, calm down and tell me what happened," I say in the nicest voice I can, considering I'm dying inside. Vivs and Laura have moved to stand behind Max in an attempt to make this moment more private. Ron has joined me on the floor.

"We . . . we . . . were at the mini r-r-ropes course." He's having trouble getting his words out. "And G-g-graydon wanted to do the grown-up r-r-ropes course . . ." He takes a deep breath as I rub his arms. "And they said no and Graydon said this is the worst party he has ever been to." Max starts up a fresh round of sobs.

"He *what*?" I can see Shirleen charging over to where I'm kneeling with my son. Max moves into the safety of my arms.

"Shirleen, it's okay. I'm handling it." I'm hoping my look conveys how much I don't want her to interfere. Apparently it doesn't.

"Where is Graydon now, Max?" He shrugs. She stomps out of the party room.

"Is Graydon going to get in trouble?" Max asks, wiping his nose on his sleeve.

"I think he might, buddy," Ron says.

"Good," Max says firmly. "He says mean things."

"Why don't you hang in here, sweetie? The pizza is coming out soon."

I hug him and get up off my knees to see that Nina and Garth have arrived, gifts for Max in hand.

"Hey, you guys! I'm so glad you could come. Max, look, Aunt Nina and Garth are here." I send him over to give them a hug, which gives me the opportunity to take a huge "serenity now" breath. Ron puts his arm around my shoulder and gives me a squeeze.

"Best mom ever," he whispers in my ear.

Hardly, I think, but I take the compliment with a smile.

Brandon and Kayla arrive with the pizza just as the boys are coming back from the play area and the mothers return from their fake visit to the bathroom. Last to arrive is Shirleen, followed by Graydon.

"Jennifer, there has been a misunderstanding. Graydon didn't say it was the worst party he's ever been to."

"Yes, he did." Max comes running back to me.

"He's lying," says Graydon. "He lies a lot."

Whoa. Hold on there, bubble boy. You are in dangerous territory. I'm about to say something, but Max decides to come to his own defense.

"I don't lie," he says. "Almost never," he adds with conviction.

"You lied about the one-armed man," Graydon counters.

At this point, the entire room's focus is on these two little boys. Even Shirleen is hanging back.

"I didn't lie about him! He's real. Zach B. saw him, too."

Zach B. looks up and nods. He seems pleased to have been brought into the drama.

"Well, I don't believe you." Graydon folds his arms in front of his chest in an exact imitation of his mother. I almost burst out laughing.

"Wait a minute." Garth steps in. I want to wave him off, but stop myself.

"Do you mean *this* one-armed guy?" He reaches into the gift bag he's holding, pulls out a picture frame, and turns to the picture toward Graydon. From where I'm standing, I can see it's a photo of Jack, from the day of the indoor mudder. He has his one arm around both boys, and they are all smiling.

"Yes!" Max yells as if he has won the lottery . . . or a good game of Lego Indiana Jones. He runs to hug Garth and takes the picture. "See, Graydon? I told you I wasn't lying." He is beaming.

"*We* told you." Zach B. puts his arm around Max.

Graydon walks closer to the boys for a better look at the picture. After studying it for about ten seconds, he hands it back to Max.

"Cool. Mom, what can I eat here?"

If I was hoping for an apology, I was going to be disappointed. That "cool" was all the ground Graydon was ever going to give. I look at Garth.

"You are my hero," I mouth to him. He nods and winks. Nina blows me a kiss.

The kids have already moved on and are scarfing down pizza like it's the first and last time they will ever have it. I'm sitting with the moms, enjoying chicken Caesar salad and a delicious cup of smugness. Shirleen sits down beside me.

"Well, I'm sure glad the boys hashed that out. It's good to get to the truth, I always say."

Clearly, she doesn't notice the slice of humble pie in front of her. There are many ways I could respond, but I go with a nod and a smile.

18

As the famous anorexic Karen Carpenter once said, "Rainy days and Mondays always get me down." Man alive, we have had a lot of precipitation these past few weeks. It's either rain or sleet or snow or hail that has me scraping off or digging out the minivan every day. Oh, well. At least the mail is getting delivered . . . or so they say.

On this particular freezing rainy Monday I'm meeting Asami (*please, not the duck hat; please, not the duck hat*) to unveil my master plan to get to the bottom of the Sasha and Nadine Lewicki mystery/ Asami obsession. As I'm driving to Starbucks, my cell phone rings. I hit the Answer button on the steering wheel.

"Jen's Nail Salon; how can I help you?"

"On a scale of one to ten, what is your mood right now?" It's Ron.

"Is ten the best or the worst?" I ask.

"Whatever makes you happier."

"Well, then, I guess I'd say I'm about a five, and you can do the math."

"I just got offered tickets to watch the Roller Warriors play tonight."

"Okay . . . the roller whats?" I can hear Ron's eyes rolling on the other end of the line.

"Kansas City's roller derby team."

"You like roller derby?" I'm wondering how he got through the vetting process without this little nugget of information coming out.

"I'm trying to make a deal to supply all their skates for the next five seasons. The manager offered me tickets, so I think it would be good for me to go."

"Why are you even asking me? Of course it would be good for you to go."

"I kind of want to bring Max."

"In God's name, why?"

"I think he'll really enjoy it. It's a lot of fun to watch."

I turn into the Starbucks parking lot and find a spot.

"I'll have to take your word for it." I smile to myself, thinking how many questions Max is going to have.

"So, when you pick him up from school, can you drop him at the store? I'll get him dinner and we'll go from here."

"Sure, babe. I'll see you in about an hour."

"Perfect, thanks."

I press the button on the steering wheel again to hang up and have a good laugh. Watch *this* be the sport Max falls in love with.

Starbucks smells like roasted coffee and something else . . . a croissant being baked? Asami and her hat are already on the love seat, patiently waiting for me.

I've had quite enough caffeine already today, so I opt for a calm tea and one of those yummy cake pops. I choose the one with nuts, reasoning that it is healthier.

As I settle in across from Asami, I can tell she's dying to know what I have come up with, so I don't waste time with pleasantries.

"So, remember when the FBI did that huge Mafia sting a bunch of years ago?"

"No."

"Well, a bunch of Mafia guys had gone into hiding and the FBI couldn't find them anywhere. So they sent out letters to the Mafiosos' last known addresses, saying they had won some really big prize but they had to show up at a certain warehouse to claim it." I'm pretty sure I'm fudging some of the facts.

"Did they go?"

"Yes. A lot of them did and were arrested. Maybe if Sasha thinks she has won money or something, she will show up to get it."

Asami's face is pinched in irritation.

"What's wrong?" I tear into my cake pop.

"Well, it's just so . . . simple. It's such an obvious plan. I'm mad I didn't think of it myself."

It isn't that *obvious*, I think but do not say. "So, do you want to try it?"

"Of course! What should we say she has won?"

"How about a car? Or fifty thousand bucks?"

"Perfect. You should send the letter out today."

"Me? No, no. This is all you, partner."

"Don't you want to see who shows up?"

"I look forward to you telling me all about it," I assure Asami.

I sit back and we sip our respective drinks for a minute.

"So is your daughter still dating the boy in Jeen's band?" Asami is trying to make actual conversation with me. I'm touched.

"Travis, yes. They seem very fond of each other. How is Jeen doing?"

"Fine. He really loves school."

"That's great."

Awkward pause while I realize we have both run out of small talk. That's fine. It's time to go, anyway.

"I'm heading out to get Max. Good luck with your Sasha hunt."

Asami turns her determined eyes to me and nods. Whoever Sasha Lewicki is, I can't help but feel sorry for her.

On my way out the door, I bump into Suchafox heading in. I haven't seen him in ages—not even at pickup. He gives me a quick hug and the Polo wafts over me.

"So you really *do* drink coffee, just not with me!" he says light-heartedly.

"Ha, ha. Yes! How are you?"

"Good. Do you have time for a chat?"

I look at my phone. "No, I've got pickup in five minutes; don't you?"

His face falls a bit. "No, Ali does pickup now."

"Oh" is all I can think of to say. I'd love to know more, but I hate not being there when Max comes out. I was five minutes late to Scouts once and he was convinced I was never coming back for him.

"Gotta run. See you soon." I dash out to the minivan and as I'm getting in I turn to see Don still watching me from the door. He looks really sad. I make a mental note to reach out to him later.

✦ ✦ ✦

Don't ever tell Ron this, but I love a night to myself. After dropping a very confused but excited Max off at the store, I stop to pick up some groceries, then drive home. I know exactly how I want to spend my evening. An uninterrupted bath is unspeakable luxury when you are a mom. The knowledge that no one is going to bother me is intoxicating. I fill the deep claw-foot tub in our master bath with the hottest water I can stand and add an entire bag of Dr. Teal's Epsom salts. It's not exactly "Calgon, take me away," but they do have a nice lavender scent. I light a few candles, get myself a generous glass of Oregon pinot noir, and connect my iPhone to the Bluetooth speaker. I put my phone beside the bed and think about texting Don to see if he's okay, but decide to do it later. I don't want anything distracting me from my bliss.

As you know, my heart belongs to rock and roll, but when I'm trying to relax I like to switch it up with a little smooth jazz on Pandora. Anita Baker starts to sing.

So here I sit, and you couldn't find a happier person on the planet at this moment.

When I first hit the water, it feels like a thousand tiny needles piercing my body, but once I submerge, the pain dissolves with the salt.

I close my eyes and start to visualize the mud course. I take myself through each phase—the run, the wall, the pegs, the steep ramp, the freezing water, the ring of fire, and finally the crawl through the mud to the finish line. Two months to go, but I wish it were tomorrow. I'm so ready. I'm so ready. . . .

My eyes snap open. The bath water is cold and I'm shivering.

I must have dozed off. I stand up quickly and throw one leg over the tub while I reach for a towel. I must lean too far because the next thing I know, my foot on the floor is slipping forward and my other leg isn't out of the bath yet. I'm forced into a split that crashes my vagina into the side of the tub. I feel a snap in my groin, followed by eye-watering pain.

"Shit, fuck, ow, crap, goddammit!" I roll onto my side and back and force my other leg out of the tub.

"Son of a bitch, mother fuck." I start to cry. I can't believe how much my groin hurts. I have no idea how I'm going to get up. I'm shivering, so I pull the towel over me for warmth and put my head down on the fluffy white bath mat. When I've calmed down I start crawling to the bathroom door. I need to get to a phone and call someone. The bottom half of my body is useless, so I rely on my arms and pull myself along the floor.

Is it shallow that even in my excruciating pain, I can't help but notice how strong my upper body is? Go me! Argghhhh! My groin is throbbing.

I slither to the door of the bathroom, grab the knob, and yank it open enough to crawl through. God, I'm cold! Bone cold, as my mom would say. I've never fallen asleep in the bathtub, and now I know why it's not recommended.

I can only imagine the spectacle that Ron is treated to when he walks in a minute later as I'm making my way to my cell phone by the bed, naked, towel barely around me, crying and swearing at the same time.

"Jesus, Jen!" He runs to my side and is down on the carpet with me in a nanosecond.

"I f-f-fell in the t-t-tub," I manage to sob out before I collapse into his body.

"Where's Mommy?" I hear Max yelling from downstairs.

"Oh, my God. He can't see this. He'll have nightmares for years."

"Hang on, buddy. She's in the bathroom," Ron calls to him. "Get your PJs on and brush your teeth." He looks at me. "What hurts? Did you break anything? Do you need an ambulance?"

"I don't think so. It's just my groin." I'm shivering uncontrollably.

Ron appraises the situation and decides to scoop me up and onto the bed. He grabs a sweatshirt out of my drawers and helps me put it on. I welcome the feel of my pillows as I lean back and Ron pulls the duvet over me. My vagina is still throbbing, but my shivers are starting to die down.

"I'll be right back." He kisses my head and runs out of the room. I can hear him talking to Max in a low voice and then going down-stairs. When he returns, he has one of the ice packs I keep at the ready in the freezer, a glass of water, and two ibuprofen.

"Can I take a look?"

I nod and help him pull the duvet aside. He hisses when he sees my upper legs. I look down: there is already the beginning of a bruise right where my leg meets my hip. It's hard to tell if my vulva is also bruised, because I've gone native down there, but it feels like it is.

"Shit," I say, and my eyes fill with tears again. I shove the pills in my mouth and take a gulp of water. After I swallow, a sob escapes my throat.

"Shhh. It's okay. Let's get the ice on it." Ron places the pack gently at the top of my leg. I wince at first, but soon the cold pack brings relief to the ache.

"Is Max okay?" I sniffle. "How was roller derby?"

"Max is watching TV and roller derby was fine. Tell me what hap-pened here." Ron's velvet voice is rich with concern.

"I was taking a bath and I fell asleep. When I woke up, I was cold, so I got out too fast and I slipped with one leg out and landed on my bun," I say, using the word for vagina that came into our house via the wisdom of Graydon Cobb. (Max was thrilled to come home one day and tell me that Graydon says boys have hot dogs and girls have buns.) "I felt my groin snap and the pain was mind-blowing."

"Oh, babe, I'm so sorry. I think you should go for an X-ray tomorrow."

I nod, but suddenly realize I'm too tired to talk anymore. My eyes close without any effort on my part.

"Do you have Garth tomorrow? I should call and cancel."

I hear Ron's words, but they take a few seconds to sink in. Garth, training, mudder. Mudder!

"Oh my God," I groan.

"What?"

"All my training." I take a deep breath and start crying yet again.

"Hey, hey, hey." Ron rubs my head. "It's okay."

"Why are you crying?" says a little voice from the door.

I quickly cover up the ice pack and look around Ron at Max. He's wearing his "Where's Waldo?" PJs, hat, and glasses.

"Come here, sweetie." I hold out my arms and he walks into them while still standing beside the bed.

"Why are you crying? Did you miss us?"

Only a child would see it like that.

"I did miss you, but I also got a little boo-boo on my thigh and it hurts a bit."

"Do you want me to kiss it and make it better?"

"That's okay, Daddy already did. How was roller derby?"

Max stands up, eyes shining.

"It was so funny! These ladies roller-skate around in a circle and try to knock each other over. I didn't like it at first, but Daddy says it's all pretend and they don't really get hurt when they fall."

I raise my eyebrow at Ron. He shrugs.

"The other team was called the Roller City Rats."

"Yeah, Max loves that name." Ron smirks.

"Well, I'm glad you had fun, but it's way past your bedtime. Give me a hug and let Daddy put you to bed so I can rest my boo-boo." I hold out my arms again.

Max snuggles into me. "But I hate when Daddy puts me to bed," he whines. "He always falls asleep before I do."

"Not tonight, buddy!" Ron assures him as he swings Max over his shoulder.

"Good night, baby." I sigh and lie back down on my pillow. I'm asleep before Ron comes back to bed.

19

Four hours at Overland Park Regional Medical Center later, I learn I haven't cracked or broken anything. I have a badly pulled groin muscle and a beauty of a bruise. As stupid as this sounds, I'm a bit disappointed. I mean, if I'm going to go through something *this* painful, I'd like to have bragging rights to a cracked pelvis, not a bruised front bum. Dr. Sintay, the man on duty this morning, tells me I'm lucky I didn't have a more serious injury. "The bathroom is a very dangerous place, Mrs. Dixon."

Especially after my husband has been in there, I think but do not say.

Ron brings me home with my filled prescription of painkillers; after I assure him I'll be fine, he heads off to the store. He has left me propped up on the comfy couch with ice on my crotch and the remote in my hand. Who could ask for more? Peetsa is taking Max to her place after school, so I am a lady of leisure for a few hours. I pick up the phone and call Garth.

"What did the doctor say?" is how he greets me.

"No breaks or cracks, just a pulled ligament and a really bad bruise."

"Oh, Lordy, thank goodness. Did he say when you could start training again?"

"Nothing for three weeks; then we'll see. That will give us three until the race."

Silence.

"What is it?"

"Jen, we may want to rethink the mud run for April."

"Are you crazy? It's just a bruise. I'm fine!" I'm practically yelling.

"Take it easy." Garth's voice is annoyingly calm. "Hear me out."

I let out an audible sigh and give the phone the finger. "Okay, what?"

"You have done great work. I can't believe how far we've come over the past six months."

"Garth, don't handle me, please. Just spit it out." I'm speaking more harshly than I mean to, but my patience has already been taxed by twenty minutes of medical attention spread out over four hours at the hospital.

"Okay, here it is. If you're benched for the next three weeks, you will not be ready for the mud run. You think you'll be back where you left off, but you won't—you'll be out of shape. It won't take you long to get back to peak performance, but I'd rather you not risk another injury. There is another run in Springfield in August. We can aim for that."

He's right. I know he's right.

"But I feel so ready. That's exactly what I was thinking in the bath last night. I was wishing the race was today."

"Well, be thankful that it isn't. We can reevaluate in a month, but right now I say we take it off the table."

"I'll agree to reevaluate in a month," I concede, stubborn to the end. "What can I do right now, while I'm recovering?"

"Rest, Jen. That's the best medicine. Don't jump the gun, or you'll be on your butt for another month. I'll come and see you tomorrow." I hear a voice screaming in the background. "And Nina says you're a spaz."

"Ha! Tell her to call me later. I'm going to take a nap." I stifle a yawn.

"Good girl. See you tomorrow."

I hang up with Garth and snuggle down into the comfy couch. Just as I'm nodding off, my cell phone buzzes. It's a text from Asami.

Can you meet?

Oh, God, I'm so not in the mood for her brand of crazy right now. I decide to ignore it.

The phone buzzes twice more in quick succession.

Hello?

Can you meet?

I growl and type a quick reply.

Not feeling well. Let's try next week.

Of course, Asami is back at me in seconds. She must have twenty fingers.

It's important.

I know I can't do anything today, but I might be able to see her tomorrow, so I text her as much.

Where?

My house at 1.

I don't get another text, but I can imagine Asami firmly nodding to herself.

✦ ✦ ✦

The next day at one sharp, Asami rings my doorbell. Nina and Garth had come earlier to bring me lunch (Taco Bell, my favorite binge) so I asked them to let her in on their way out. I hear an exchange of greetings and a little mumbling; then Asami joins me in the living room.

"I had no idea you had an accident." I think I hear genuine concern in her voice, and I'm touched.

"Yup. I slipped getting out of the bathtub." The more I say it, the more of an idiot I feel like.

"Did you yell, 'I've fallen and I can't get up'?" Asami asks. It takes me a moment to realize this is her idea of a joke. I smile.

"Good one. So what's up?"

"Well . . ." She sits in the chair across from me and undoes her coat. No duck hat today, sadly. I would have loved for Nina to see it. "I hate to kick you when you're down, so to speak, but your idea didn't work."

"My idea about . . ." I leave the question hanging. I know what she's talking about, but I need to make her pay for her joke.

She frowns at me.

"Your idea of telling Sasha Lewicki that she had won something, so she would show up and claim it. It didn't work. No one showed up."

"You sent her an email?"

Asami nods.

"Using a fake address?"

She nods again.

"And told her she won . . ."

"Ten thousand dollars."

"Really? Where did you tell her she could collect it?"

"The food court at the mall. In front of the Wok and Roll."

No wonder it didn't work.

"Why there?"

"I wanted a crowd around in case something unexpected happened."

"Like what?"

Asami shrugs.

"I don't know. I just wanted witnesses."

I shift on the couch and wince in pain. I should really take another painkiller but I'll hold off until Asami leaves, although this conversation might be more enjoyable if I were a bit high.

"How long did you wait?"

"Five hours."

"And no one showed. Did you see anyone you know?"

"I saw a lot of people from school."

"Did you talk to anyone?"

"Not really." Asami looks a little embarrassed. "Some people waved, though."

"Well, it's very possible that she did show up and saw you and maybe some other people from the class, and she got spooked. Or she did show up, but you know her by another name. Who did you see?"

Asami closes her eyes and thinks for a moment.

"I saw Principal Jakowski, Peetsa, Kim Fancy and her daughter, um . . . and Zach Elder's mother."

"Trudy."

"Right, yes. Trudy. That was pretty much it."

"Huh. Well, I don't know what to say. I'm sure she'll show herself at some point." I stifle a yawn. "Sorry. I'm still a little dopey."

Asami jumps up the way Max does when I tell him dinner's ready.

"Oh, I'm sorry. I should go. Thanks for hearing me out." I can tell she's a bit bummed by this setback in her investigation.

She pulls on her coat and starts toward the door.

"Can I get you anything before I go?"

"No, I'm fine, but thank you. And don't worry, Asami. There's probably a really simple explanation for this whole thing."

Asami gives me the firm nod that I now associate only with her and leaves me to my painkillers.

✦ ✦ ✦

The aftermath of my bathroom hijinks brings forth some good news and some bad news. The bad news was that Dr. Sintay says I definitely should not go on our spring break family ski trip out west. The good news? I'm staying home alone for a week. Well, not completely alone. Nina will move in with me, and Chyna will take my place on the slopes.

I know I should be more upset about this, but I can't seem to muster the sadness. I love the place we always go—a little hidden gem in Utah called Solitude that totally lives up to its name. I swear there has never been a lift line even if we are skiing the busiest week of the year. It's populated mostly by locals who want to avoid the craziness of Park City, and I absolutely love going there . . . usually.

But since the accident, all I can think of is the sheer felicity of time to myself. What, oh what, will I do to fill the days that are usually taken up with errands and housecleaning and laundry and Max and Ron and their various time-sucking wants and needs? Don't for one minute think I don't absolutely adore my life as a wife and mom. But even the best lives need a vacation and, let's face it, renting a house with your family at a ski resort is *not* a vacation. It's basically moving your life from one location to another. Unless someone else is making the beds, doing the laundry, and cooking, it's just the same old life with the added inconvenience of not knowing where anything is in the kitchen.

My convalescence is going more slowly than I thought it would, so I am completely useless when it comes to packing Ron and Max for the trip. Max is only capable of loading up the toys he wants, and Ron hasn't packed a bag since the day he said "I do." It's nothing short of torture for me to sit in bed while he ransacks the storage bins and throws things willy-nilly into suitcases.

"Sweetie, you may want to have Max try on some of his ski clothes before you pack them."

Since this is about the thirtieth time I have butted into his business, Ron is done with me. He pauses on his way out the door.

"I love you, but if you say one more thing to me about packing, I'm going to hide your pain meds."

I don't tell him I switched to Aleve two days ago because the painkillers were interfering with my wine drinking. I stay mute for the rest of the morning, knowing full well that Max's toothbrush and toothpaste will never make it into the suitcase.

And now I sit on my super-comfy couch with six days stretching out in front of me like a red carpet of possibilities. Scrumptious smells are coming from my kitchen, where Nina is cooking dinner, and a fine glass of wine is within reach. If it weren't for the constant ache *down there*, life would be pretty perfect.

I grab my laptop from the side table and open it up. There is a joke email from Peetsa with the subject line "15 Ways to Make Everything Awkward," the usual spate of crap from the Gap, Zappos, Pottery Barn, and Weight Watchers, and a note from my mother.

> *To: JDixon*
> *From: KHoward*
> *Date: 3/26*
> *Subject: How are you feeling?*
>
> *Honey,*
>
> *How are you feeling? Better, I hope. I would call, but ever since I woke you up in the middle of the day I'm worried I'll do it again and I know how you need your sleep. But please call me whenever you want, oh but not for the next few days. Dad and I are heading out of town to our post–St. Patrick's Day drying-out retreat. Half of our congregation is still loaded.*
> > *Feel better, sweetheart.*
>
> > > > > *Love,*
> > > > > *Your Mother*

I'm just about to close my computer when an email pops up from Miss Ward.

> *To: JDixon*
> *From: PWard*
> *Date: 3/26*
> *Subject: Spring break*
>
> *Hello, Jenny,*
>
> *Haven't seen you in a while and then someone told me about your accident. Hope you are feeling better.*
> > *On April 12, we will be taking a class trip to the Elbow Chocolate factory. I think the children will enjoy seeing how chocolate bunnies are made.*

> *I will need 3 mothers to go with us. Can you and Asami send out a note?*
>
> *Thanks,*
> *Peggy*

Well, this is pretty odd, considering we had our Easter celebration just before the break. But mine is not to reason why. The clown car that is the inner workings of Miss Ward's mind will remain an enigma to me. Oh, and by the way, I'll be skipping that field trip, thank you very much. Putting me in a chocolate factory is like putting an alcoholic in a whiskey distillery. I have a serious addiction and the only way I can keep it in check is complete abstinence. There were some dark (chocolate) days when I first returned from Europe and realized full-on what my life was going to be like (a) living with my parents and two small daughters and (b) working at a crappy job. Things looked pretty bleak, so I turned to my one constant source of sunshine . . . chocolate. I got quite a taste for the good stuff while I was chasing bands overseas. Ever have a Milka Bar? INXS used to insist on having them in the green room at their concerts. My mouth waters just thinking about it. I am not exaggerating when I say I ate that sweet devil for breakfast, lunch, and dinner every day for about six months. I couldn't stop, nor did I want to. Chocolate made me happy—fat and happy, and then just fat. I remember vividly the day I took Vivs and Laura for their flu shots. I asked the nurse to give me one, too. She looked me up and down and said, "Let me ask the doctor. I'm not sure it's okay in your condition. How far along are you?"

That was it. I went home, threw out a good ten pounds of Milka Bars a friend and fellow band stalker had sent me, and have almost never touched chocolate again. I think that's one of the reasons I hate Halloween—all that chocolate coming into my house unprotected and available.

I need to email the class immediately to start trolling for volunteers.

To: Miss Ward's Class
From: JDixon
Date: 3/26
Subject: Chocolate, anyone?

Hello, classmates!

Happy spring break! Hope you are all having a nice week off. Obviously, I'm still on duty as your trusty class mom. It's a 24/7 job that knows no rest. You're welcome.

Miss Ward wanted Asami and me to let you know our kids will be going on a field trip to the Elbow Chocolate factory on April 12. Yes, I realize we have already had our class Easter party, but Miss Ward has arranged for them to learn how to make chocolate bunnies so that next year they will be ready! Anyhoo, I need 3 parent volunteers to help chaperone the trip.

I know many of you have yet to volunteer for a field trip and I have no problem calling you out in the parking lot at pickup if I have to. My advice is to jump on this bandwagon. It's chocolate, for God's sake. It doesn't get much better than that.

Response times will be noted.

I remain forever your girl,
Jen (and Asami in spirit)

I close my laptop and sigh. I wonder how the ski trip is going. It's only been a couple of days, but I miss my crew and wonder how they're getting on without the shoemaker's elf (that's me). I'm fairly certain Vivs and Laura are helping Ron with everything and not just playing house with their boyfriends. They had the fear of God put in them at a very early age. I worry most about Max, because I know he's going to miss me. I tucked a few love notes into his suitcase for him to find randomly, just to let him know I'm thinking of him. I would have done the same for Ron but my poor baby has hidden-note PTSD from his crazy ex-wife. Cindy used to put a couple of dozen notes into his bag whenever he went away for a boys' weekend or a sporting-goods expo. He had to open each note at a certain time on a certain day, and she would call to make sure he was doing it. Every note ended the same way: "Don't you dare cheat on me. I will know if you do. All my love, Cindy."

"Dinner's ready." Nina sashays over to the comfy couch to help me get up. I can walk, but getting up and down is still painful.

"Sure you don't want to eat in the living room?" she asks.

"Nah." I grab her arm, and together we hoist me up. "I need a change of scenery." As I stand, my 'gines starts to throb and my eyes water from the pain. But I suck it up, make my way to the table, and ease onto one of the padded dining room chairs. Dinner looks great.

"What is this? It smells delicious."

"Curried chicken, mango chutney, green beans with pesto and parmesan, and basmati rice." Nina sits at the head of the table and raises her wineglass to me.

"You found all that in *my* kitchen?"

"You have a lot of great stuff in your cupboards. You guys must get a lot of gift baskets, because you have all these little jars of gourmet ingredients that I know damn well you didn't buy yourself."

"Like what?" I'm trying not to be insulted.

"Uh, caviar, pralines, chili pepper jam, vacuum-packed Israeli dates, cornichons." Nina counts them off on her fingers.

"Okay, okay." I take a bite of the chicken and savor it. "Oh, my God. This is so good." I raise my wineglass. "Here's to the chef."

Nina clinks my glass.

"And thank you for staying with me. I really owe you."

Nina waves my gratitude aside. "Are you kidding? I'm loving this. I hope you don't mind if Garth comes over sometimes."

"Not at all. I'm hoping he'll start me on some stretches or something. I have quite a little food baby, thanks to not working out for two weeks." I pat my stomach for effect.

Nina gives me the "You're nuts" look and continues eating. I decide now is a good time to spring an idea on her that I have had brewing for a couple of weeks.

"So, what's the word on Sid?"

She raises her eyebrows.

"Um . . . not much. I finally blocked him on Facebook. I'm guessing he got the message. Why?"

"Well, I've been thinking that he hasn't suffered nearly enough for being such a world-class douchebag to you."

Nina shrugs. "I'm over it." Jeez, doesn't anyone hold a grudge anymore? She is living proof that nothing makes you forget an old love faster than a new love.

"Well, I care. That guy needs to suffer for his sins."

Nina sits back with her wine and a curious look on her face.

"And how do you propose he suffer?" She picks a piece of rice out of her teeth.

"We spam him." I grab my wine and take a sip.

"We what?"

"Spam him. Sign him up for every stupid spam email possible."

"Seriously?"

I can tell by Nina's face she doesn't think much of my idea.

"Think about it. There is nothing more annoying than having your In box jammed with hundreds of messages from every website in the world. I propose we sign him up for everything from Jehovah's Witnesses to the Kardashian fan page."

Nina starts to giggle. "Or a Green Bay Packers fan site. He hates that team so much."

"Okay, good. Now you're talking. What else does he hate?"

"He hates ABBA."

"The band?"

"Yup."

"Who the hell hates ABBA? Okay, what else?"

"Um . . . Oh, God, I haven't really thought about this."

"Take your time—"

"Richard Simmons! He hates Richard Simmons—the workout guy. And scary movies—he was always such a wimp. Do they have a website for that?"

"Darling, they have a website for everything."

Nina grabs my computer from the comfy couch and we pass the next hour listing everything Sid doesn't like and finding websites we can sign him up for. When Nina runs out of memories, I just start signing him up to get emails from local politicians and the NRA. He's not going to know what hit him. Is what we are doing small and petty? Yes. Is it an abuse of the Internet? Absolutely. Do I feel bad about it? Not one bit. I hope Sid chokes on his In box.

While we are executing our attack, FaceTime rings, and my two favorite men pop up on my screen. They both have red faces and look exhausted.

"Hey there!"

"Hi, Mommy! How are you feeling?"

"I'm better. How was skiing today?"

"It was cold. Are you feeling better enough to come skiing?"

"Not quite, sweetie, sorry. How long did you ski? Did you go on any blue runs?"

"Nope. Dad says that's tomorrow. But I don't want to ski tomorrow. I was so cold," he starts to whine.

"How cold is it up there?" I direct my question to Ron.

"Today is supposed to be the worst day. It will be high twenties tomorrow. Thirties at the bottom of the mountain," he assures me, but I'm skeptical. Ron always has a tough-it-out mentality when it comes to Max. I personally hate skiing when it's really cold, and if I were there I wouldn't have made Max go out. It's one of the fundamental differences between Ron's parenting style and mine. I am much more prone to baby my baby.

"Where are the kids?" I ask, to keep the conversation on a positive note.

"They're all out for dinner, except Chyna. She's running Max's bath."

Just then a disembodied voice yells out, "Max, have we found your toothbrush yet?" I debate telling them that I know exactly where it is, but decide against saying anything. According to my mother, it's not nice to gloat.

"Go get in your bath, Maxi. That will warm you up for tomorrow."

"Okay. Bye!" He jumps off Ron's lap and away from my screen.

Ron looks surprised. "That was easy."

"Only till he gets out of the bath and realizes I'm not on the computer anymore."

He lets out a big sigh. "He really misses you. We all do."

I'd be flattered, but I know that most of what they miss is everything I do for them. I'm not being cynical. I just know my customers.

"I miss you guys, too. It's so damn quiet here. How did everyone ski today?"

"Great! Well, except for Travis. I don't think he's ever skied before."

"Oh, no! Did he take a lesson?"

"Actually, Vivs is a pretty good teacher. She got him up and going, and then we each took an hour with him on the bunny hill. Max loved that he wasn't the slowest one on the hill. He insisted on teaching Travis pizza and french fries."

He's referring to the way instructors teach little kids how to snowplow and slalom. I can just picture him.

"Please make sure he's bundled up tomorrow. You'll never keep him out there if he's cold."

"I will. I promise. How's your 'gines?"

"Getting there. I'm walking pretty well, but getting up and down is still a bitch. I think Garth is going to give me some light stretches to do later this week."

"Just take it easy, please."

"I will. Give the girls my love." I blow a kiss to the screen. "Love you."

"Love you, too," Ron answers, and then the screen goes black.

✦ ✦ ✦

"Just a little more, Jen. Take a deep breath. You're doing great."

Garth and I have reached a new level of intimacy. He is doing something called Thai massage on me. We are currently on the rug in my living room; Garth is sitting snugly behind me with his arms wrapped around my arms, which are wrapped around my torso. Allegedly, he is stretching me using his own body to enhance the stretch, but I can't help feeling like this is a joke he and Nina cooked up.

I take yet another deep breath as Garth gently releases me from the "stretch." I actually feel really good, so I try to override the feelings of weirdness that keep popping up. It doesn't help that Nina is sitting right in front of us, watching and no doubt having threesome fantasies.

"Wow. That felt great. Thank you." I look at Nina. "Has he done this to you?"

She smirks. "He does me a little differently."

Garth blushes and stands up. "Okey-dokey. That should really help with your stiffness, Jen."

"Does it help with your stiffness, Garth?" I ask with as straight a face as I can muster. Nina bursts out laughing.

"You two are lethal. My gosh, five days together and you have your pay-per-view special all scripted."

"You should hear what we say when you're not here," I kid.

"No, thanks. I don't think I could take it and I was in the military."

Nina stands, too. "What time do you think they're going to get here?" She's asking about our intrepid skiers, who are due back this afternoon.

"Ron says . . ." I grab for my phone and check my texts. "ETA is around six, assuming they land on time. Do you guys want to stay for dinner? We can order in."

"No, thanks," they say in unison. Nina continues: "I want to get

Chyna home and unpacked. But you guys should be able to have a major leftover binge with all the stuff I've cooked this week."

"You are a rock star. I can't thank you enough." I really mean it. Nina and I had so much fun—actually, just the right amount of fun. I needed this week of convalescence, but now I'm totally ready to have my Dixon men back.

You can imagine how thrilled I am to be touring the Elbow Chocolate factory on this fine April morning. Oh, I got my three volunteers from the email I sent out, so I figured I was home free. That is, until Trudy Elder called me *this morning* to back out . . . something about Zach having Coxsackie. Oh, isn't *that* convenient. Hey, lady, some of us just suck it up and honor our commitments.

So here I stand in a hell that involves a still-sore groin, the futility of making chocolate bunnies, and the torture of those sweet sirens (milk and dark) being created right in front of my face. I have said, "No, thank you," at least ten times to samples passed my way. I wish there was a Nobel Prize for self-denial.

The kids are having a ball watching chocolate turn into bunnies. I guess I suffer from a tragic lack of curiosity, because I have never wondered how they make the hollow ones, but it's actually knowledge I am now happy to have.

Our guide this morning is Jacques (effectively morphed from his real name, Jack, to make our chocolatier experience that much more exotic) and he has already showed us how to pour just the right amount of chocolate into the bunny mold and then twist it around until all the sides are evenly covered and there is no excess chocolate, all while flirting with Miss Ward in a disturbingly obvious way.

I mean, jeez, there are kids watching! Enough with the double entendres, Jacques.

Joining me on my chocolate journey this morning are Jill Kaplan and JJ Aikens, who was much friendlier than I expected when I showed up instead of Trudy.

She and I are standing on the periphery of the chocolate inner circle and have a distant but effective view of the Jacques show.

"Now, who wants a solid bunny tail to bite into?" he asks the children in an accent that can only have been acquired by watching Maurice Chevalier movies and spending time in North Dakota. We see him wink at Miss Ward, and she giggles.

"Can you believe her?" JJ says out of the side of her mouth, in case there are any lip-readers in the vicinity.

"Well, they've definitely got a little something going on," I counter in a low voice.

"Uh, yeah, they do. How do you think we got this private tour?"

"I'm sorry, what?"

"I hear she's sleeping with him!" JJ side-talks to me again.

"Are you sure?" I turn to see if she is kidding.

"Well, I wasn't *there*, but Kim told me."

"Was *she* there?"

I'm rewarded with a barking laugh from JJ. That's a first.

"You never know." JJ sounds a little bitter.

I'm trying to play catch-up with all this new info being launched my way. Jacques and Miss Ward are having a fling, and Kim Fancy knows all about it. Kim Fancy who (and I wouldn't believe it if I hadn't seen it) slapped Miss Ward across the face two months ago. I need to know more. I regard JJ and wonder just how much truth serum she has taken today.

"I haven't seen you and Kim together much lately," I fish with small bait.

JJ looks at me like I'm a drink of water in the desert. "Thank you! I know. I feel very pushed aside."

"Pushed aside by who?" I fake genuine concern. "Miss Ward?"

"What? No," she scoffs. "By her training."

"Her training?"

"Yeah. She's spent the last few months training to do a mud run this month."

Mud run? I get a little sick to my stomach.

"She's obsessed with it. She's working with a trainer and everything."

This news hits me like a punch in the gut. Why, I do not know. I mean, who cares if Kim Fancy is doing the same mud run that I am? It doesn't make me any less special.

Yes it does! screams the cocktail party in my head.

I see Jill Kaplan waving frantically at me from the other side of the chocolate river.

"We better join them," I say to JJ.

As we walk toward where the kids are going to decorate their bunnies, I pull myself together. Jacques has lined up fifteen small bunnies, one for each of the kids to personalize and take home. There are candy eyes, candy bows, candy hats, and even candy carrots for them to have fun with. I notice Max trying to put the candy carrot on the bunny's nose like he would make a snowman nose, but he can't get it to stick, so he eats it.

"Hey, no eating the accessories, buddy," I admonish him.

"What's the assesories?"

"The decorations." There is a lull in the constant chatter as the kids busy themselves with their task. I glance up to see Miss Ward and Jacques standing in the corner whispering while they watch.

"Could she be any more obvious?" JJ sidles up to me to continue her bitch session. I find myself wondering if Miss Ward did indeed whore herself out for a free class tour of the chocolate factory and decide that if she did, she's a better woman than I am.

"You know, I've been training for a mud run, too," I tell JJ as a way to change the subject. "I wonder if it's the same one Kim is doing."

"You are?" JJ's tone is a little more incredulous than I would like.

"Yeah. I've been training since September."

"Wow, I had no idea mud runs are so in vogue." She seems baffled that she would be out of the loop on something popular.

"Oh, yes. All the middle-aged housewives are doing it."

"Really?"

I smile. "No, I'm just kidding. Do you know which race Kim is planning to run?"

"Uh, it's here in April. That's all I know. Is that the one you are doing?"

"I think so. I had an accident a few weeks ago and it put me on the disabled list. I get to start training again next week." As I say this, it starts to throb down there and I realize starting to work out again is going to be a bitch. I'm still tender, plus I'm out of shape. Garth is going to have an "I told you so" field day.

"Maybe I should do it, too." JJ jostles me out of my thoughts.

My God, does this woman ever do anything on her own? She is a professional bandwagon-jumper-on, if there is such a thing.

"Absolutely. Give it a go," is all I say to her.

"Less chitchat, please, moms." Miss Ward has extracted herself from Jacques and joined us without JJ or me noticing. I ignore the reprimand.

"Looks like you and Jacques have made a love connection," I comment.

Miss Ward makes the face I make when I have smelled bad cheese.

"He's not my type at all."

I look at JJ and she rolls her eyes.

"Okay, it's time to get the kids into their coats and back on the bus." Miss Ward pulls her purse over her shoulder.

As the little ones load onto the bus, clutching their bunnies, each one wrapped in cellophane, I give Max a hug and thank JJ and Jill for chaperoning.

My phone buzzes while I'm starting up the trusty minivan. God, it feels good to sit down! It's a text from Ron.

Want a night off from cooking? Let's go to Garozzo's for dinner.

Oh, he read my mind.

Max too?

Already got Chyna to sit with him, so it's just you and me, babe.

Sounds like just what I need.

Sometimes I can't believe how lucky I got. I did kiss a lot of frogs, but it was worth it to end up with this prince of a man.

My phone buzzes again.

You look great today.

Dinner and flattery? Hm . . . something's up.

Thanks! You always look great.

Seriously? I didn't think you noticed.

How can I not?

Glad you like what you see.

Typical Ron. He has no idea how cute he is.

I do indeed.

You're making me smile.

I want to do more than that.

Aren't you frisky today!

You are, too.

What do you want to do about it?

I text him my sign for boobs since they're his favorite part of my body. The poor man hasn't had sex since my accident. He's been so patient. Then I have an idea.

How about we take a little bathroom break at Garozzo's tonight?

Really?

Really. You've waited long enough.

Wow. I don't know what to say.

Say you'll see me at 7, dummy!

Okay.

I laugh as I start the minivan and pull into traffic. Ron and I used to flirt-text all the time. It's been too long. Tonight should be fun. I haven't had bathroom sex in ages.

+ + +

Ron has a last-minute work crisis, so I end up meeting him at the restaurant. He is waiting for me in his car and jumps out when I pull up. He seems a bit preoccupied, so to cheer him up I give him a huge hug and let him know I've gone commando tonight.

"Really? Wow. That's unexpected." He grins like a goof.

"I thought I'd make it as convenient as possible." I squeeze his butt.

"It?" He squeezes mine back.

"Yes, it."

"Well, this is a nice surprise."

"Really?" I stop walking and look at him. "We planned it earlier."

"We did? When?"

"Today. You were flirty-texting me." I reach into my purse to show him my phone and when I look up I see Don Burgess coming around the corner. He stops short when he sees us. Complete and utter horror washes over me as I realize what I'm going to see when I look at my texts. Don. Ron. Shit. I seriously need to think about getting glasses.

"What are you talking about? Let me see." He reaches for my cell and I consider making a run for it. But in the end I know this will all go better if I just 'fess up.

Don is frozen in place, looking very confused. I'm guessing he's trying to assess the situation.

Ron finishes reading and looks first at me and then notices Don.

"Don. What's up? Having dinner here tonight?" Ron's voice is way too calm for my comfort.

"Uh, yeah." Don, to his credit, looks confused and uncomfortable. "You guys, too?"

"We sure are. Who are you eating with?" Ron crosses his arms and takes a wide stance, like he's a bouncer.

"Okay, okay, let's not make this awkward," I say, as though it isn't already. I stand between the two of them. Don and Ron. Jeez, what are the odds?

"Did you come here to have sex with my wife in the bathroom?" Ron's velvet voice is about an octave lower than usual.

Don's face shows no sign of the panic that is ripping through me.

"Um, no. I came here to tell her I *couldn't* have sex with her in the bathroom."

"What?" Ron and I say at the same time. I'm a little insulted. He'd be lucky to have sex with me anywhere, especially a bathroom. I realize this wouldn't be a smart thing to say right now, so I force out a laugh.

"It's all a big misunderstanding." I put my hand on Ron's arm. "It's actually really funny when you think about it."

"It *would* be funny if this guy hadn't shown up thinking he was going to screw my wife." Ron yanks his arm away and glares at Don.

"Hey, whoa," says Don. "That's not why I came." He puts his hands up and starts to walk backward. Not a great idea as he only has about two feet before he falls over a planter filled with super-tunias and lands flat on his back.

"Are you okay?" I start toward him, but Ron holds me back.

"He's fine." He leads us both into the restaurant. I mouth, "I'm sorry," to Don as I'm pulled through the door.

"Hi, Mr. and Mrs. Dixon."

Irina greets us from behind her podium. I call her the hostess with the moistest because her hands are always wet. She is one of our favorite people at Garozzo's, and normally I would ask how her kids are and take a few moments to chat, but tonight I don't dare do anything except give her a quick smile and nod.

Ron takes the wheel.

"Irina, can we get the table in the back by the small window?"

She gives him a puzzled look, but only says, "Sure thing, follow me."

She gathers up a couple of menus and leads us through the half-full restaurant to what is generally known as the crappiest table at Garozzo's because it has the distinct honor of being both by the bathroom and near the place where the waiters congregate to place their orders. If Ron is trying to punish me, mission accomplished.

As we sit down, I open my mouth to start explaining, but Ron, who still has my phone, is busy scrolling through my texts with Don. *Oh, shit.* He finally looks up at me.

"What the fuck is going on?"

Uh-oh. Ron never drops the f-bomb. This is bad.

"Sweetie, I'm sorry. You saw the texts. You know it was a mistake."

"For *you*, it was. But he thought it was real. Why the fuck would he think you'd invite him to screw you at a restaurant?" He pauses. "Are you having an affair?"

"No!" I say as emphatically as I can. "No. No. Never. I would never do that."

"Oh, come on, Jen!" Ron snaps at me. I look over his shoulder and notice we're drawing looks from some of the customers. "You've been texting with this guy since the beginning of the school year."

"Yes, but it's just texting. Stupid, mindless texting that means nothing." I'm trying to remember just how bad the flirting got.

"Why would you write 'Do you mean coffee or COFFEE' in capital letters? If some woman texted that to me, I'd think she was coming on to me."

"Would you like to hear the specials?" Our waitress makes an untimely entrance.

"Can I have a glass of red wine?" I ask.

"Me, too." Ron rubs his hands over his eyes.

She nods and walks away. I look at Ron, and he takes a deep breath.

"I just meant to be funny, I wasn't coming on to him. You need to believe that."

Ron shakes his head and looks at the table.

The wine arrives, and we both take a huge gulp. I can tell Ron doesn't know what to say, so I keep going.

"You know, it probably wouldn't have happened if you hadn't told him I had a crush on him in high school."

"Oh, please, he already knew that."

"Trust me, he had no idea."

"What about your big hookup in the P.E. laundry room?"

"We didn't hook up!" I suddenly realize I've never told him the story. "I walked in on him going down on the girls' volleyball coach."

Ron raises his eyebrows.

"Really?"

"I was in detention and they used to make us help out the custodial staff. I was given a bunch of uniforms to wash. So I went to the P.E. building, walked in the laundry room, and got an eyeful of Don having a box lunch."

"Wow. Did they see you?"

"Unfortunately, yes."

"Did the teacher get fired?"

"I don't know. The only real conversation Don and I ever had in high school was when he asked me not to say anything. He said they were in love, if you can believe it."

Ron smirks, and I think I can see a thaw coming. But then his brows come together again.

"But none of this explains why he came here tonight." He runs his hands through his hair and scratches really hard. "I mean, Jesus. He thought he was going to have sex with you. There must be something else."

"Well, technically, he says he came here *not* to have sex with me, so . . ."

Ron scowls at me. I heave a deep breath trying to slow my heart beat down. We drink our wine in silence until Ron finally says, "I've lost my appetite." He gets up and puts some money on the table.

"I'll see you at home." As he walks away, I can barely see him through the tears welling up in my eyes.

✦ ✦ ✦

I finish both glasses of wine at the table by myself. I have a headache from trying not to cry, so when I get to the minivan I let loose and sob for a good ten minutes. Ron has never walked out on a fight before. That's usually my job—I'm the runner, he's the chaser. I have no idea how to make things right. I'm really hoping he just needs time to cool down.

I drive home in a fog. My stomach is queasy and my head is still pounding despite my sobfest—most likely because I haven't had anything to eat since two o'clock. As I pull up to our house, I see about five cars in the driveway; all are familiar, and I'm immediately panic-stricken. I leap out of the minivan and run to the front door, where I'm greeted by a burst of laughter coming from my living room. *WTF?*

When I walk into the room, my family and friends are sitting in a circle playing Apples to Apples. My mother looks up at me.

"Well, finally. We thought you guys would never get here."

"What are you all doing here?" I ask with no social grace whatsoever.

"Ask your husband," my mom suggests.

"Is he here?"

"He's supposed to be with you." Nina stands and walks toward me. "What's wrong?" She knows me better than anyone. Not to mention my eyes probably look like I've gone five rounds with Muhammad Ali.

"He left the restaurant before me, that's all. What are you guys doing here?" I ask again.

"We came to talk to you," Laura says as she starts to clean up the card game.

"About what? What's wrong? Why are you two not at school?"

"We're heading back tonight, don't have a cow." Vivs frowns. "Why isn't Ron here, is the real question. He called this powwow."

"I need some water," I say, and head to the kitchen. What the hell are all these people doing in my house? I'm so not in the mood for this. Chyna walks in as I'm chugging my drink.

"Max is on your bed watching TV," she tells me. "Do you want me to stay with him?"

"Would you mind, sweetie? I need to deal with what's going on in my living room."

"Sure, good luck." She gives me what looks like a pitying smile and heads back upstairs.

I start for the living room, but my mother cuts me off in the hallway and drags me back to the kitchen. She backs me up against the counter and looks at every square inch of my face. Finally she speaks, in the kindest voice I think I have ever heard her use.

"What's wrong, honey?"

"Oh, Mom." I dissolve into tears and throw my arms around her.

"Shhh. Okay, okay. Let it out."

When I can finally calm down enough to get a coherent sentence out, I briefly tell her the whole sordid tale, starting with when I first saw Don at curriculum night and ending with this evening's fiasco.

"I thought it was just fun, you know? It made me feel giddy. But I never ever would have taken it anywhere. I love Ron and I'm happier than most married people I know. Why would I put any of that at risk just to have a laugh? What is wrong with me?"

"Oh, sweetheart, there's nothing wrong with you. You're just mourning your youth."

Great, my mother's calling me old. I say as much to her.

"Jennifer Rose, that is not what I said. Of course you're not old, but you're also not that twenty-two-year-old girl traipsing through Europe throwing her cat around."

"Mom!"

"No, listen to me." She leads me to the kitchen table and pulls out two chairs for us.

"You did it all and had a great time, and don't ever tell your father this, but I'm glad you had a little fun. We got married right out of high school, and he's the only man I have ever kissed, let alone . . . you know." She looks at her lap.

I let that little overshare sink in for a minute.

"Are you saying you regret only being with Dad?"

"No, I'm saying it's okay to realize that the really fun part of your life just might be behind you. Be sad that it's over, and then move on. Those years aren't coming back, no matter how young a little flirting makes you feel. And believe me, there's a whole lot of good stuff still to come."

I look at my mother and try to see her not as my mom, but as a woman. It's not something we often do as daughters. Then something occurs to me.

"So, did you ever have a little flirtation with someone?"

She gives me a worldly grin. "Now, sweetheart, you don't think I went to bingo all those years because I loved playing it, do you?"

I crack up at this and continue to laugh until I start crying again. Ugh.

My mom hands me a paper napkin from the holder on the table and waits for me to calm down.

When I do, I ask her to tell me why everyone is here.

"Oh, my goodness. I forgot about them. We should get back in there."

She holds her hand out for me, the way she used to when I was a child. I happily take it.

"But *why* are they here?" I ask again.

"You'll see. It was Ron's idea."

At the mention of his name, my stomach does a high dive. I wonder when he'll be home.

That question is answered as we enter the living room; he's sitting with my dad, my daughters, Nina, and Garth, quietly waiting for something to happen.

"So, what's going on?" I say to no one and everyone.

My mother, who has joined my father on the couch by this time, nods to Ron, who nods back; then she stands up and takes a piece of paper out of her bra. Nice, Mom. Way to keep it classy.

"Jennifer, I just want to start by saying we are so proud of you. I mean, let's face it, you weren't exactly on the fast track to success after your little trip to Europe."

That elicits a good laugh from the crowd.

"But you pulled yourself together and have created a beautiful life."

"Thanks, Mom." My eyes start to well up again, and so do hers. She hands the paper to my father, sits down, and blows her nose into the tissue that permanently lives in her sleeve.

My father stands and clears his throat.

"We have really enjoyed watching you get yourself back into shape and, honey, you really look terrific. Not that you weren't always a beauty, but you have a real nice healthy glow these days."

"Um, thanks, Dad." Why are they saying all these nice things? My birthday isn't for, like, two weeks.

Nina goes next.

"Girl, you know how I love to bust you about your training, but I know you've really put your heart and soul into it. I wish I had the discipline to go the distance like you have. You're my hero." She raises her glass to me in salute.

My eyes are misty with tears that just won't stop. I can't believe all the love I'm receiving. It's too much, considering the emotional tsunami I have already been through today.

"My turn!" Vivs stands up and makes everyone laugh.

"Mom, you are without a doubt one of the most insane people I know. Nobody I know has a mom like you. You taught Laurs and me to be strong, independent women, but you also forced us to learn how to do laundry and cook. I swear I'm the only one of my friends who knows how to sew a button."

"Well, that's just shameful," my mother interjects. The lack of domestic capability among the younger generation really grinds her gears.

"Anyway, we love you and we are really proud of you, no matter what."

No matter what?

As I'm pondering this last line, Laura takes the wheel.

"You have been the best mother ever. Even when you did things like hit us with your shoe when you were driving—"

"That was one time!" I feel the need to defend myself.

"I know! I'm just saying that even though you lost your temper and were really mean sometimes—"

"Laura, stop talking." Vivs takes her by the arm and pulls her down.

"She knows I love her," Laura protests, but remains seated.

Garth stands up beside Nina and gives me that great megawatt smile I remember so well from the first time I met him.

"Jen, you are a rock star. You took a chance on an old has-been trainer like me, and I have enjoyed the last six months so very much. Becoming your friend has just been icing on an already frosted cake."

"Thanks, Garth, I feel the same way."

"But here's the thing."

Ah! The thing. Finally we get to the thing.

"I don't think you should attempt a mud run for the next few months."

I'm surprised I didn't put this together sooner. I mean, my dad talked about what a nice body I have now. When would that ever come up in a happy-birthday speech?

Everyone is watching to see what my reaction will be. If they had caught me on another night, I might have argued with them, but tonight the fight is all out of me, so I just shrug.

"I don't really know what to say. I can see you've put a lot of thought into this, and clearly you have had meetings behind my back."

"Just one," Laura assures me.

I wink at her; then I look straight at Garth.

"Really?"

He smiles sheepishly. "We'll do this, I promise. I just don't think you're ready. You were, believe me. But missing these last three weeks has put you off schedule for the one in April. I've told you before, August will be your shining moment."

"But in the meantime . . ." Ron stands up. I haven't been able to make eye contact with him this whole time. "I want you to think about doing the mini event at my store." His monotone feels like a slap in the face after all the love I've been getting.

"You're doing that event again?"

He nods. "The governor's office called us last week and asked if we would participate again."

I look at Garth, who gives me a thumbs-up.

"Back to the scene of the crime, huh?"

"This time you'll crush it," Vivs assures me. Everyone nods in agreement.

I'm suddenly overwhelmed by the events of the night. I can't help it. I start to cry yet again.

Laura and Vivs get out of their chairs and rush over to awkwardly hug me. How did they know that's just what I needed?

✦ ✦ ✦

On my way to bed that night, I tiptoe into Max's room to kiss him good night and find him still awake.

"Can't you sleep, buddy?" I sit down on his bed and brush the hair from his eyes.

"No. I think I ate too much bunny," he mumbles.

I suppress a smile.

"I'm surprised Chyna let you eat it."

"She didn't really know," he whispers. "She thinks I just ate the ears."

"Well, that's not cool. Just because I'm not home doesn't mean you can break the rules."

"I know." He yawns. "I'm sorry. Will you lie down with me?"

I know I should go into the bedroom and try to talk to Ron, but I really don't feel like being iced again. After everyone left, he went upstairs without a word. And anyway, who could refuse such an offer? I cram myself into the race-car bed and Max snuggles into me.

21

To: Ms. Ward's Class
From: JDixon
Date: 4/8
Subject: Ye Olde Parent/Teacher Conferences

Good morrow, good friends!

I was going to do the whole email in olden speak but I'm already bored with it, so I'm switching to acerbic.

Can you believe it's conference time again? I feel like we just went through this whole rigmarole. I mean, my God, how much more can we talk about our kids?

Apparently Miss Ward has a lot to say, so we will be squeezing our butts back into those little chairs come April 27 and 28.

My plan is to use the same schedule as I did in September. I have attached it below. If you have a problem, keep it to yourself or tell Asami. She has a much more sympathetic ear.

Conference Schedule:
Thursday, April 27
     12:30 Lewicki
     1:00 Fancy
     1:30 Aikens
     2:00 Zalis
     2:30 Alexander
     3:00 Kaplan

Friday, April 28
     8:00 Cobb
     8:30 Dixon
     9:00 Westman
     9:30 Baton
     10:30 Tucci
     11:00 Elder
     11:30 Wolffe
     1:00 Gordon/Burgess
     1:30 Chang
     2:00 Brown

By the way, on April 29 there will be a mini mud run at my husband's store (the Fitting Room, on Drummond St.) to help raise awareness for the governor's "Get Fit" campaign. If anyone would like to participate, email me and let me know. I can bring five people.

    That's it. Move along. Nothing to see here.

Jen (and Asami in spirit)

✦ ✦ ✦

I can tell Garth is taking it a bit easy on me, and frankly, I'm glad. How sad is it that it takes six months to get into shape and basically six days to fall out of shape?

He's keeping away from anything that might tax my groin area, which unfortunately doesn't exclude burpees. After five, I cry uncle and he gives me a breather. We have already done push-ups and sit-ups and a bit of jump rope cardio, but I had to stop because the blood was pumping a little too enthusiastically through my downtown area. We're only twenty minutes into the workout and I'm already done.

"Looking good, Jen."

"Oh, please, Garth! I'm like a newbie. When was the last time I quit after five burpees?"

"Give yourself a break. We have two and a half weeks to get you back in fighting shape, and it's not going to happen in one day. I want to work your cardio a little more, so why don't we fast-walk on the treadmill? I'll give you a bit of an angle so it feels like a hill."

I sigh and hoist myself off the floor of Ron's Gym and Tan. I haven't been down here in a few weeks and I forgot all the little changes I made to the décor over the winter. The is now a red Nike poster with black letters that says, "If no one thinks you can, then you have to." It was a Christmas gift from Peetsa and I love it. I also put in a decorative basket of towels for when I sweat, and a pitcher of water, which sometimes has lemons in it and sometimes cucumbers. I usually light a Bay Breeze Yankee Candle, too. All in all, it's a nice place to work out.

"What are you doing for your birthday?" Garth asks as he pushes the buttons on our treadmill.

"I'm not sure." I'm fast-walking but I sneak a look at Garth. "Why? Is Ron planning something?"

I sound a bit desperate. Things at home have been pretty tense for the past week. I hope Max isn't picking up on it. I mean, we still eat dinner together and hang out, but Ron has a force field around him when it comes to me. We talked the morning after the weird intervention thing, when he found me sleeping in Max's bed. Ron said he just needed time and space and would I just please give it to him, which I have, but it's been really hard. I just want to say over and over how sorry I am and how much I love him, but he won't give me the chance.

"Not that I know of," Garth says in answer to my birthday plans question, and I'm sure he's right. He slows down the treadmill and looks at me thoughtfully.

"Are you okay with just doing the store's mini mudder?"

"Totally okay." I huff and puff. "I'm so out of shape, I'll be lucky to get through it."

"I'm going to make sure you are more than ready."

✦ ✦ ✦

After Garth leaves, I sit down at the kitchen-counter office with ice on my groin to check my emails.

I have a lot of responses, so I don't even bother opening Sasha Lewicki's. I don't really need to know when she will be out of the office until.

To: JDixon
From: AChang
Date: 4/8
Subject: Ye Olde Parent/Teacher Conference

Jennifer,

I have not seen you in a while. I assume you have recovered from your accident.

Thank you for taking care of the conference schedule. Can you meet me for tea before pickup tomorrow? I have a new theory about you-know-who.

Asami

Oh, for the love of God, woman, give it up. I'm going to have to shut her down. I email that I will meet her at Starbucks tomorrow at two. She needs a reality check.

To: JDixon

From: KFancy

Date: 4/8

Subject: Ye Olde Parent/Teacher Conference

Hi, Jen,

Well, it's lucky I didn't plan a trip back to Manhattan, or I would have been in trouble again. My conference time is fine.

By the way, I would love to participate in the mud run at your husband's store. What a cute idea. It will be nice and easy after I do the real KC mud run the week before. Will you be doing it too?

Thanks,

Kim

I figured she would take the bait. Kim Fancy is just the incentive I need to truly rock the store's mud run.

To: JDixon

From MJBaton

Date: 4/8

Subject: Ye Olde Parent/Teacher Conference

Dear Jen,

Our conference time is great and Jean-Luc would like to participate in the mud run at your husband's store. Would that be okay?

Thanks,

Mary Jo

Jean-Luc Baton wearing shorts and working out? Uh, yes, please. Then I open Shirleen Cobb's response and it gives me the only good laugh I've had in days.

To: JDixon
From: SCobb
Date: 4/8
Subject: Ye Olde Parent/Teacher Conference

Jennifer,

Conference time is fine. I would like to have helped you and your husband out with the mud run thingy but I have been training at Curves for about two months and I don't want to do anything that might interfere with my progress.

Shirleen

Much to my surprise, no one had a problem with their conference time *and* I filled all five spots for the mini mud run. Besides Kim and Jean-Luc, Hunter's two moms signed up, and so did Ali Gordon.

When I see her email, it reminds me that I owe Don one. The morning after Flirty-Text-Gate, he wrote me a very nice note explaining that he showed up at Garozzo's to let me know that he thinks I'm awesome, but not in that way. Apparently he's been trying to get back together with Ali and all his romantic focus has been on that. He said he really had wanted to meet me for coffee all those times but just to talk to me about *her*. He told me he loved our texting banter, but never thought of it going beyond that.

> *When I got your invitation for sex, I was surprised and flattered. I mean, really flattered. But I knew there was no way it was going to happen. I wanted to talk to you about it in person and not just leave you hanging alone at the restaurant. You're a great girl and I was worried I had done something to lead you on. Now that I know the texts weren't meant for me, it all makes sense.*
>
> *I hope you and Ron were able to laugh it off. He didn't look too happy, but I'm sure once you explained it to him, he was fine. If not, I'd be happy to talk to him and set him straight.*
>
> *Cheers,*
> *Don*

Is he kidding me? This is the guy who said he wanted to help me work out. If that's not flirting, then someone hand me a dictionary. That's such a guy's way out. *Oh, you didn't want to have sex with me? Yeah, me either. It was just banter.* Right, Don, hold on to that.

I'm not going to lie. Finding out that my little crush was possibly only one-sided all along was a real punch in the boob. I know I said the texts didn't mean anything and they were just for fun, but the sad truth is that, once again, Don Burgess is not interested in me. At least this time we're friends—or we *were* friends; I'm not sure what we are now.

I write Don back a note saying all is well and wasn't that hilarious and blah blah blah. I wish him luck with Ali and say I'll see him around.

Good-bye, Suchafox! It was fun while it lasted.

✦ ✦ ✦

April is my favorite month, and not just because it's my birthday. I love the way the air smells of mud created by the ground thawing. It's one of the first signs of spring and always makes me think of my childhood.

I take a deep breath before I head into Starbucks for my Asami intervention. I spot her standing in line to order, so I walk up beside her and say, "Okay, what's your new theory?"

I kind of like the way my relationship with Asami works. There's no preamble, no fake kisses and chitchat. We just get right down to it.

"It's Miss Ward," Asami blurts.

Oh, Jesus, this is going to be worse than I thought.

"My treat today," she continues. "What would you like?"

"Wow, thanks. I'll have a tall Peach Tranquility. I'll go grab the couch for us."

I settle in and check my phone for messages, hoping for something from Ron, but no luck. He's still being chilly. When Asami joins me, she places a giant cookie between us. Chocolate may be a no-no for me but I never say no to a chocolate chip cookie.

"Help yourself," she says as she takes off her sweater.

Who is this woman? Or maybe this has been the real Asami all along and I just never saw it. I decide I need to be kind but firm about her crazy witch-hunt.

"I have to say something to you and I hope you hear me," I begin. "I really think you're barking at the moon. I know it's a bit of a mystery, who this Sasha Lewicki woman really is, but in the grander scheme of things, who cares? Is it hurting Suni in any way? Is it affecting the quality of your day-to-day life? Probably not, so why don't you just drop it?"

I silently give myself props for my nice little speech. I see that Asami's frown has formed a small "v" on her forehead and her mouth is poised in an "o." I take this moment to break off a bit of the cookie and pop it in my mouth, but find to my horror that it's filled with raisins, not chocolate chips. There are few things in life more disappointing. I would spit it out if that was socially acceptable.

Asami still hasn't said anything, but she is looking at me.

"I'm sorry. I hope I didn't hurt your feelings. I just think there are more important things to worry about."

She nods. "You're right, there are. I'm not sure why I'm so focused on it."

"Well, it will definitely go down as one of the great mysteries of room 147," I proclaim. "That and how Mary Jo Baton landed Jean-Luc for a husband."

She smiles at my little joke. I think there's hope for Asami's sense of humor after all.

✦ ✦ ✦

I gratefully lower myself into bed and place a big bag of ice on my groin. It only bothers me after a long day like the one I just had. Usually Ron would want to fool around tonight, because, just like every man in the world, he thinks sex is the perfect gift to give your wife on her birthday. But the way things have been, I'm really not sure. He was very sweet this morning when he and Max gave me breakfast in bed, but then I didn't hear from him all day. It was actually fine. I was unexpectedly busy. The girls surprised me on FaceTime by singing the Beatles' version of "Happy Birthday" with Travis on bass and Raj on tambourine. Later I had lunch with Nina, Peetsa, and Ravi at the place with the signs (Stu's Diner), where we pigged out on homemade chili and Steph gave me a whole apple pie to take home. Stu's only had one new sign—a small one hanging over the front door. It said,

"If I Wanted to Listen to an Asshole, I'd Fart"

I spent the rest of the afternoon getting my hair cut and blown out, and topped the day off having a really fun dinner with my folks and Max and Ron at Minsky's. They have the best pizza in KC. Some might say Waldo's is better, but we're a Minsky's family from way back. We always order the same thing—a Papa Minsky's with pepperoni, Italian sausage, salami, and roasted red peppers. You don't want to be sleeping with any of us on a Minsky's night, let me tell you.

So this is forty-eight. All things considered, I'll take it over twenty-eight any day. Especially *my* twenty-eight, which saw me living with my parents and raising two small kids. As the great Billy Joel once said, "It's some kind of miracle that I survived." This is definitely my time to remember.

22

I wake up way before my seven a.m. alarm. I'm beyond excited, but before I jump out of bed I force myself to do my morning bed stretches and affirmations. This is something Garth made me start while I was injured. Here goes.

"My mind and body are in perfect balance. I am unlimited."

Nice, right? Loving myself isn't really up my alley, but I find this very empowering. It's better than the mantra I used to have, which was "Get your fat ass out of bed."

I know today is just a store-sponsored mini mud run, but to me it's the Olympic Decathlon and the Super Bowl rolled into one and placed in a large bag of chips. My nerves are crack-a-lacking. I'm going back to the scene of my crushing defeat—my complete and utter breakdown in the face of physical challenge. That was a bad bad day. The only thing that could have made it worse would have been shitting myself while trying to get over the wall.

But today, that wall is mine. "My mind and body are in perfect balance. I am unlimited."

I hoist my fat ass out of bed and drag it to the shower. Max is still sleeping. I can only assume Ron is already at the store supervising the setup. I don't have to be there until nine.

God, I wish I had slept longer; I was up so late. I lean against the shower wall for support. As luck would have it, Ron and I chose last night to finally hash out Textgate. Things had certainly been lightening up between us, but we hadn't had a real discussion about it. After I put Max to bed, I joined Ron in our bedroom and caught him reading something on my phone.

"Is that my phone?" I tried not to sound too indignant, because we've always had an open-phone policy in our marriage. But seeing him scrolling without even asking kind of set me on edge.

"Yeah, it is," he answered without any guilt in his voice. "I was rereading those texts you had with Don."

Okay, so we're doing this. I girded my loins and jumped in.

"See anything you missed the first time around?" I asked.

"Yeah, a lot. You guys were really chatting it up."

"Just about stupid stuff." I walked over and sat on the bed beside him.

"I can see that." He continued to look at my phone and not me.

I touched his arm. "Ron, I'm sorry. I really am."

"I still don't understand why you felt the need to have such a back-and-forth with this guy. Am I not interesting enough?"

I sighed. How could I say, "It's not you, it's me," without sounding trite?

"Sweetie, this is all on me. You are more than enough of everything I could possibly want in life. But according to my mother, I'm having a bit of a midlife crisis."

Finally Ron looked at me.

"What's the crisis?"

"Uh, I'm forty-eight, my best years are behind me, and I'm going to be a grandmother."

Alarmed, he sat up. "What? Who's pregnant?"

"Well, no one yet, but it's coming just like everything else."

"Jesus, Jen, you nearly gave me a heart attack."

"Sorry. It's just what I think about."

"What else do you think about?" He seemed leery of my answer.

I lay back on the bed and closed my eyes. Cripes, what don't I think about?

"I think about how I look just a little less attractive every day. I think that when I'm sixty, Max will just be finishing high school. I wonder if I should have had a career instead of a bunch of jobs. I wonder why you love me and when you might stop. I worry that I'm not a good enough wife, daughter, mother, and friend. And I worry that if this is it, this is my whole life, will it be enough?"

There was a long pause, and then my husband said, "That's it?"

It took me a moment to realize he was joking. I started to belly-laugh. He lay down beside me.

"So this is why you started flirting with an old boyfriend?"

"He was never my boyfriend. But . . ." I was trying to nail down what had been driving me this whole time.

"But . . . it made you feel young?"

Ding ding ding! Ron for the win.

"I guess in a way it did. I mean, he knew me before college, before kids . . . before you."

"Well, he knew the young you, but not the best you, as far as I'm concerned. I don't know if I would have liked seventeen-year-old Jen as much as forty-seven-year-old Jen."

"Forty-eight," I corrected him.

"Right, forty-eight. I'm sorry you're having a midlife crisis about getting old, but you need to see yourself through our eyes."

"*Our* eyes?"

"Mine and Max's. We love you and think you're amazing. That ski trip was no fun without you, and not just because no one made skillet tacos or us."

I started to say something, but Ron cut me off.

"Let me finish. You are everything to us . . . to me. But if we aren't enough for you, then that scares me."

I sat up on the bed. "You are! You are! I love my life with you guys and with the girls. It's just hard getting older. I'm not the prettiest girl at the party anymore, and I need to adjust to that."

Ron sat up beside me and pulled me into his arms.

"You will always be the prettiest girl at my party. Don't ever doubt it."

Corny, right? But it was music to my ears, and the makeup sex really burst the dam of tension between us. I'm so glad we had it out. I just wish it hadn't been the night before the mini mud run, because now I'm physically and mentally wiped.

Out of the shower I grab my cell phone and check the weather. Sunny, with a high of 67 degrees: perfect.

I put on a pair of Lululemon cropped yoga pants, my favorite workout bra, and one of the Fitting Room T-shirts Ron had made for the event. I run a brush through my hair and decide a ponytail will be my best bet.

I'm humming the *Rocky* theme as I run down to the kitchen and whip up some scrambled egg on Ezekiel bread with ketchup—my breakfast of champions.

It's 7:30 and I'm ready to go. Shit. I need a distraction, so I go into Max's bedroom and rumble around until he wakes up from the noise.

"Hi, Mommy," he says through a yawn.

"Hey, buddy." I curl up in his race-car bed with him and snuggle.

"Is your run today?" he asks.

"Yup."

"Are you going to win?"

"I will win just by finishing the course."

He grabs my face so I'm looking right at him.

"Mommy. Winning is winning." He sounds like Ron.

"No, sweetie, winning is doing your best." I pull him into a hug.

"Want to hear my song about winning?"

"Sure." I stifle a yawn. "Lay it on me."

"Winning, winning, winning, winning, winning," he sings softly, to the tune of absolutely nothing recognizable. I shut my eyes and sigh with happiness.

"Mommy!"

I open my eyes and something has changed. The light in the room is different, and Max smells like cheese.

"What time is it?" I ask.

"I don't know." He goes over to his iPad Mini and opens it. "It's eight-five-five."

"What the fu . . . dge." I scramble off the bed. "Did I fall asleep?"

"Yeah, when I was singing. So I went down and made my own breakfast without using the oven or the microwave." He sounds so proud of himself.

Boy, nothing good ever comes from me dozing off. I start pulling clothes out of the dresser and throwing them on his bed. "Sweetie, we have to get going. Can you get yourself dressed?"

"But *Teenage Mutant Ninja Turtles* is on."

"Max, you knew you were going to miss it today. Please get dressed and meet me in the kitchen."

"I don't feel like it." He's pouting *and* whining now.

"Max, please! This is my big day. I need full cooperation. Lock and load, let's go." I start pulling his PJs off.

"No! Stop it! Don't! Hands are not for hitting!" he yells.

"I'm not hitting you. I'm undressing you. Stop fussing around!" I'm inches from losing it. "What is *wrong* with you?"

And as I say it, I know.

"What did you make yourself for breakfast?"

"Cheez Whiz," he grumbles.

He's hungry.

"Buddy, how about you get dressed and I'll let you have two Pop-Tarts for breakfast. Then you can watch a DVD in the car on the way to the store."

Threats and bribes are the only two ways I know how to parent. Luckily, this bribe works and before you can say, "Jen's a crappy mom," Max and I are in the minivan and speeding downtown to the store.

As we pull into the parking lot, it looks like the circus has come to town. There is a big orange tent where people are gathering. A large blue, orange, and white banner has been hung on the building welcoming everyone to the Governor's Get Fit Mini Mud Run sponsored by the Fitting Room.

"Max, look at that!" I yell so he can hear me over the headphones. The sight is impressive enough to tear him away from his movie.

"Whoa!" he yells. "Cool."

And indeed it is cool. Ron's team has done an amazing job putting together a fierce-but-not-too-fierce obstacle course, which covers half the parking lot and the adjoining field. It takes me a minute to register that, much to my horror, a fire obstacle has been included. They've really upped the ante from last year.

There is no room for cars in the lot, so I have to park down the street. Max and I rush back to the parking lot and wend our way through the crowd to where Ron is registering participants and getting liability waivers signed.

"Hey, sorry we're late."

"Are you late?" Ron doesn't even look up. I can tell he is overwhelmed by the turnout. I know it's a big day for him, but it's a big one for me, too.

I leave Max to hang with his dad and the rest of the team behind the desk. In the parking lot, I bump into Hunter's two moms. Kim and Carol are dressed in matching shorts and homemade T-shirts that say "Team Hunter." I give them both a hug.

"You guys look great!"

"Thanks. I can't believe that obstacle course!" says Kim or Carol. "I'm a little intimidated."

"It's bigger than the one they had last year," I tell them.

"Did you do it last year?"

"Uh, you could say that." I really don't want to relive the shame of last year's failed attempt. I spot Garth, Nina, and Chyna over by the door to the store and excuse myself.

"How are you feeling?" Garth asks after I hug all of them.

"I'm a little frazzled. I fell back asleep and woke up, like, fifteen minutes ago," I tell them. "Chyna, sweetie, want to make twenty bucks the hard way?"

She smiles and walks toward the tent where Max is.

"I already told her that's what she's here for," Nina assures me. "How are you and Ron doing?"

"We finally talked about it last night."

Nina raises her perfect eyebrows. "Boy, when Ron says he needs time and space, he isn't joking."

"I know, right?"

"So, are you forgiven?"

"You could say that." I blush, thinking once again about our makeup sex. "I think he was determined to prove that my reality is better than any fantasy."

Nina smiles. "Pulled out all the stops, did he?"

I lean in and tell her she'll get all the details later. Right now I need to focus.

I turn to Garth.

"As soon as I saw the course, my groin started to hurt. Is that normal?"

"You'll be fine. It's a great course. I'm looking forward to it."

"And I'm looking forward to seeing you in action." Nina gives his arm a squeeze.

"Me, too," I purr.

"All right. Cut it out right now. Jeez." Garth is blushing at our now ongoing joke.

Hot Dad Jean-Luc and Kim Fancy are having a tête-à-tête over by the Gatorade stand, which is right in my line of vision. Kim is wearing a long-sleeved black unitard that makes her already thin body seem emaciated. Jean-Luc is looking mighty fine in thigh-length running shorts and a hoodie. I look down at my T-shirt and leggings and realize I should have put a little more thought into my outfit.

I wave to them both and start to walk over. Don Burgess's baby mama, Ali, falls into step with me; I completely forgot she'd signed up. I wonder if she knows about the texting drama, or if she would care.

"Hey there. Thanks for letting me do this," she says, panting a little. "My New Year's resolution was to dump my bad habits and get back into shape. That course looks really scary."

She stops walking to catch her breath; I wonder how well she's going to do, given she can't even keep up a brisk walk without huffing and puffing.

"Did Don come out to watch you?"

"Oh, God, I hope not," Ali replies, then puts her hand over her mouth. "Sorry. That was an overshare."

"Not at all. Do you not like when he watches you do things?"

She shakes her head. "It's hard to explain."

I frown to show her I have no idea what she's talking about, but just as she's about to continue I see Kim and Jean-Luc coming toward us, so I touch her arm and ask her to hang on.

"Thanks so much for coming!" I enthuse to them. "Kim and Carol are by the tent, so it looks like room 147 is here to represent!"

"I'll say," a voice behind me chimes in.

I turn, and of all people in the world, you'll never guess who's there. Well, maybe you will, but it shocks the shit out of me.

Miss Ward is standing there in a pink warm-up jacket and shorts. Her blond hair is done in two braids and she's wearing a white do-rag.

There are cries of "Miss Ward!" and "Peggy!" as everyone in the group greets her in their own way.

"Here to cheer us on?" I ask.

"I'm here to do more than that. I'm going to do the course."

"Good for you." Jean-Luc seems disproportionately happy to hear this news. I, however, have gone into silent panic mode. I flash back to when I told Ron I was going to invite some people to do the course. We were in the kitchen, cleaning up the dinner dishes.

"Uh, I'm not sure." He seemed less than thrilled.

"Or maybe I won't."

"It's just that we've had a huge response this year. I put a poster up in the store two weeks ago, and I already have a hundred and seventy-five people signed up to participate. I'm just wondering how many can do it in three hours."

"Well, if they're anything like I was last year, you can bet on thirty seconds before they collapse in defeat."

Normally that would have made him smile, but because we were still in the ice age, all I got was the back of his head.

"So you'd rather I didn't ask anyone?"

"No, you can, but just keep it to five max, okay?"

"Okay."

Not wanting to rock the boat, I took his request very seriously.

And now here's Miss Ward, assuming she can just tag along. I take her arm and lead her away from the other parents.

"Did you sign up through the store?" I ask, as politely as I can.

"No." She frowns. "I saw it in your email."

"Well, you didn't RSVP, and I said we could only have five spots. I don't know if they can squeeze you in." *How did she see the email?*

"But I did RSVP, Jen. In fact, I was probably the first to RSVP."

I give her a quizzical look. Her gaze is steady.

"I'm *always* the first one to respond."

And in that moment, I feel a huge shift in my equilibrium. I'm off balance for a nanosecond but quickly steady myself. *Oh. My. God.* I take a breath.

"Sasha Lewicki, I presume."

"In the flesh."

Pieces of the puzzle start to click into place. Miss Ward is the only one who has ever seen Sasha and her daughter, Nadine; she isn't on the class email list and yet always knows what the emails say. Oh, my God, Asami was right! She is going to lord this over me for the rest of my life.

I'm about to launch into a hundred questions, the first one being "In God's name, why?," but I'm interrupted by the loudspeaker announcement that participants should start making their way to the course.

Suddenly Garth is at my elbow. "I think we should watch a few people before we do it." I nod and allow him to lead me away. I'm completely floored, but I remember my manners and invite the group from 147 to follow us.

"Are you okay?" Garth asks as we head to the starting line.

"Yes, why?"

"You just have a really strange look on your face."

"Just nervous, I guess." I could tell him about the big mystery I just solved, but I don't think he'd get it.

We all gather in line to do the course. I turn and look at my group. Kim and Carol have joined us and are giving each other a pep talk. Dr. Evil has her game face on and Ali is biting her nails.

She is the one I can relate most to. Jean-Luc Baton is doing some last-minute stretches, but is momentarily distracted when Miss Ward takes off her warm-up jacket. I'm with him. Her boobs truly defy gravity. I take a moment to admire them before I turn my attention to the course.

"This is going to be fun," Garth enthuses as we watch the first people take off. They are letting groups of two go every two minutes. The first up are two middle-aged women who I may or may not recognize from Curves. They can't get over the wall, so they do something that never would have occurred to me: they walk around it.

The course is pretty basic, but that doesn't mean it's easy. Just like last year, the six-foot wall is the first obstacle. Then you have to carry a tire about fifty yards, then run a hundred yards, and then crawl under a net through a long mud patch. After that comes a set of monkey bars, and a fake hill to climb and then slide down the other side. Then you run through some sprinklers to get wet, and jump over the line of fire and race to the finish line.

Adrenaline is pulsing through my veins as Garth and I get closer to the starting line. I want to scream, "I'm not ready yet!," but the truth is, I am. At this point I just want to get it over with. Especially that damn wall. I look around for Ron, hoping he realizes that I'm about to go, but I only see Chyna and Max waving at me from the sidelines.

I turn to Team 147. I see Kim Fancy and Miss Ward/Sasha Lewicki have paired up to do the course together. Huh. I thought they were mortal enemies, what with the slap and all. Competition makes for strange bedfellows. I shake my head to clear it. I can't lose focus.

"Good luck, you guys!" I say to everyone. They all smile and give a thumbs-up. As I'm taking a last look around for Ron, some guy at the starting line tells Garth and me that we're next. Garth takes my hand.

"You got this, Jen." He winks at me, and then we're off.

We run to the six-foot wall. Scenes from last year flash through my mind, and I immediately fall into my old, bad habit of trying to hoist myself over using my arms.

"Use your legs!" Garth yells to me from the top of the wall. Jesus, he's already up there?

I remember what he's taught me about saving my arm strength and using my legs. I grab the top of the wall and, keeping my arms straight, I frog-jump up the wall with my legs until I can hook my foot over the top and follow it with my body. I jump down the other side and wince with pain.

Garth jumps down, too.

"All good?" he asks. I nod.

We run toward the tires and each pick one up. It's heavy but not unmanageable—more awkward than anything. I can't run with it, but I walk as quickly as I can and am more than happy to see the place where you drop them. Garth, of course, is carrying two.

"Doing great," he puffs as he throws his tires on the pile and we take off on the hundred-yard run. "How's your groin?"

It's actually hurting, but there's no way I'm telling him that.

"Good. Fine," I pant.

At the end of our sprint is the mud patch. We get down on our bellies and crawl through what seems like five miles of muck but in reality is only about fifty yards. I'm exhilarated as I come to the end. I jump to my feet and high-five Garth, who naturally is right there waiting for me.

The monkey bars are next. Without thinking, I jump up and grab the first one; immediately, my hands slip off and I land on my butt.

"Wipe your hands on the grass or you'll never get a grip!" Garth yells while sailing across with ease. I rub my hands on the grass try-ing to get as much mud off as possible. When I grab the bars again, my hands hold tight and I scramble across.

Garth and I run up the manmade hill and then slide down the other side, which is all mud. As we do, I realize we are coming to the end. We run through the line of sprinklers to wet ourselves down and then hold hands as we jump over the fire line. I don't even feel the heat.

As we jog to the finish line, I see my whole heart waiting for me.

Mom, Dad, Max, the girls, their boyfriends, Nina, and, right in front, Ron holding an ice pack.

I run straight into the group with my arms open wide in the hopes of embracing all of them at once. There is laughter and tears and congratulations and screams of "You're getting me dirty!" from my mother. I gratefully take the ice pack from Ron and hold it between my legs.

"I love you so much," I tell him with tears in my eyes.

"I know." He hugs me.

We have to make room for the other racers, so we herd ourselves over to the side and chat while we cheer on the rest of Team 147 as they cross the finish line.

Kim and Carol are first. They hold hands while they run, smiling the whole way. They seem to have a really nice marriage. As they complete the course, Carol lifts Kim into her arms and swings her around in a big hug. Well, now we know who's the bitch and who's the butch. Another mystery solved!

Next I see Jean-Luc running with Ali, both covered in mud but only one of them looking like he just finished a *Men's Health* photo shoot. Beside him, Ali is struggling to keep pace and looks happy to see the finish line. As they cross, Jean-Luc picks her up and swings her around. Is this some kind of ritual I wasn't made aware of?

Last but not least from our little team come Kim Fancy and Miss Ward—covered in mud and running like they are racing each other. I'm not kidding. They are neck and neck and running so close together that one of them could easily take the other out with a good shove. I'm thinking Kim Fancy for the win, but they actually cross the finish line together, clasp hands, and run toward the side of the building where the Porta Potties are located.

"When you gotta go, you gotta go," my mom says.

"I want to do it again," I say to Ron. "It went by so fast." I hug him and reach my arm out for Max. "You guys are the best cheering section in the world." I turn to my family and friends. "I can't believe you all came for this." They are all talking to each other and completely ignore me.

"I've got to get back to work." Ron extracts himself from Max's and my hug. "Are you going to hang out, or what?"

"The first thing I have to do is pee. I'll come and find you." I hand him my ice pack and take off toward the side of the building. I'm so happy, I'm practically flying. But when I turn the corner of the building, I stop short, because I'm treated to the sight of Miss Ward and Kim Fancy over by the side of the Porta Potties, *making out*! I mean, really going at it. Kim has our kindergarten teacher backed against the toilet, and Miss Ward has one leg wrapped around her like a rope. They don't see me, so I immediately backtrack around the corner and wonder if I have just imagined the whole thing. A quick second glance confirms that I have not. This is too much to take in. Miss Ward is Sasha Lewicki *and* she's Kim Fancy's secret lover? I feel like I'm in a movie. A really dirty one.

I still have to pee, but I decide to use the bathroom inside the store. I walk back through the parking lot, only semi-aware that people are still doing the obstacle course. My mind is trying to put together all I know about Miss Ward and Kim Fancy. How long has this been going on? Did Miss Ward *not* have an affair with the dashing David Fancy? I had been so sure about that, especially after the Christmas party–turned–jewelry show. I mean, Miss Ward had obviously taken her dress off at some point and then put it on backward. I always assumed she had hooked up with the dashing David in the bathroom for a quickie and that was why Kim slapped her, back in February. *That slap!* What was that all about? A lovers' quarrel? Foreplay?

I walk into the store, grateful for the relative quiet. This is a terrific event, but I'm not sure what it does for Ron's business. Everyone is outside having fun, not inside buying things.

I wave to Kendra, the salesgirl behind the counter, and head to the bathroom, which is on the left side of the store right near the jockstraps and sports bras. I lock myself in because I need to think, plus it's nice to sit down for a minute. I feel like I have been at Mach 10 with my hair on fire ever since I woke up for the second time this morning.

Usually, I do some of my best thinking on the toilet, but today all I come up with is more questions. So I flush and wash my hands. A glance in the mirror shows I have the battle scars of a mud warrior all over me and I feel all kinds of cool as I head back to the parking lot. I look at my watch and can't believe it is only 10:15. All this has happened in an hour? It makes me think of the army slogan, "We do more before nine a.m. than most people do all day."

I find Max and Chyna at the Gatorade table, passing out cups to people.

"Mommy, Garth is looking for you," Max informs me, handing me a cup of orange Gatorade.

"Okay, thanks. Are you guys having fun?"

"Dad says I can play in the mud when everyone is done and swing on the monkey bars."

"He did, huh? You are so lucky."

"He said I could try to do the course, too," Chyna tells me. "If it's okay with you."

"Of course. But maybe get Garth to help you. Any idea where he and your mom are?"

"I think they went to talk to the guy from the governor's office."

"Where is he?"

"Sitting with the guy making all the announcements." She points to a table set up near the starting line.

"Max, want to come with me or stay with Chyna?"

"Mommy, I'm working."

"Righty-o! I'll be back in a little while."

On my walk over to the table, I am stopped at least a dozen times by friends and customers all congratulating me on the success of the day, as though I had anything to do with it. I promise to pass along their compliments to Ron, if I ever see him again. Finally, I spy the announcer's table and Garth chatting up some guy in a suit. I wait until he sees me, then I wave him over. I'm not in the mood to press any more flesh.

"There you are! I was looking for you. You must have really had to pee."

"You have no idea," I respond. "Where's Nina?"

"She's getting something from the car. How are you feeling?" He puts his arm around me.

"I feel great! That was a breeze. I wanted to go right back and do it again. How did I look?"

"Like a girl who's ready for a bigger challenge, that's for sure. I'm so proud of you. You must be on such a high."

Well, I was, I think but do not say. The whole Miss Ward/Kim Fancy drama has really pulled me off track. Garth is right—I should be walking on air. Instead, all I want is to find Nina and tell her everything. But Garth doesn't need to know any of this.

"I am. It was amazing and I owe it all to you." I give him a hug.

I can tell Garth is happy. "And we aren't finished yet. August, baby. That's when the real deal will happen. We need to keep training all summer."

"I'm ready," I tell him. I spot Nina walking toward us. "I'm going to steal your girl for a few minutes." He smiles and waves me on.

I grab Nina's arm and redirect her to a bench near the street.

"Looks like you and Ron—"

I cut her off immediately.

"I have to tell you something, but you can't tell anyone else."

"Okay." Nina seems more dubious than curious.

"Swear on Chyna's life that you won't say anything."

"Uh, no. But I'll swear on our friendship, if that makes you feel any better."

I regard her for a moment, then nod.

"Good enough." I take a deep breath. "I just saw Miss Ward and Kim Fancy making out by the Porta Potties." I wait for a reaction, and Nina doesn't disappoint. Her eyes nearly pop out of her head.

"Are you shitting me?"

"Nope."

"Didn't you tell me one of them *slapped* the other?"

"Yup."

"Are you sure they were making out? Maybe they were just hugging."

"With their tongues?"

"Oh, my God, seriously?"

"Yup."

"Was it hot?"

"No!" I laugh. Only Nina.

"I'm just sayin'—they're both good-looking women. Would a guy think it was hot?"

"Probably. Not really the point I was getting at, though."

"This is seriously good gossip."

"You promised you wouldn't say anything," I remind her.

"I won't. Wait, can I tell Garth?"

"Of course." I know I'll be giving Ron a play-by-play later.

Nina looks past me toward the parking lot.

"We should get back. Garth is giving me the 'Mayday' sign."

While Nina goes to rescue Garth, I check in with Max, who is still manning the Gatorade table with Chyna.

"Hey, guys. Having fun?"

"Mom, I'm hungry. Can Chyna and I go to McDonald's?" I can see Max is losing interest in his job, and the golden arches next door are acting like a bat signal on him. Let's see, Pop Tarts for breakfast and now McDonald's for lunch. I hope Child Protective Services isn't watching.

"I guess so," I say. "But I don't have my purse with me."

"I have money from my mom," Chyna assures me.

"Okay. Well, don't eat too much if you're going to do the course later."

"We won't," they say together, and head off.

The event is going strong. People are still lined up to do the course, and the announcer has started to play great motivational tunes like "We Will Rock You" by Queen. I smile to myself, because I'm happy for Ron. This is a real win for him.

I pass Ali Gordon limping to her car and realize we'd never finished our conversation.

"Are you okay?" I ask her.

"Yeah, I'm fine, it's just my calves are starting to seize up. I think I should have trained a bit for this."

"As someone who did nothing but train, I'm going to agree with you. Need some help?" I lean toward her.

She gives a resigned laugh and puts her arm over my shoulder. "I guess I do, thanks."

I support her around the waist and we start walking. I'm generally a nice and helpful person, but I'm not going to pretend I don't have an ulterior motive. I want to see if I can get Ali to spill the beans about her and Don. I'm in no shape to be clever or crafty, so I just come straight out with it.

"So, what's your deal with Don?"

She sags a bit more into me.

"I'm sorry I said that earlier. I just get frustrated sometimes."

"Why?"

She sighs. "Look, he's a good guy. He's just really . . ." She's searching for a word, but I don't have any suggestions.

"He's Peter Pan," she finishes.

"He dresses in green and flies around the city?" It's a joke, but apparently not to Ali.

"I mean, he has Peter Pan syndrome. He doesn't want to grow up."

"Really? I don't get that from him at all."

"Why would you? You haven't had to raise a kid with him."

I think about that for a second.

"Is he not involved with Lulu's life? I mean, he shows up for all the school stuff."

"Yeah, that's a recent development. Now that she walks and talks and communicates, all of a sudden he wants to be Dad. When she was a baby, forget it."

"That's rough. Why did you guys have a kid to begin with?"

She gives a bitter guffaw.

"The condom broke."

"No!" I gasp. "Oh, my God, that actually happens? I always think of it as an urban myth like the alligators that live in the New York sewers."

This she does laugh at. "Nope. Not a myth. We had only been dating a few months when it happened. That's my car." She points to a beige Hyundai parked on the corner. She takes her arm from around my neck and fishes her key fob out of her fanny pack. But I'm not letting her leave just yet.

"And you wanted to keep the baby, of course."

"We both did. I mean, Don was forty-two at the time and I was in my late thirties, so we thought why not, you know? He wanted to get married, but I held off on that, thank God. I was like, 'What's the rush?' Don was really into it until Lulu was born, and then reality set in."

"Oh, God," is all I can think of to say.

"He freaked out." She sighs and leans against her car. "He was actually jealous of all the attention Lulu got. He really didn't get it. We started fighting all the time, so I told him if he couldn't accept that he wasn't the child anymore then he should just stay away."

"And did he?"

"Yes!" she yells. "Can you believe it? I didn't see him for, like, three years."

"What an asshat." I can't help but think how lucky I am to have Ron "I'll change the diaper" Dixon.

"My parents live in Des Moines, so they weren't much help. I was on welfare for a while. I mean, it really sucked."

"When did he come back?" This conversation is making me remember how tough it was carting Vivs around Europe while I was pregnant with Laura. Now there's a book I should write.

"You won't believe me."

"Try me."

"We met speed dating."

"What?"

She nods her head with wide eyes.

"Of all the gin joints, right? When he sat down in front of me I nearly spat my drink out."

"What did you say to him?" I'm completely spellbound.

"I actually said, 'Of all the gin joints.'" She shrugs. "We agreed to meet afterward, and he claimed he wanted back in Lulu's life."

"So you let him?"

"Not right away. I mean, the guy was AWOL for three years. If he'd wanted back in so badly, he could have called or emailed anytime. I always wonder what would have happened if I hadn't gone to that stupid dating thing."

I give her another way to look at it.

"But it's kind of romantic. Like it was meant to be."

"I guess. He's been around a lot. It's been great having help with Lulu, especially money help. And, I don't know if you know this, but he's really good with kids."

"I actually witnessed that firsthand on a field trip."

"He's a natural. It makes me sad for him that he missed all those years with Lulu."

"Do you guys date other people?"

"I'm not sure what he does, but I haven't had a date in two years. That's why I want to get in shape, you know? Stop looking like something the cat dragged in."

I definitely knew where she was coming from. After I had Max, "dumpy" was the only real way to describe me. That's why I joined Curves. I consider suggesting it to Ali.

"You're hardly something the cat dragged in," I assure her. "Have you guys ever considered getting back together?"

Ali opens her car door and groans loudly as she eases herself into the driver's seat. "Don talks about it, but I don't know. I'm still getting over being mad at him."

I nod.

She starts her car. "Thanks for the help."

"Epsom salt bath and Advil," I advise. "For the pain."

23

You'd think with all my newfound knowledge I would have been out there like a bumblebee pollinating all of William Taft Elementary with news of Miss Ward, Kim Fancy, and the phantom Sasha Lewicki. But I didn't. I sat on all of it, which if you ask me shows Herculean restraint. Ron thinks I'm just scared of the fallout, and maybe I am. This isn't just "I saw her bingeing on ice cream at Ben and Jerry's" gossip. This is information that has the potential to hurt people and change lives. I keep thinking about Nancy Fancy and how she will have to deal with everything if this comes out. And poor little Nadine Lewicki! Oh, wait, she's not real.

I know I should at least let Asami know she was right all along and put her out of her misery, but I don't know what she'll do with the information, so I simply go on with my life.

The mud run at Ron's store was a huge success. It was even on the front page of the *Kansas City Star,* albeit below the fold. The picture they used was of Garth just getting out of the mud. You can actually see my elbow in the shot! The lieutenant governor called Ron personally to thank him. They want him to start thinking about next year and maybe doing a cross-promotion with one of the TV stations.

It's mid-May, so Vivs and Laura are done with school for the year, but both have opted to stay on campus and work rather than come home. I can't say I'm surprised. Love is definitely in the air in Manhattan, Kansas. They *are* both coming home for Max's last day of school, which to my shock and awe is only two weeks away. Normally, the kids would be in classes until the third week of June, but apparently the school board has scheduled good old William Taft for a facelift, so they're shelving those oh-so-critical last two weeks when the kids do nothing but play games and go on field trips.

I realize I should email Miss Ward to find out if she wants to have a year-end party. The last day of school isn't a Hallmark holiday, is it?

I get up from folding laundry and head to the kitchen-counter office to send her an email. When I log on I notice that Shirleen Cobb, Nina, and Miss Ward have all emailed me. Aren't I the popular one today! Just for shits and giggles, I read Shirleen's first.

To: JDixon
From: SCobb
Date: 5/23
Subject: Play date

Jen,

Apparently Graydon would like to have a play date with Max. I'd like to have it at my house so I can monitor what Graydon eats. How about this Saturday?

Shirleen

Yes, Graydon and Max are friends again. The whole "You're a liar" incident is long forgotten . . . by some. I'm just glad Shirleen wants to host. I already have more gum than I can chew. Worrying about Graydon's list of dos and don'ts just might push me over the edge. I email her back telling her it's fine and move on.

> *To: JDixon*
> *From: NGrandish*
> *Date: 5/23*
> *Subject: Hey*
> *Breaking news from the principal's office! Call me.*
>
> *Xo*

Just then my phone buzzes and I see that Nina has texted me the same thing. I think I know what it is. She has been making noise about stepping down as PTA president, but I always assumed she was all hat and no horse. Wow, I guess she finally did it. I'll call her later.

> *To: JDixon*
> *From: PWard*
> *Date: 5/24*
> *Subject: Today*
>
> *Hi, Jenny,*
>
> *I know we're coming up to the long weekend, but could you meet me in the classroom after school today at 3?*
>
> *Thanks,*
> *Peggy*

Finally! The universe has rewarded my patience and cowardliness. Miss Ward wants a meeting. I'll seriously die if Kim Fancy is there, too.

I type back a quick affirmative reply to Miss Ward, then text Peetsa and ask if she can take Max home with her after school.

I just have time to run up and take a mini shower (no hair washing), put on a fresh mom uniform, and head to Starbucks before my meeting. Peetsa has responded that she will take Max with her and Zach while they go grocery shopping for their Memorial Day barbecue, which we're invited to. I really owe her one. Taking two six-year-olds grocery shopping is only slightly easier than herding cats.

"You look good, Mama," I say to her at pickup. It's a sunny spring day and Peetsa has busted out a short pleated skirt and a light blouse for the occasion. She looks so pretty.

"I thought you weren't going to be here." She squints at me.

"Miss Ward asked to meet with me."

"About what?"

I shrug. "No idea." I hate lying to her. Fortunately, Ravi comes up to us, and the subject turns to summer and what we're going to do with the boys. We're trying to formulate some kind of shared schedule when the school bell rings. The good weather has infected the kids and there is extra noise and activity as they pour out of the building.

I wave Max over and give him a hug. He smells like dirt, so I can tell they were outside a lot today.

"Hey, buddy, do you mind going with Zach T. for a while? I need to meet with Miss Ward."

"Are you going to talk about me?" He looks worried.

"Nope. We're going to talk about the super big end-of-the-year party we're going to have for you guys." Peetsa raises her eyebrows at me, and I shrug.

"Can we get a bouncy castle?" Max asks.

"And cotton candy," Zach T. adds.

"It's not a carnival, guys, it's just a party. I'll see you later." I wave to Ali and Lulu as I walk toward the school. My phone rings just as I am walking in. It's Nina.

"I'm sorry, I meant to call you earlier. Did you do it? Did you quit?"

"I was going to, but I'm having second thoughts. But I did overhear something that you'll be interested in."

"What?" I pause in the lobby because I don't want my voice echoing down the empty hall on my way to room 147.

"Miss Ward resigned."

"What?"

"Yup. Apparently she told Jakowski she's leaving. I don't know anything else."

"I'm actually on my way to a meeting with her right now." I whisper even though there is no one around.

"Oh, my God. Go find out what's going on and call me right back." Nina hangs up before I can even say good-bye.

I put my phone in my purse and hurry to the classroom, where I find Miss Ward sitting at her desk, humming a kids' song and organizing some papers. When she sees me, she jumps up much the way she did on curriculum night, oh so many months ago.

"Jenny!" She hugs me. "Thanks for coming. Sit down. I have some news for you." She hops up to sit on her desk, leaving me with either one of the kids' tables or one of their chairs. I choose a table and just hope it holds me.

"What's up?" I ask as casually as I can.

"I wanted to let you know that I have resigned."

"Really?" I act genuinely surprised, or at least I hope I do. "Why?"

I think she's going to confess that she got caught inventing a fake student and parent and they asked her to leave. But once again, she surprises me.

"The private school I used to work at in New Jersey really wants me to come back, and they've made me a great offer."

"Really? Wow. Good for you," is all I can think of to say. And then something occurs to me. "You could have just emailed me the news. Why did you want to meet?" Bold, I know. But I'm not walking away without answers.

She looks at me slyly. "I thought you might have some questions for me."

"I do, actually. Did you want to have an end-of-year party? I meant to email you about it."

"Sure." She waves her hand at me. "Anything you want. I'll leave it to your imagination. Anything else?"

I sigh. She clearly wants me to ask.

"Why did you make up Sasha and Nadine Lewicki?" There, it's out.

She gives me a smile that lets me know she thinks she has won some kind of standoff.

"Well, I was new here, and I wanted to keep tabs on the class without anyone knowing it. I loved your emails, by the way. You're very funny."

"Thanks. Is that the only reason?" I ask.

"I've had some bad experiences with class parents in the past. Mothers can be so catty sometimes."

I look at her, but don't say anything. She shrugs.

"What other reason would there be?"

I'm feeling very unsatisfied. It's like having an itch in the middle of your back that you can't quite reach.

"I don't know. You went to a lot of trouble just to spy on your own class. I would have cc'd you on the emails if you wanted."

"Yes, but they wouldn't have been the same, now would they? I wanted the real flavor of the class."

"Oh, well, okay. Good. I'm glad it worked for you. I'm just happy there isn't a terribly neglected sick little girl with a workaholic mother out there."

She laughs. "I know, right? Hello, Child Services?"

I'm positive there's more to the story, but I've heard all I want to.

"Okay, so I'll arrange for the party on the last day of school. Maybe we can play freeze tag on the grass behind the school."

"I don't need to know the details, Jenny. I'm sure it will be great."

This is my cue to leave. As I open the door, Miss Ward is right behind me, pulling me into an awkward hug.

"Thanks, Jenny. You were a good friend this year."

I really don't know what to say to that, so I just hug her back and walk away.

On my way back to the car, I dial Nina. She answers on the first ring.

"What happened?"

"Well, you were right—she's leaving."

"Did she tell you why?"

"She said her old school in New Jersey wants her back and made her a great offer."

"Do you believe her?"

"I do. Why would she make that up? The bigger question is, does Kim Fancy know, and how is she taking it?"

"Are you friendly with her at all?"

"Not even a bit," I admit.

I unlock the minivan and slide into the driver's seat.

"So is this public knowledge?" Nina asks.

"Well, she didn't say to keep it quiet, so I guess it is. I'm feeling a little bad. She might have been crazy, but Miss Ward was a good teacher. Maxi is going to miss her."

"Oh, he'll fall in love with his next teacher. They always do."

We make plans to see each other over the long weekend. As I pull out of the parking lot, I see a red Grand Cherokee with the hood up on the side of the road. I slow down to see if they need help and regret the impulse immediately when I see JJ Aikens. I roll down my window.

"Hey, JJ, need any help?"

She looks up, confused, then walks from her car over to mine.

"No, thanks." She sighs. "I'm just waiting for Triple A. I *told* my husband the transmission was going on this thing."

"Do you have Kit with you? I can drop her somewhere if you like."

"It's okay. She's playing on my phone and it shouldn't be too much longer." She looks at her watch.

She seems disproportionately sad, even for someone with a broken-down car. I decide to tell her the big news about our teacher to take her mind off her troubles.

"Miss Ward just told me she's leaving the school and going back to New Jersey."

JJ doesn't seem a bit surprised. But what happens next really startles me.

"So is Kim," she says in a weird, squeaky voice. She then screws up her face and bursts into tears.

"She is?" I say a bit too loudly. This makes JJ cry harder.

I throw the minivan into Park and get out. I walk over to her and put my arm around her shoulder.

"I'm so sorry. I know you guys are good friends."

She shrugs off my semi-hug and looks at me like *I'm* the crazy one.

"Do you think I'm sad? I'm not sad, I'm *mad*!" She wipes her apparent tears of anger away and looks me straight in the eye. "You have no idea what I have put up with from her."

I'm so confused. "What are you talking about?"

"I can't tell you. I'm not supposed to tell anyone."

"Tell anyone what?" I lob out there to see if she'll bite.

She shakes her head. "For almost three years I've kept her secrets and supported her stupid ideas." She is speaking more to herself than me. "Did you know she's always trying to have stuff delivered, because I guess people in New York don't go out and do their own shopping?"

"You mean *Manhattan*," I say, trying to lighten her up.

"Manhattan," JJ sneers. "New Jersey is more like it."

"She's from Jersey?" I ask, genuinely surprised.

JJ looks panic-stricken. "Oh, my God, don't tell her I told you."

"Told me what?" I wink at her. "But is she really?"

JJ wipes her nose with her hand and nods.

"A place called Edgewater." She shrugs. "It's supposed to be nice."

"So why all the talk about Manhattan?"

"She wanted to make herself sound more important. *I* didn't even know the truth until this year when that woman showed up."

I frown. "You mean the jewelry designer?"

"No, Miss Ward!"

"She knew Miss Ward from New Jersey?"

There's that panic-stricken look again.

"Oh, my God. Don't say anything. No one's supposed to know."

I'm trying to remain cool and calm, but my heart is racing.

"Why would it be a secret that they knew each other in New Jersey?"

"I'm not supposed to tell anyone," JJ whispers.

Yeah, you're a real gatekeeper,

As bad timing goes, Triple A showing up right then counts as a winner. JJ is immediately pulled out of our conversation cocoon when Dusty (according to his name tag) walks up and asks what the problem is.

As JJ takes him to the front of the car, I debate whether I should stay and push my luck, or cut and run with what I have.

The decision is made when JJ calls out to me asking if I can drive her and Kit home.

"I'm happy to," I answer with a smile. I jump in my driver's seat and pray for lots of traffic.

✦ ✦ ✦

"I don't think I've ever been to your house," I tell JJ. I know damn well I haven't.

"I'm off Trail's End, right by the mall."

"Gotcha." I pull into the street and calculate that with traffic I will have about fifteen minutes to glean as much information from her as possible, unless we get lucky and there's a three-car pileup. Kit is sitting in Max's car seat happily watching one of his movies with the headphones on.

"So . . ." I lead off, hoping JJ will pick up the ball.

She turns her whole body to me.

"You have to promise you'll never tell anyone what I told you," she begs.

"You've only told me that Miss Ward and Kim knew each other from New Jersey. I won't say anything, but I think I'd have a hard time finding someone who cares."

"It's not that they know each other, it's *how* they know each other."

We're at a stoplight, so I turn and give her my best "confused" look, which isn't hard because I am still pretty confused.

JJ gives an exasperated sigh.

"Look, if I tell you, you can't tell anyone."

"I won't."

"Swear on Max's life."

Funny, I had just asked Nina to swear on her kid's life, and she had refused. I'm not sure it's wise to bet Max's life on my ability to keep my yap shut, but I'm too damn curious not to.

"Okay. I swear."

"On Max's life."

I grimace.

"On Max's life." Now I know I won't tell anyone. I look at JJ expectantly.

"Well, from what I know, Kim moved here to get away from Peggy."

I try to keep my eyes on the road but I have to look over to see if she's serious.

"When I first met Kim at preschool, we hung out all the time because we had to be there to help the kids with separation. You weren't there, were you?"

Am I that forgettable?

"I didn't do preschool for Max."

I want to slap the judgmental look she gives me right off her face.

"Kim told me back then that they'd moved for David's job, but also because he'd had an affair and they needed a fresh start. They seemed to really be trying. They used to take these romantic weekends. We watched Nancy a few times."

"How does Miss Ward fit in to all this?"

"When we first got the letter from the school telling us who the kindergarten teacher was, Kim totally wigged out." JJ laughs humorlessly at the memory. "She told me this was the woman David had the affair with and she had obviously followed them here. She was really unhinged and I felt bad for her. She even went to Principal Jakowski and tried to have her fired before school started."

"I'm surprised she didn't manage to," I say, thinking about how relentless Kim Fancy can be when she wants something.

"Turn left here," JJ directs. We are now on Trail's End, fairly close to our destination.

"She couldn't, though. Have you ever seen Miss Ward's résumé?"

I shake my head no.

"She has a doctorate in early childhood education from Columbia and she started her career pioneering a 'Mandarin for toddlers' program for the state of New Jersey. There was no way Jakowski was going to turn her away."

"That's crazy," is all I can think of to say.

"That's my house at the end of the block, with the blue mailbox," JJ tells me. Shit! I'm not ready to let her go yet. I pull into her driveway and put the minivan in Park.

"So, is this like a stalking situation? She followed them here to boil a bunny on their stove?"

"What?" JJ clearly doesn't get the reference to my favorite movie of all time, *Fatal Attraction*.

"Nothing. So she moves here supposedly to win David back, and what? Try to get him to leave Kim?"

"That's what I thought, but it turns out it was *Kim* who had the affair, and *Kim* who she came here to win back." She shakes her head in disbelief. "And now she has."

"When did you find out all this?"

"Two weeks ago. Until then I thought David had had the affair with her, and I felt so bad for Kim to have to see this woman. She bad-mouthed her constantly, but then would go and have"—she makes air quotes—"'meetings' with her. I thought she was trying to save her marriage. But then I walked in on them making out in Kim's backyard. I think it was just after that event at your husband's store."

We both sit in silence for a moment. Miss Ward moves to Kansas to follow her heart and ultimately wins the girl. Huh. It's kind of romantic, in a crazy-bitch sort of way. Then I frown.

"So what's going to happen to Nancy and David?"

JJ shrugs. "No idea. Do you think he would go back to New Jersey with them?"

"I can't even pretend to know what these people would do." I laugh. Boy, nothing like this ever happened when I was class mom for Vivs and Laura.

"God, it feels good to talk about this," JJ admits. "I've been keeping a lot of secrets this year." She starts gathering up her bags and tells Kit to get ready. "Thanks so much for the ride."

"Any time."

"It was nice to talk to you. I used to have a lot of friends, but after Kim moved here I became kind of obsessed with her and I lost most of them." She opens the minivan door and gets out, but pauses before she closes it.

"Maybe I was a little in love with her, too."

And with that slight overshare, she closes the door and heads up her front walkway with Kit.

"Remember," she turns and yells, although I can barely hear her through my closed car windows. "You can't tell anyone."

24

To: The Soon-to-Be 1st Grade Parents
From: JDixon
Date: 6/8
Subject: HAGS! As the kids would say

Dear Formerly Miss Ward's Class,

I just want to give a third and final reminder to everyone that tomorrow is the last day of school for our kindergarteners and everyone is invited to our field day/picnic, which takes place from 10 a.m. to 2 p.m. on the west side of the field behind the school.

Thanks to everyone who volunteered to bring food and drinks. I'm happy to report that we have a new winner in our speedy response category. Since Sasha Lewicki's automated reply has left the class, Ravi Brown leads the pack with an impressive 58 seconds, but you should know that all responses came in at under ten minutes. I couldn't be prouder.

I also want to thank everyone for pitching in these last two weeks and helping Principal Jakowski manage our class. Miss Ward's untimely

> *departure could have been a disaster, but we all pulled together and made it work. Special shout-out to Ali Gordon and Don Burgess. You guys are amazing with kids! You should be teachers.*
>
> *Hope to see you tomorrow, but if I don't, then HAGS (which I think is a truly horrible acronym for Have a Great Summer, but the kids seem to love it).*
>
> *Over and out for good!*
>
> *Jen (and Asami in spirit)*

✦ ✦ ✦

And there it is, my last official email as class mom. After tomorrow, I'm a free woman. Well, "free" is a relative term, I guess, since I'm still a mom and I now have an active little boy home with me all day, every day. Thank goodness for play dates. I already have Max scheduled through July Fourth weekend.

These last two weeks have been what my mother would call a mare's nest. Miss Ward never came back after Memorial Day weekend, if you can believe it. She must have been planning all along to leave then. I should have known from that hug.

The children were very confused when they wandered into room 147 on the Tuesday after the long weekend and found a note from Miss Ward written on the Smart Board. Only about a third of them could actually understand it. According to Max, Suni Chang saved the day by reading it aloud to the class. The note explained that her work here was done, that they were all going to be wonderful first-graders and she had to move on to a new group of kindergarteners who needed her . . . just like Mary Poppins. She wrote that! *Just like Mary Poppins.* Go fly a kite, Miss Ward.

The school had to scramble to make sure her class was covered for the final two weeks. Most of the moms took a turn co-teaching with Principal Jakowski, who showed no indication that he had ever spent any real time in a classroom. My shout-out to Ali and Don was from the heart. They came in together, which I was surprised and happy to see, and the kids loved them. They created all these amazing learning games that were really fun (all this according to Max, whose favorite was something called What's in the Bag?). I can't help but wonder if my chat with Ali kick-started a little something between them. Probably not, but it's more fun for me to think that it did.

I found it a bit out of character for Miss Ward to leave without giving the kids any kind of closure. I've said it before, she was a bit of a wack-job but a *great* teacher. The kids were sad that they didn't get a chance to say good-bye to her or their beloved classmate Nancy Fancy, who (big shocker!) didn't come back, either. I can only assume they're all happily ensconced somewhere in Manhattan or New Jersey.

I kept the promise I made on Max's life, but about a week after JJ Aikens swore me to secrecy, she started telling anyone who would listen. It was quite the topic at the klatch, let me tell you. And, like any good story, it got better with each telling. My personal favorite was when Shirleen Cobb said *she* heard that Miss Ward and the Fancys were making porn together. When I asked her what kind of porn, she said, "The un-American kind."

The only secret that actually stayed a secret was the real identity of Sasha Lewicki. Of course, I did tell Asami (I mean, who else would really care?), and she could not have been more magnanimous when she said, "I told you so." I have to give her full props. She totally called it.

Right now I have to dash to Party City to get water balloons for one of the games we'll be playing at the picnic tomorrow. That party will be my final duty as class mom and, I have to admit, the thought chokes me up a little bit.

I debate sharing this with Nina when I see her at the picnic tomorrow. Ever since she re-upped as PTA president, she has been dropping little hints about me being a class mom again. She hasn't come right out and asked me yet, but I know she will. And when she does, I'm pretty sure I know what I'll tell her.

"Absofuckinglutely not!"

To: The parents of Mrs. Peele's 1st grade class

From: JDixon

Date: 8/30

Subject: I'm your class mom!

Dear Parents,

For those of you who don't know me, my name is Jennifer Dixon, and it is my pleasure (wink) to be your class mom for this coming year.

To the parents who were with me last year in kindergarten, all I can say is you've made it through boot camp already. You know the rules and you can stop reading this now. See you on curriculum night, which is (see below).

To the rest of you, make sure to read every damn word of this email . . .

Acknowledgments

First and foremost, I'd like to acknowledge Beinstock/UTA super-agent Paul Fedorko, who convinced me that all my whining about being a class parent might actually make a good book. Thank you for not only encouraging me but also shaming me by saying "Danielle Steel isn't too busy to write and she has more kids than you."

While writing *Class Mom*, I had no idea that the five most dreaded words a friend of the author can hear are "Will you read my book?" Thankfully, I had a bevy of generous souls who were more than willing to read various drafts and give me feedback, and for that I am grateful. The most loyal of these was my paid professional friend Gabrielle Maertz. If Gabby hadn't laughed in all the right places, I never would have kept writing beyond the first forty pages. Others who gave me their time and wisdom: My forever sister/friends Maria Crocitto, Nancy Bennet and Cindy Vervaeke. Alison Cody who lived the whole nightmare with me. Jessica Aguirre who printed out all 360 pages and lugged it around until she finished it, God bless her. Paige Baldwin, who told me that Jen needed a goal. Sheri Impemba who was the first to read it and ask me if she could let her friends read it too. Jan Weiner who let me use a very sweet story about her son Caden, and Caroline Rhea, who gave me the funniest line in the book ("I'll let you decide which one it is).

Thank you to Serena Jones, my editor at Holt, who had the scary task of telling me that the fruits of my two-year labor of love needed rewrites. There is an old joke that goes, "How many writers does it take to change a lightbulb?" Answer: "It doesn't need changing!" But indeed it did, and Serena's razor-sharp insights and gentle nudging made *Class Mom* a much better story.

And finally, thank you to the Starbucks at Eighty-Eighth and Broadway for allowing me to use your café as my writing room and for always having the PB-and-J lunchbox and iced green tea that fueled my creativity.

About the Author

LAURIE GELMAN was born and raised in the Great White North. She spent twenty-five years as a broadcaster in both Canada and the United States before trying her hand at writing novels. Laurie lives in New York City with her husband, Michael Gelman, and two teenage daughters. *Class Mom* is her first book.